DON'T HATE
THE PLAYER

DON'T HATE THE PLAYER

ALEXIS NEDD

BLOOMSBURY

NEW YORK LONDON OXFORD NEW DELHI SYDNEY

BLOOMSBURY YA
Bloomsbury Publishing Inc., part of Bloomsbury Publishing Plc
1385 Broadway, New York, NY 10018
29 Earlsfort Terrace, Dublin 2, Ireland

BLOOMSBURY and the Diana logo are trademarks of Bloomsbury Publishing Plc

First published in the United States of America in June 2021 by Bloomsbury YA

Text copyright © 2021 by Assemble Media
For more information about Assemble Media, go to www.AssembleMedia.com

Bloomsbury books may be purchased for business or promotional use. For information on bulk purchases
please contact Macmillan Corporate and Premium Sales Department at specialmarkets@macmillan.com

Library of Congress Cataloging-in-Publication Data
Names: Nedd, Alexis, author.
Title: Don't hate the player / Alexis Nedd.
Other titles: Do not hate the player
Description: New York : Bloomsbury Children's Book, 2021.
Summary: Sixteen-year-old Emilia, secretly a dedicated gamer, competes with her elite team in a major
tournament at the same time she and her best friend are running for class president and vice president.
Identifiers: LCCN 2020040664
ISBN 978-1-5476-0502-6 (hardcover) • ISBN 978-1-5476-0503-3 (e-book)
Subjects: CYAC: eSports (Contests)—Fiction. | High schools—Fiction. | Schools—Fiction. |
Best friends—Fiction. | Friendship—Fiction. | Hispanic Americans—Fiction.
Classification: LCC PZ7.1.N386 Don 2021 | DDC [Fic]—dc23
LC record available at https://lccn.loc.gov/2020040664

Book design by John Candell
Typeset by Westchester Publishing Services
Printed and bound in the U.S.A. by Berryville Graphics Inc., Berryville, Virginia
2 4 6 8 10 9 7 5 3 1

To find out more about our authors and books visit www.bloomsbury.com and sign up for our newsletters.

To Bryan Cruz. It runs in the family.

PART I

Jake

NOBODY ACTUALLY LIKED Emmett Franklin, but his birthday party was the most well-attended event on the fourth-grade social calendar. It didn't matter that Emmett was kind of a dick or that he only ever hung out with Connor D. and Matt P. at school. What mattered was that every year, his parents shelled out for an entire Saturday afternoon at the Hillford Mall Arcade, which meant everyone who showed up got two fat rolls of tokens and all the pizza they could eat for what might be the greatest five hours of their young lives.

Jake Hooper knew he was only invited to Emmett's birthday because their class had a rule that party invitations had to be given to every student in his homeroom. Even if he felt sheepish showing up somewhere he wasn't wanted, the possibility of finally beating the high score on *Knights of Darkness* was too delicious to pass up. His mom was thrilled he'd been invited and encouraged him to make some friends at the party, but the moment Jake stepped onto the arcade's sticky carpet, he zeroed in on the big blue machine in the back—the one that would soon display HIGH SCORE: JCH on an infinite, glowing scroll for everyone in the mall to see. That machine was his ticket to glory.

A ticket to glory that was, as Jake would soon discover, made out to someone else.

He could tell from the back of her head that she didn't go to his school. Jake always sat in the back of the classroom and had gotten unusually good at telling people apart by their hairdos. This girl had brown, poofy hair like no one in Mrs. Ripton's class, so Jake immediately knew he didn't know her. She might have been in a different class or gone to a different school, but either way she was at the party, outside of the "everyone gets an invite" rule. Emmett must have liked her. If Emmett liked her, Jake was sure he didn't.

But Jake Hooper wasn't a quitter. Games were his thing, maybe the only thing he was serious about. His classmates called him weird and loud, and his teachers wrote on his report card that he was "distractible," but Jake felt better about all of that when he played games. He liked the ones where he got to be a hero, kicking down bad guys and overpowering crowds of undead with a well-timed blast of fire magic. He also liked it when he got to play with his friends, who lived in other places but teamed up with him for crypt raids and group challenges. It was better, Jake thought, to win when other people could share it.

That was why Jake panicked when he got closer to the *Knights of Darkness* machine. He couldn't see the girl's face as she played, but he could tell she was concentrating hard on landing her combos and smashing through the wights that swarmed out from the castle on the side of the screen. Thanks to his new glasses, Jake saw from a short distance that her kill tally was edging dangerously close to his own personal best, the fifth-place high score that got him on the leaderboard the last time he played.

Sometimes Jake's mom told him to be careful of other people's personal space. He had a habit of leaning and squinting—that was how she knew he needed glasses—and even though his vision was better now, Jake still found himself getting close to things he was interested in. In his curiosity he forgot that most people don't really like it when they glance to the side and see a person they don't know staring over their shoulder.

The girl noticed and did not like it. She only twitched a little, as if someone had poked her in her side, but it was enough to make her finger slip off the attack button and miss landing a powerful finishing move. After that there was no way she could catch up the flow she had going before.

"No, no, no, wait, wait, wait—UGH!"

It was like watching a car crash in a movie. In slow motion, her holy knight avatar's health chipped down to almost nothing as her attacks failed to keep up with the game's defending forces. Jake winced every time the squelchy sound of stabbing punctuated the enemy's hits on the knight until the fateful phrase YOU DIED flashed across the screen. GAME OVER.

Jake was no stranger to making people lose games (that was kind of the point of going player versus player), but he'd never physically watched someone wipe out because of something he did. The girl smacked the machine with both hands and looked over at him with the same expression his dad made when Jake dropped a dinner plate or forgot to close the screen door all the way. The look said it was impossible for Jake to be as dumb as he just acted, like how was he even alive if he was going to be *that* stupid.

It was suddenly very hot in the arcade, especially under Jake's hair.

"You messed me up!" the girl hissed, apparently not trying to bring more attention to their shared shame than was absolutely necessary. "Why are you standing so close to me?"

If only Jake had a reason that didn't sound silly. He could have said that he was nearsighted and wanted to watch her play, but his glasses gave that away as a lie. He also could have said that someone told him to tell her it was time for pizza, which was only true in the sense that it was technically time for pizza but was also mostly a lie. He defaulted to the magic word, which, if Jake had ever made a list of the words he said most often, would definitely be at the very top by thousands and thousands of points.

"Sorry."

Next to them both, *Knights of Darkness* reset to the title screen and flashed bright with the game's opening cinematic. The knight looked up at the castle, which was encased in a purple swirl of dark magic. INSERT TOKEN. The evil sorcerer stood in a graveyard and raised his hands, casting the spell that would reanimate his undead army. INSERT TOKEN.

"*Sorry?* I was gonna get on the board, and now I have to start over and *can you step back, please*?"

Jake felt like stepping all the way out of the mall and into the reservoir across from the parking lot, but in the interest of trying to make things right, he only moved away enough to give her what his mom would consider a normal amount of space.

"Here," he said and dug around in the front pocket of his sweatshirt. He pulled out one of his two rolls of arcade tokens and held it out to her, desperate for that to be enough to make up for his existence. One half of his perfect afternoon, traded for peace. "I just—You're really good. You were doing really good, and I was watching. You're definitely gonna get on the leaderboard, but I feel bad for distracting you."

The girl picked up the roll and looked at Jake like he was an alien, which was an improvement on her looking at him like he was stupid. She glanced back at the *Knights of Darkness* screen, then back at Jake.

"I'm not going to take your whole roll," she said after

clearly weighing the option in her mind. "I mean I wouldn't be mad if you gave me a coin, but not the whole thing." She cracked the cardboard tube in half, shook out one token, and handed the rest back to Jake. "Seriously, it's weird that you just gave me the whole thing."

Jake was used to being called weird, but the way she said it, with a smile that brought him into the joke, made him feel like she wasn't making fun of him. Now that he knew she wasn't going to ruin the rest of Emmett's party for him, she sounded really nice.

"Sorry," he said again, "for being weird." And then, with a boldness he didn't know he had, he asked if he could watch her play the next game. "I can never get that shield combo to work and you just did it, like, five times in a row. It was awesome."

The girl smiled wider, apparently happy that he noticed her skills. "It's not hard if you kind of count between the attacks; it'll beep right before the shield is ready, so you have to listen, but yeah, once you hear it you gotta pull the stick right away so the knight jumps belove and abow it really fast."

Jake had no idea what the curly-haired girl just said. "Sorry, 'belove and abow'?"

The girl smacked her forehead with her palm. "I talk too fast. He goes above"—she pulled the stick to show Jake the move—"and below. I can show you, but you gotta stop saying sorry."

"Really?"

"I'm in if you are. Let's play after pizza."

Right. Pizza. Eating food with the other kids, including Emmett and Connor and Matt. Jake looked over at the party tables covered in plastic tablecloths and hoped that he would find somewhere to eat where no one would bug him. Probably by the time he finished eating, the girl would forget she'd ever talked to him and he'd never learn that shield combo or see her ever again.

"Are you coming?"

The girl was ahead of him, gunning for the pizza table, which was already crowded with the kids from Jake's class. She'd stopped and was waiting for him to join her. Huh. People never waited on Jake to do anything. This girl was actually kind of nice. After they got their slices, she even sat next to him while they ate.

Her name was Emilia Romero, her friends called her Em, and she was Emmett's new next-door neighbor. She went to the Monteronni elementary school, which explained why she wasn't in Jake and Emmett's class. She liked *Knights of Darkness* and a few other games but didn't have a console at home. She had poofy hair because her parents were from Puerto Rico, and she had a pet bird named Cloud, and she talked a *lot*, which was great because Jake wasn't sure what he'd even want to say back to her. He liked her immediately and very, very much. It felt impossible not to.

After the pizza, Jake and Emilia did play co-op on *Knights of Darkness* and she taught him how to do the shield combo. He told her how to press the side buttons in the right order to unlock the secret black armor; she screamed and played as the unlockable dark knight for the rest of the day. Each time they lost, they put their heads together to strategize how to get further next time and took turns feeding the machine until they snagged the second-place high score and were down to one last token.

The party ended before they could get the top spot. Well, to be fair, the party ended sometime after they got the third-place score, but when Jake's mom arrived to pick him up, he begged her to let them try for second. Their partnership ended when Emilia's dad came and motioned for her to leave *Knights of Darkness* alone. Jake was left to tap their initials—ENJ for Em 'n' Jake—in second place.

"Can we try again soon?" Jake asked as they split the contents of the party's last, lonely goody bag (some jerk must have taken two).

Emilia looked back at her dad and shrugged. "I don't get to play a lot, but I hope when I do, you're here," she answered. Then she left.

Jake still had one token and looked back at *Knights of Darkness*. He was probably warmed up enough to get the solo high score, but getting home late would make his dad angry. The last coin went into his pocket.

He saw Emilia again the next year at Emmett's eleventh birthday party, which was at the Franklins' house and not the arcade. They snuck onto the swinging bench on the back deck and played *Pokémon Black* on Jake's 3DS. In seventh grade, Jake's friend Todd knew Emilia from Monteronni and had her over for Halloween, where Emilia and Jake coincidentally dressed as Iron (Wo)man and Captain America. The two of them faced off on *Guitar Hero Live* in the basement while Todd, who was fun but a little perverted, tried to organize his first game of spin the bottle.

Every time Jake ran into Emilia, he liked her more. She never treated him like he was weird or made fun of his glasses. They might have been friends if Jake had just asked for her Snapchat or something. He never did. Stuff always got in the way, and the older they got, the more there was for him to think about.

By the time Jake's mom left and he moved with his dad to the apartment on the other side of town, it was almost too overwhelming to think about anything. He couldn't bring himself to care that moving meant he had to go to a new school for tenth grade, or that his mom hadn't asked for custody, or how crummy he was doing in school. He did play more games, though. And he got really, really good.

For some reason, Jake always held on to that Hillbrook Mall Arcade token. He hadn't seen Emilia in years, but there was always a chance they'd make it to the top of the leaderboard.

CHAPTER ONE

Emilia, Monday, Week I

I'M JUST SAYING that the worst thing to ever happen to me was *Guardians League Online* changing their meta to make my main completely useless in competition. I played as Condor, poison damage MVP of *GLO*'s entire character lineup, for years—literal, actual years—and now there isn't a single respectable team using him in their comp. And yes, I checked the character compositions of every other top-tier team. They're a Condor-free zone and have been since Wizzard "updated" the game with a new patch, new math, and an all-new meta.

I should have expected something like this would happen. The second anyone gets comfortable with the way damage, defense, and magic works in any Wizzard game, the studio goes back to the drawing board for some big surprise release that, to be fair, usually makes the game more fun. It's just this time the sea change is rocking the hell out of my boat.

Before Wizzard introduced the new meta in their September patch, I was unstoppable. Condor was my main character, and I got so high on the leaderboard for the Philadelphia server that Byunki asked me to start practicing with Team Fury, the group he's shuffled and reshuffled a dozen times before settling on a winning lineup for online competition. *The Byunki.* Server legend, ruthless captain, and, judging by the Team Fury smackdown compilations on YouTube, one of the best playing tanks in all of *GLO*. He's played with some of the best damage-dealing DPS players in the game and picked out the fastest, most brilliant healers to shore up his defense.

Fury is so good that I've gotten better just from playing alongside them for a few months. *GLO*'s competition mode is like capture the flag on steroids, with five players on each team whaling on one another to capture a payload of treasure. When I played Condor, my job as a DPS was to cram enough poison damage on our enemies. Now that Condor's damage is garbage, I have to relearn how to get good on Pharaoh, a magic character whose skills and cooldowns are so much harder to nail than Condor's ever were.

I also had something of a handle on my junior year at Hillford West even with my parents reminding me every day of summer vacation that this year was "the big one" and "the one that counts." I'd done the math and balanced it all out perfectly: school, field hockey, college visitation spreadsheets, keeping up appearances with Penny and the rest of my friends, sort of (maybe) starting to date Connor Dimeo, which is wild, all while making sure nothing from the real, 3D part of my life ever touched the part where I spend every night playing a team-based, multiplayer shooter with a bunch of people I've never met. Team Fury doesn't know who I am in real life. And if anyone who actually knows me found out about *GLO* . . .

It's going to be okay. It has to be, so it's going to be. I'm only jumbled up because it's Monday, I was up way too late getting my butt kicked in practice matches with Fury, and I haven't shaken the jittery feeling that comes when I play too long and start seeing hit counts and usernames floating around whenever I close my eyes. I was so off my game last night that Byunki sent me a DM asking if I'd been practicing with Pharaoh outside of team scrimmages, which I absolutely have been but not as much as I have in previous weeks. He could tell, and he told me to shape the hell up via DM:

> Fury isn't about excuses. Fury is about winning. If
> you're not going to win, you don't belong on Fury.

"Yes, sir. Loud and clear, sir. Let me just go scream into a pillow real quick, and I'll be back with those insanely difficult crossbow ranged kills you requested, sir."

I did not say that in response to Byunki's DM. I am saying it now, out loud to myself while finishing my makeup in the mirror of my car. Not while I'm driving. I don't have a death wish; I just need a few minutes to get my face and/or life together before I have to endure another day at school. The student parking lot is good for that. Everyone's already inside, and I have first period free today. No one's going to bug me here. I breathe in. I breathe out. I scratch a tiny crumb of mascara off my eyelid with the tip of my fingernail. Everyone has a process.

Looking at my reflection, I can see my concealer is doing god's work on the dark circles under my eyes. By god, I mean Rihanna. The Fenty was a gift from my mom, who handed it to me before I left for school this morning. She didn't have to tell me why. I looked tired and have been looking tired since I joined Fury.

"Just a tap; blend it over your cheekbone so they don't see the work," she said twenty minutes ago or every day of my sixteen years on Earth. "They only get to see the results."

"Only the results," I agree quietly in my car as I stare at those results in the mirror. Cat eye, thickened lashes, everything on my exhausted brown face cranked a notch and a half above normal. Hiding the struggle is what I do best. "Come on, Emilia," I mutter when I finally feel ready to face the day, "let's get this bread."

"Who ya talking to?" Sweet Christmas, I was so in my head that I didn't even notice Connor pulling into the parking space behind me. His windows are rolled down, and he's using his soccer captain voice to project through the glass of my very closed door.

Conner used to park a lot farther away. He bribed another junior to switch spots with him and acts like he made a great sacrifice, saying nothing of the part where I didn't ask him to do that for me. It's clear that his love language is being directly in my face as much as possible, whereas mine is something I've yet to discover.

"Hey! No one!" I shout back. The curtain rises on today's performance. I get out of the car and meet him out in the lot.

I liked Connor a lot more before I knew he liked me. He's a good guy, a Hillford West athlete who drinks that respect women juice (eh, maybe a respect women juice concentrate), and I could probably do a lot worse. It's just that now that he's asked me out and we've gone on a grand total of two dates since the school year started, I'm learning what it's like to be the single object in Sauron's all-seeing eye. Not in a "destroy Middle-earth" way, just the red-hot inescapable attention of it all. No one's ever tried to be my boyfriend before this, and it's freaking exhausting.

And okay, Connor does look like one of those impossibly sculpted twenty-four-year-olds they cast to play high schoolers on the CW, except he's actually in high school and just looks like that, so that's nice. I'm not afraid to admit that it's nice. Especially when he's playing soccer and his shirt is off and he looks all . . . shiny. Let she among us who wouldn't get a little stupid around IRL Archie Andrews cast the first stone.

"Gotcha matcha," he says when I emerge from the space

between our cars. He's holding two matching Starbucks cups that undoubtedly contain a matcha latte for me and a whatever-the-hell he likes for him. This is unbelievably nice of him, but also not what I need this morning.

"Thanks. Sorry I was so zoned out just now. I was up forever." I sniff the latte before I try to take a sip. It smells like hot, fresh grass cuttings. I don't remember ever telling Connor I liked matcha lattes, but I'm too far in to say anything now. Who knows? Maybe I'll come around on him. Them. Maybe I'll come around on *them*.

"Studying for the English quiz?"

"English quiz? I don't have an—*English quiz!*" Frick. I knew there was something I was forgetting. I'm usually so much better about this! Fricking Wizzard and fricking Pharaoh. I'm completely off my game in more ways than one.

"You're not telling me you forgot? Do you want me to help you study before? I took American lit last year, and I still remember some stuff. What are you reading now?"

The idea of spending the rest of my free period with Connor poring over . . . whatever book we're reading in class is already giving me a headache. Last year it would have been fine; over this summer we texted about summer reading, and that was fine too. When he asked to hang out at the diner last month, I'd assumed it was a pre–junior year group hang thing. It was actually, in his mind, our first "date." And yes, in retrospect it was obvious what he was up to—no one texts a girl his thoughts on *The Picture of Dorian Gray* ("yo, these bros are totally banging") for a month solely because he's super into Wilde, but I still felt trapped. I almost didn't say yes to the second date, but having the excuse of talking to boys is a better cover for *GLO* than holing up in my room with the lights off for no discernable reason, so I went along with it.

Dating Connor has its perks at school too. He shines so bright in the Hillford West constellation of stars that the details of my life look dim in comparison. We're only a few weeks into the school year, and all anyone wants to know is if we're dating. He's concealer for my less respectable habits.

"I didn't forget the quiz," I say quickly. "I studied last night. So much, like all night. Obviously that's what I was doing. But you know me! I love grades. And I promised Penny I'd go over some chapters with her. Gotta get to the library right now, actually."

"Yeah, sure." He nods. "Tell Penny I say hi."

"Of course!" I shout back, leaving him in my dust. "Thanks for the coffee!"

I think he finds this charming in a "there she goes again, the girl who is always running away from me" sort of way.

The hallways are pretty deserted since most students are in class by now. I don't have a ton of time to refresh my memory for this quiz, so I'm grateful not to have to stop to talk with anyone else on my way to the library. Hillford gives at least one free period to everyone except freshmen, but only a few of us were lucky enough to get free period first—the library is mostly empty except for a few scattered seniors flopped on the couches in the lounge area and a handful of nerds huddled around a box of cupcakes near the old computer lab, which no one but the gaming club uses. Must be someone's birthday.

Just beyond them is Penny. She's alone at a study table, not because no one wants to sit near her, but because they know better. Penny Darwin has ruled our year since middle school with the fierceness of a Habsburg empress and the fear-inducing poise of a lioness. She's top five in our class, the lead in every school musical, and has more Instagram followers than anyone I've ever met in person. Penny is terrifying. She is my best friend in the world.

"Hey, I got you a latte." I slide Connor's unloved gift onto the table in front of Penny, a tithe for the queen. She gives me a look that says I'm full of shit, but she's never said no to a Connor matcha before.

"You know if you actually try one of these, you might like it." She says that but licks the rim so I can't take the latte back even if I want to.

"Pretty sure you said that about Connor too. Also, what are we reading in English right now?"

Penny rolls her eyes at me and picks up the book in front of her on the table. *"The Great Gatsby,* you ding-dong. You didn't read it?"

Gatsby, Gatsby . . . I pull a notebook out of my backpack

and riffle through it. Right, the rich guy who wants to marry that Nazi's dumb wife. I find the pages I'm looking for and sit down.

"Of course I read it. I just read it in, like, July when I read everything else. It's been a minute. Let me see what I've got."

My collection of five subject notebooks is the key to keeping my academic life together during gaming season. I prep during the day all summer, reading the books on the English syllabus, copying down calc formulas, and running through everything I'm supposed to learn that year in advance, which makes going to school more of a refresher course than an actual learning experience. My notes on *The Great Gatsby* are thankfully thorough enough to jog my memory.

"Okay, we got the green light, can't change the past. Giant golfer lady? That must have been from the movie."

"That movie was terrible."

"I thought it was fun. Why did I write 'The American Dream' surrounded by a bunch of sad face emojis?"

"Because social mobility in the 1920s made white people scared they weren't special, so they constructed class barriers to keep immigrants and new money out, and nothing has changed since."

I have no idea what I would do without Penny. I can feel myself remembering enough about *Gatsby* to get through my English quiz and close the notebook.

"Okay, I'm good. How are you, boo?"

Penny pulls a flyer out of her backpack and slides it over to me. It says, and I'm not making this up, "#DARWINNING" in huge block letters and has a photo of Penny looking pretty in a red, white, and blue crop top. "Vote Penny Darwin for President" is in much smaller text on the bottom.

She leans in toward me and whispers conspiratorially, "She's running."

"She's running! Principal Klein approved your platform? Oh my god, you worked so hard on that, congratulations! You totally have my vote and the whole field hockey team, if I can swing it."

Penny takes her flyer back and admires her own picture. "How about you guarantee it? Run with me. Be the Biden to my Obama. The, ah shoot—Who ran with Hillary?"

"Kaine."

"I never remember that guy. The Kaine to my Clinton."

"Penny, I—" I love Penny, I really do. We've been best friends since I moved here in the fourth grade, and I would do anything for her. And my mom would be over the moon if I could add student council to my resume for college. I wouldn't have to do it next year, just long enough to have "Junior Year Vice President" as a nice little bullet point and drop it if she runs for senior class next year. Vice presidents don't really do anything anyway, right?

I mean Dick Cheney shot that guy in the face and beefed up the military-industrial complex to, like, catastrophic efficiency, but he didn't have Penny Darwin in the executive's chair. She wouldn't even let me touch the real work. I'd just have to stick out the campaign while being field hockey captain and a Model UN delegate and volunteering while maintaining my GPA and playing an undead necromagical warlock with an elite team of competitive gamers every night under cover of darkness so no one finds out.

It's just one more thing, for a little while. I'll do it for Penny. It's just practice with Fury for now, and the campaign will only last up until homecoming in October.

"Yeah," I tell Penny once my mind is made up. "Yes! I do."

"It's a campaign, not a proposal."

"Is it? Whatever. I accept your nomination."

"Yay!" Penny claps in glee. She draws attention from a couple of the guys having breakfast cupcakes at the gamer table, who look over at her like she's a colorful, exotic bird. One of them even turns to look at me, squinting through thick glasses and a curtain of messy black hair. Relax, nerd, I don't want your cupcake.

Once he gets a look at my mean mug, he turns away immediately. That's right, shoo.

"I'm so stoked you said that," Penny continues, "because your name is already on the paperwork. Had to turn it in before Klein signed off on it. Behold, the first Black-Latinx presidential ticket in the history of Hillford West."

"Are we really the first?"

"Bitch, probably. Smile." Penny holds her phone up to take a selfie of the both of us holding her flyer up. I'm grateful all over again for this morning's concealer gift. She won't have to fix any of my tired eye nonsense with an app before she posts.

"Sleepy eyes; you have sleepy eyes, Lia, wake up." Never mind.

"Boo, you. I was up late."

"Yeah, I know, up late not reading *The Great Gatsby*. Here, close your eyes, and when I count to three, open them wide. Pageant trick I saw on YouTube. One . . . two . . ."

On three I force my eyes open and smize for the angels. Please let it be enough this time; my cheeks are starting to hurt.

"Hold . . . hold . . . amazing. I'm sending it to my moms too. You know they love you."

I love Penny's moms too. They let her be excellent without interfering too much, and the result is my unstoppable BFF.

"So why were you up late if it wasn't for the quiz?" Penny asks when she's texted and posted the campaign announcement everywhere it needs to go. "Were you talking to Connor? Did he take his shirt off on FaceTime?"

"I was not talking to Connor," I admit. "I mean, yes, he does take his shirt off on FaceTime sometimes. I was . . ."

See, I wish I could just tell Penny about *Guardians League Online*. If anyone in my life deserves to know how dork-ass crazy I am about this game, it's her. We share everything else in common except this. She's not into video games, but even if she were, I don't want to get her involved with that part of my life. It's not that I don't trust her. It's more complicated than that.

A buzz from my pocket interrupts my train of thought and gives me an excuse not to answer Penny right away.

"Did you just text me the photo?" I ask.

"Not yet, I'll tag you."

"Oh, wait a second then—" I pull my phone out of my pocket and feel my stomach do a flip. It's a notification from the Team Fury Discord. Byunki never does the @everyone thing unless it's really important.

FURY. URGENT. READ.

Not good. Or maybe really good? I don't like the word "urgent." Urgent can mean too many things, and I prefer clarity in virtually everything. There's a wall of text in the chat that looks like a press release:

Wizzard Games and Claricom are proud to announce their dual ownership of the East Coast's first all-Esports stadium venue. Just a few steps from the Wells Fargo Center in Philadelphia, Pennsylvania, the Wizzard-Claricom Arena will host team and individual Esports tournaments in a fully interactive, 3,000-seat video theater.

In honor of the Wizzard-Claricom partnership,
Wizzard Games invites Diamond-Tier amateur teams
from the studio's flagship *Guardians League Online*
franchise to participate in the arena's first live *GLO*
tournament. Teams will be chosen with local and
leaderboard preference and will compete for a grand
prize of $200,000.

Whoa. Team Fury is the top-ranked team on all Philly-based servers, so local and leaderboard preference means we're a lock for the tournament, right? We have to be. Fury Discord is exploding with responses from my team members, and in the middle of the eighteen straight lines of party parrots, there is Byunki with my answer.

Wizzard contacted me this morning. Meeting
tonight on the Fury server. Get ready to win.

A live tournament. Winning two hundred thousand dollars. I'm so excited at the idea of competing with Fury that it takes my brain a moment to catch up to the fact that live means *live*. In person. With my face in front of people.

"Lia, you okay? You look really awake now compared to, like, five seconds ago."

"All good. Family stuff. News," I mutter. "Hey, Penny, I need a second."

"Fine with me. I'm gonna go make copies of the flyer. If you want to talk, though, I'm here."

She doesn't press the matter any further and gathers her books into her backpack. On her way out of the library, Penny struts past the gamers, and I see her ask for (more like demand) a cupcake to go with her latte, which is so on brand I have to laugh. The guy who was looking at me earlier gives one to her without question. I kind of feel bad for glaring at him now. Happy birthday, dork.

Another buzz from my phone reminds me to keep checking the Fury Discord. Byunki wants our full names, addresses, phone numbers, all the stuff he'll have to put on the competition paperwork to get us submitted as a team. The other guys are chucking their info in main chat as fast as they can type, but I click through to send Byunki a DM instead.

Can I get that to you tonight? I type. I don't want to test his patience, but I need time to think, or plan, or . . . something before I agree to competing live.

Are you in or not? he responds.

Come on. Byunki of all people should know why I would hesitate. He knows that I don't give out any info or even go on voice chat when I play with anyone besides our team. When he tapped me for Team Fury, I had to explain everything that had happened, and he said he would give me a chance anyway.

Not hard to find another DPS, he follows up. There are a million of you and only one Fury.

And only one shot at winning two hundred stacks on the biggest *GLO* stage ever created. This tournament is about more than the money. It's glory. It's going from being a nobody to being a legend at something I really, really love to do. Fury's famous enough for their dominance in online tournaments, but this would catapult them to a whole different level. They'll make it there with me or without me.

I want them to do it with me, though. I don't think I've wanted anything more in the history of my life, ever. To hell with the consequences. Not gonna pass this up.

I'm in, I tap with quivering thumbs. I'm Fury all the way.

My phone buzzes in my hand again, not from the Fury Discord. I have been tagged in a photo on Instagram. Penny worked her filtering magic so our campaign announcement matches the rest of her grid, and our smiles make us look like we know we've already won the election. The end of her caption catches my eye—Make sure to vote on October 13th!

If we start now, the campaign should last four weeks, right? Something about that doesn't sit right with me, so I reopen my Discord to check if the heavy sense of dread I'm beginning to feel is justified. The first round of the *GLO* tournament is this weekend, and then the tournament itself will last . . . yup, those exact four weeks.

Back on Instagram, the likes and comments are rolling in on Penny's post: "queens," "voting 4 u," "omg perfect," "flawless," "women! in! the! sequel!" with clap hands between each word. Every stupid heart feels like someone's flicking me on the side of my head. Penny needs me to win her election, and I need to win the tournament with Fury at the exact same time. How the hell is this going to work?

I'm going to need a dump truck of concealer to hide what the next four weeks will do to me. Penny and Fury both want results.

CHAPTER TWO

Team Unity, Monday

*[**JHoops** has logged into GLO Chat: Team Unity]*

shineedancer: Jake!

ElementalP: jake jake jake jake

BobTheeQ: Fooooooooorrrrrrrrrrrr

JHoops: oh please don't

shineedancer: he's a jolly good fellow

ElementalP: FOR HE'S A JOLLY GOOD FELLOW FOR HE'S A JOLLY GOOD FELLOW

BobTheeQ: Which nobody can deny <3

shineedancer: sweet birthday babyyy

JHoops: thanks yinz

shineedancer: did you eat cake you deserve cake

ElementalP: the biggest possible cake

JHoops: I had a cupcake, the smallest possible cake

JHoops: it was actually really nice. the gaming club got them for me even though I've only been in school with them for a few weeks

ElementalP: omg you're already making friends at
your new school I'm crying

BobTheeQ: I got you a present.

BobTheeQ: It's a surprise.

BobTheeQ: Just for you.

JHoops: is it about the tournament

BobTheeQ: But we have to wait for Muddy.

shineedancer: muddy's always late

JHoops: leave muddy alone! I can wait

shineedancer: since we're waiting . . . did the
bday boy do the thing today

JHoops: shinee. ki. pls

ElementalP: oh ya did you talk to her?

JHoops: no and i shan't

BobTheeQ: Why not, you're a treasure.

ElementalP: just a little jewelry box of a person

JHoops: it's been too long and it's weird now.
i don't want to be weird

shineedancer: we believe in love, love's not weird

ElementalP: we believe in YOU, you're weird but
we're still on board

JHoops: she doesn't even remember me, she looked
right at me today and it was like -_-

JHoops: which is cool it's cool i'll live i got
stuff to do

shineedancer: can i give you some feminine advice

ElementalP: can I give you more, different feminine advice

JHoops: do you guys want to coordinate before or

shineedancer: talk to her

ElementalP: TALK TO HER

BobTheeQ: Can't argue with all caps ¯_(ツ)_/¯

ElementalP: You've been talking about her since you started this year

shineedancer: it was way before that

BobTheeQ: Remember the Knights of Darkness story. Love a story that starts with KOD.

shineedancer: it was a fight-cute

BobTheeQ: We just want you to be happy, Jacob.

JHoops: oh jacob is my father, call me jake

JHoops: and don't bring KOD up again I'm trying to have a nice birthday

ElementalP: One day moratorium on KOD, aka mystery girl, aka one half of my OTP. Only cuz it's your birthday

JHoops: where the hell is muddy i want my surprise

[LanguageBot:] language.

JHoops: sorry languagebot

*[**MUDD** has logged into GLO Chat: Team Unity]*

JHoops: thank god

MUDD: did jake talk to her

JHoops: oh come ON

MUDD: taking that as a no

shineedancer: lol you are correct sir

JHoops: HEY BOB WHAT'S MY PRESENT

BobTheeQ: Soooo

BobTheeQ: We all saw about the tournament.

ElementalP: I CRIED, DID WE RANK?

BobTheeQ: . . .

BobTheeQ: We ranked.

JHoops: omg

BobTheeQ: It was tight, we're not as high on the main boards as some of the other teams but we got local preference.

shineedancer: praise be to gritty

ElementalP: Are THEY in

BobTheeQ: They're in.

MUDD: holy shit

[LanguageBot: LANGUAGE!]

MUDD: sorry languagebot:(

ElementalP: REVENGE IS OURS

BobTheeQ: They're seeded much higher than us for obvious reasons

MUDD: because they blew the wizzard execs

BobTheeQ: Because they're Fury and they're legends.

JHoops: we have the advantage though

MUDD: lol do we

JHoops: low profile means no one knows what to expect

BobTheeQ: Birthday Jake is right. Fury showboats. They stream, they have their YouTube channel. We can see them but they can't see us. The new meta has everyone on edge so we have to crunch some numbers and sharpen up.

ElementalP: LEEEROYYY

MUDD: don't.

ElementalP: ok

BobTheeQ: I know we feel morally obligated to murder Fury.

JHoops: we really really do

BobTheeQ: But I'm keeping an eye on them. And their new member.

ElementalP: Do you know who he is? Did they recruit from the philly server?

BobTheeQ: Not that I can tell but I'm working on it. We need to focus on us though. And before I forget . . . we got merch.

JHoops: UNITY for the win!!!!

JHoops: omg was that my present

BobTheeQ: Yes my son.

MUDD: that's not your son.

BobTheeQ: First up—shirts and badges. They got our logo and everything.

ElementalP: BLUE CROSS. BLACK SHIELD. CAN'T LOSE.

BobTheeQ: Packages are in the mail, feel free to

wear them around, spread the word and look fly but make sure they're clean for the first round.

MUDD: deputizing myself to bring the lint roller

BobTheeQ: Granted. Ok buddies and muddies. Time to get on voice chat.

shineedancer: oh you mean your old man analog chat fetish won't work in-game? groundbreaking

BobTheeQ: I like having a pregame chat log. And you love playing with the bots I make for it. Anyway. We're starting on the Lakeport map for practice tonight. Let's rock and roll.

shineedancer: you sound like my dad

MUDD: hbd jake

[Team Unity is Queued for Battle]

CHAPTER THREE

Emilia, Thursday

MY CONSULTATION BINDER is, if I may say so myself, a thing of beauty. I'm talking table of contents, color coded, transcripts printed on extra-thick paper, and a fully signed list of teachers who have already agreed to write letters of recommendation for me. My mom made me promise to tell whichever college counselor I get that I plan on applying early admission so he or she has a better idea of what the numbers game will look like for me, because that was definitely something I was going to forget after putting all of this together for the past, oh, *seven years*.

I hope I get Mr. Grimes. He's supposed to be the nice one. Also he's new, so he hasn't had two exhausting years of my mother hounding him about my college prospects, two years in which I'm sure he would grow to despise me as a spoiled overachiever whose parents will make his life a living hell unless I go straight to the Ivy League. Without that, there's a chance he might like me. I actually love it when authority figures like me.

It helps that the guy going before me is Matt Pearson, one of Connor's junior teammates on the varsity soccer team. He's never been the brightest bulb in the chandelier. Don't get me wrong; I like him a lot more than I like most of Connor's hangers-on. Matt started out as kind of a prick, but the regulating mechanism of middle school reforged him into the kind of jock teddy bear who chooses kindness more often than not. I'm not sure if he does that because of some innate goodness or if he's genuinely not smart enough to be mean. Either way, I don't mind sitting with him at Connor's lunch table.

Also, he plays *GLO*. I can't actually connect with him on that front because showing a single iota of familiarity with the game would raise too many questions, but hearing him talk about it reminds me the gaming landscape is a normal place to be and not, as my parents assume, a Hieronymus Bosch painting full of deadbeats.

The door to the admissions suite opens up, and I look over to see Matt emerge with a short stack of papers in his hand and "I just saw a naked ghost" eyes.

"Whoa, dude, you okay? Did you get Grimes? Is he the worst? You can tell me if he sucks."

Matt looks startled to see me sitting in the chair next to the door. He might have thought he was the last person in for advising since it's almost time for the school day to end, but I had my reasons for booking my appointment this late.

"Hey, Emilia! Um, nah, I got Butler. She's scary. Apparently, I'm really behind on this stuff? She gave me homework."

"Homework from an advising session, that sucks."

"I'm supposed to look up the schools on this list she gave me." He waves the papers in his hand. I can't get a good look at whatever he's holding, but for Matt's sake, I hope it's a short list.

"Um, by the way," Matt continues, "you know your mom's in there, right?"

She is *what*? I specifically picked Thursday for my advisor meeting because I knew she had booster club before field hockey this afternoon. Come on, Matt, be wrong. You're wrong so much; do it again, please. For me.

"Wait, are you sure? My mom? Mrs. Romero, Coach Romero, is in there right now?"

Matt looks back at the door like that's going to help him clarify if the woman he saw in the office was in fact my own mother. "Pretty sure. She's kinda hot, right?"

"You're gross."

"Everyone says it."

"Everyone's gross!"

Here lies another one of the downsides of having my mom be the field hockey coach at my school. Ever since she took over the job when I was in ninth grade, there's always someone who thinks I need to know what they think about her. And what they think is that she's a MILF. No, I didn't develop any issues around that. Why would anyone ask me that? It's just another way my mom dazzles the world with no effort and I have to live up to every day of my life.

"She's with Grimes, so you probably got him, if that makes you feel any better. He looks cool." Matt looks at the papers in his hand again. "Butler's not cool."

Poor baby. It's not his fault his primary talents are kicking a ball and being sweet.

"You're gonna be fine, Matt. I'm serious. There's a website where you can compare your grades with target schools. I'll text it to you tonight."

"Thanks, Lia. Good luck in there."

The admissions suite is one very big office chopped up with glass walls to create three clear boxes, like weird, little fish tanks that house frustrated adult mentor figures instead of blue tangs. When I walk in, I immediately see my mom in the tank on the left, chatting up a guy I assume is Mr. Grimes. On the desk in front of her is a black binder that is suspiciously identical to mine. If I had to guess, it's also color coded and packed with fancy thick paper. She spots me before Grimes does and waves me in.

"Emilia! Come in, I want you to meet Louis Grimes."

I should have expected this. Sure, it would have been nice to get a text or a call, but my mother's strategy when it comes to my college process (and everything else in life) is to always stay two steps ahead of me.

"Mom! What are you doing here? I thought you had booster club."

I know what she's doing here. She knows what she's doing here. The mice in the cafeteria kitchen know what she's doing here.

"I bailed," she says with a conspirator's smile. "You know how those booster parents are. This is a much better use of our time."

I learned a long time ago it's a billion times easier to just give my mom what she wants. I could whine about taking too many AP classes, or I could shut up and take the tests. I could tell her I hate everything about field hockey, or I can practice for seven years straight and let her frame my varsity patches for the wall in her office. As long as she gets results, I'm free to handle the how. Mostly.

"That's . . . great, Mom. Hi, Mr. Grimes. I'm guessing she's already told you about my schools?"

Mr. Grimes doesn't look like a "Mr. Grimes." I was expecting a weird, tired-looking dude with a bald spot and dad glasses, but he's young, with long brown hair pulled back in a man bun and a shiny beard that he clearly oils on the daily. I'm surprised the school lets him look as hip as he does. They probably wanted their new college advisor to look more accessible to the students, but he honestly looks like a drawing of White Jesus from a children's illustrated Bible.

And Jesus said, let the little children manifest their latent anxiety disorders when they don't get into NYU. Amen.

"Nice to meet you, Miss Romero." He gestures to the chair next to my mom's and—good lord—is he wearing a leather bracelet? "Your mom was just telling me about UPenn. Great school."

Ah, she did beat me to it. I don't think UPenn is a long shot, but if I had a choice I'd probably go to a different state for college. There's only so much Pennsylvania a girl can take, and I've got a year and a half left in me, tops. My parents made it my number one choice on the strength of it being my dad's alma mater.

"Right. UPenn." I take the seat Grimes offers and smile up at my mom. I had hoped to get his opinion on what other schools he thought I might qualify for, but with her here, I can tell this entire conversation is going to be about green castles and free laundry. "Do you think it's wor—"

"As I was saying, my husband is an alumnus, so we're taking Emilia to visit with some of his old professors in the spring. Her grades are on par with the last five years' accepted students list, her SATs are a little lower than their average, but we're proactive in working on it."

What's it like, I wonder, to get a word in edgewise? I've given up on knowing. My SAT score is fine. I prep on the side when I can fit it in. Besides, for admissions it's more useful to look at the median, not the average. See? I know how math works.

While I'm thinking about that particular layer of deception, Grimes is looking over the binder my mom brought. I have a sinking feeling he's not going to get anywhere near mine, which is probably a good thing considering the colleges on my list aren't something I'm ready to share with my mom.

"She's a model student, that's for sure. High grades, the right extracurriculars. I'd say she's right on target for UPenn, but there's obviously no promises."

She is sitting right in front of you, but sure, talk to my mom instead of me. It's only my future on the line here. Come on, Louis.

"Well, there's my husband," my mom repeats, as if Grimes missed the first time she name-dropped him, "and Emilia's adding student government to her resume this year. She's running for vice president with Penny Darwin." She turns to smile at me, performing the proud mama act entirely for Grimes's benefit. My mom is playing at something that I can't put my finger on. She's putting too much out there, acting overeager instead of exacting. I smile back at her. Better to play along.

"Oh, and she's junior captain of the field hockey team. Emilia's been playing since fifth grade," Mom adds.

"Field hockey is perfect." Grimes nods. "You know, my college roommate works in the athletics office at UPenn. He can get her on a preliminary recruitment list. If"—and for only the second time in this meeting, Grimes actually addresses me—"that's something you would be interested in?"

"I—"

"Of course we'd be interested! Thank you so much, Louis."

My mom lowers her eyes and looks almost embarrassed to have brought it up. If Grimes believes this, he has an eggplant for a brain. "I was reluctant to reach out considering my conflict of interest; what do you think we should do going forward? Would your friend need a highlight reel or maybe want to organize a visit?"

There it is. My mom didn't come to this meeting to impress Mr. Grimes or, god forbid, support me in my first advisor meeting. She's here to talk Grimes in circles until he does what she can't. It would look mega weird if the field hockey coach called up UPenn to advocate for her own daughter, but since parents aren't supposed to be involved in advisor meetings, Grimes can bring me up with their coach without it looking nepotistic.

I'm mad at how smart she is sometimes. I mean I had to get it from somewhere, but still, damn.

"I'd be happy to ask him what other students have submitted. A reel would certainly give Emilia an edge. As for the other schools on this list, I'm sure we'll have time to talk about them in our next meeting. I think you've laid wonderful groundwork for Emilia. I'd be surprised if she didn't make an impression in early admissions."

"That's wonderful news," my mom says, covering up my halfhearted attempt to ask about regular admission. With any luck, my mom will consider her job done after this meeting and not come to the next one, so I can actually ask Grimes the questions I have about college. I've lost this battle, though, so when Grimes stands up to shake my mom's hand (and mine, which actually surprises me), I put on my happy face and let him usher both of us out. He seems like a nice guy, and by nice guy I mean an easy mark.

"So that was slick," I say once the door to the advisors' suite is closed behind my mom and me. My mom couldn't look more pleased with herself if she had just pulled off a diamond heist. "Wait, let me figure it out. You . . . trawled his Facebook and found out his old roommate works for UPenn?"

"It's called strategy," she answers. "I hope you learned something from that."

Because I know nothing of strategy. I'm just the girl who stays up all night memorizing five-person battle formations and competition videos from rival *GLO* teams. Byunki has all of us looking over three of the teams we might run up against in the tournament. One of the teams I'm covering, Team Unity, doesn't have any video online, though, so I only have to cover two. He told me not to worry about it; Unity doesn't have a chance to make it into the finals.

But yeah, no, I'm dumb as hell. Never thought ahead a day in my life.

"Can I pick the soundtrack for my highlight reel? I'm thinking 100 gecs."

"I have no idea what that is. Your father can edit the reel once we"—Mom reaches into her Trader Joe's burlap tote bag and pulls out an expensive-looking DSLR that I'm sure is video capable and somehow written off as a business expense for my dad's VPN company—"get enough footage from practices and games."

"Oh, we're starting now? Like now, now?"

"Romeros don't lose, and we don't waste time. We'll check the light and see which side of the field you favor. And maybe record something today if you're up to it."

Fine, fine. This is all fine, as long as I'm free for the first round of the tournament this weekend. "Yeah, sure. I can bring it at practice today. I'll check a little, score a little. Whatever you want."

"That's what I like to hear. Get dressed; I'm going to stop by the end of the booster meeting and meet you outside."

All of the other girls on the team are finished getting ready by the time I hustle to the locker room, so I have a few minutes to cool off before I have to reenter the spotlight as Emilia Romero: person who cares about field hockey. I know that my mom sitting in on my first meeting with Grimes isn't the end of the world, and I'll probably have another opportunity to ask him about schools in New York and Chicago, but the fact that she was able to ambush me makes me feel stupid. If my mom were an enemy DPS in *GLO* and she pulled that kind of surprise in a match, Fury would roast me for days.

Since I know I'm going to be on camera, I pull my hair back in a ponytail instead of twisting it into a bun. Normally my curls flopping around my neck would distract me, but having a distinctive hair pattern will make me stand out more on-screen. I hate that I'm thinking about that, but it's the kind of thing my mom would suggest if she was in here helping me get ready. Better to do it now before she can correct me. I can also wear a headband since our school colors are an eye-catching light blue, but if I don't have anything in UPenn navy, I could accidentally look like I'm repping Columbia. Perish the thought.

What would my days be like if I didn't have all of this performative garbage bouncing around in my brain? Quieter, maybe. I'd probably sleep better too.

Out on the field, Mom is already set up with the camera and a tripod that she has produced out of who knows where. As far as I know, she has no prior experience with videography, but that's never stopped her from spontaneously developing a skill before.

"All right, ladies, circle up!" My mom's voice carries across the field and summons everyone to the center. The roll call confirms that we're all here—even Audra Hastings, who threatened to quit for the lacrosse team when she found out Connor asked me out. She's had an obvious crush on him forever and thinks I'm too . . . something (studious? loud? brown?) to date the guy she likes. I'm not 100 percent sure I want Connor to be my boyfriend, but if him buying me matcha pisses her off so much, I don't mind seeing where this goes. Audra can buy her own coffees and also eat shit.

My mom in coach mode is a sight to behold. She's shorter than most of the girls on the team but shouts with all the authority of a drill sergeant. A lot of the girls on the varsity team like her because she doubled our win/loss ratio in three years, but there are still a few who complain that she's harsh. To be clear, she is harsh, but you can tell the girls who don't get her are the ones who can, like, call their mom a bitch when their friends are over and feel no fear. You know. White girls.

Coach Mama separates us into two teams I can tell are set up to give my squad an advantage for the camera. She's given me Kendra, who passes to me whenever she gets the chance, and Preeti, the goalkeeper I can never score against. The other players are assigned on the same principle, so Audra (a weak link, let's be honest) is on the other side. We line up, Mom blows the whistle, and the game is on.

Like I do in *GLO*, I play offense in field hockey. Instead of calculating damage and shooting bolts at enemy tanks, my job is to pass this ball out to someone who can run it down the field and line myself up for a shot at the goal. Field hockey doesn't have healers because, uh, magic isn't real, but I guess our defense kind of does the work a healer would do on a *GLO* map. They can't make the offense any less exhausted or make it hurt less when we take a stick to the shins, but they do prioritize giving our damage dealers a shot at scoring. Aw, this metaphor is almost making me excited to play today.

So wait, if DPS is offense and healers are defense, then I guess the goalie is the tank? No, that doesn't 100 percent work. Tanks are strong-ass characters with more health and special abilities than DPSes or healers. They're really hard to kill, which is why taking an enemy tank out is an instant win in *GLO*. We call that method of winning a match a "checkmate." If someone took the other team's goalie out in field hockey, we'd call it a "homicide."

The other method of winning a *GLO* match is more mundane: you have to stake a claim on a payload that's hidden somewhere on the map and stay close enough to it to jack up enough points on a payload timer. If a team member dies or gets pushed too far from the payload, they lose points. You also need every team member alive to get a payload win. To that end, the field hockey ball is the payload. Or it would be if a field hockey ball were made of diamonds and all it took to score was to sit on it while a bunch of wizards and aliens and shit attacked you with a host of elemental magic spells whose effects can be countered with a complex strength/weakness system that depends on which character you're playing and the map's environmental factors.

Yeah, no. *GLO* is so much cooler than field hockey. I really tried something just then, but this game will never get me going the same way sniping fools as Pharaoh does. That doesn't change that I still have to play. Starting now.

I smack the ball out once the whistle goes off and pass to

Julie, who can dribble like no one else on the team, and charge forward to see if I can find a gap in the defense.

"Woo-hoo! Go, Lia! Hit her with your stick thing!"

That's Penny, who I didn't know was coming to practice but am glad to hear from the sidelines anyway. She's bouncing up and down so hard she has to hold her braids in her hand so they don't whip her in the face. I check to see if Connor is with her, but I don't see him there. That's fine. It's nice that he still does other things besides follow me around. My mom objected to me dating Connor when I told her about our accidental first date, but I think she's secretly pleased that I'm dating another varsity player. She thinks we look nice together, and we do, but IMO we looked just as nice when we were just friends hanging out with everyone else.

I quickly scan the other people watching the practice to see if there's anyone else I know. Sometimes guys show up just to watch us do things in shorts, but there aren't that many this time. Well, there's a few. A couple of dudes are camped out on the bleachers, but they're not watching the practice. One of them is Todd Price, who I've known since we were little kids pouring beans in Monteronni, and the other is a guy with dark hair, thick-rimmed glasses, and a T-shirt that— Wait a minute!

His T-shirt is black with a shield design and bluish X across the front. I know that shirt, or at least I know that cross. It doesn't look like something he got in a store; it has mesh sleeves like a sports jersey and something written on the breast pocket. Can't read it from this distance, but that symbol is *so* close to sparking something I feel like I've forgotten. Something really, really important.

I'm still staring at him when he looks back. Oof, now it's weird. I feel like I'm halfway to recognizing him, and because I've been caught, I find myself smiling. Who are you? I'm so close. What a crazy feeling! Isn't he—

That's when Audra wrecks me. Staring at the bleacher guy took longer than I thought, and I miss a pass from Kendra. I react too slowly to snag the ball with the flat of my stick, so the only thing I'm feeling now is a hard weight slamming between my shoulder blades and the muddy grass of the field coming up to meet my face. I have the sense to toss my stick away so I don't break or land on it, but the fall still knocks the wind out of me. The squelch of the wet ground in my ear is gross enough, but grosser still is rolling over and seeing Audra's blond head looming over me with the fakest apology face I have ever seen in my life. She really should stick to sports since Penny has the theater covered.

I'm still on the grass when my mom makes it over to me from the sidelines and offers a hand to pull me up.

"Can you stand? Does anything feel like you can't move it?"

I'm more worried about my wrists, which would be a big injury for field hockey and an even bigger one for *GLO*. I roll them once, twice, and then stretch my fingers. Everything feels fine. Throwing my stick away was a good call.

"We got that on camera, didn't we?" I say to show my mom I'm fine. As long as I got jokes, she'll know I'm not that hurt.

"Big time," Mom replies and peeks over to where the DSLR is still sitting on top of the tripod. I'm dazed, but I can make out the red glow where the recording light is still on. That's not making it into the highlight reel.

"You stopped midswing." She's back in coach mode, trying to make whatever just happened to me into a learning experience for the team now that she knows I haven't broken any bones. "What happened, you cramp up?"

"Yeah," I lie and take one more look at the bleachers to see if the guy in the T-shirt is still there. He's not, but Penny is, and I can hear her cussing out Audra in some gorgeously colorful terms. "My arm seized up, and I couldn't follow through, and then Au—"

Audra interrupts me to save her own butt. "I thought she was shielding and couldn't stop on time. I slid right into her, and I'm so, so sorry, Coach Romero. You sure you're okay?"

I was not shielding. Audra attacking offense from behind would be a foul and a green card in a real game. She's lucky my mom was too distracted by the camera to see what actually happened. Still, there's no point in being pulled into the athletics office for a talk about leaving drama off the field.

Nothing can make this practice go over; my time with Fury tonight is too important.

"It's cool. I didn't mean to shield; the cramp just froze me. So, you know. No harm, *no foul*."

Audra rolls her eyes at me behind my mom's back, and I give her nothing in return. She's lucky she didn't hurt my wrists and mess up my chance to play in the tournament this weekend. Whatever beef she has with me over Connor is completely one-sided, and I simply do not have the bandwidth to engage with her low-grade bitchery for the sake of a guy.

Guy! Who was that guy on the bleachers? Preeti helps me up, and the first thing I do is scan again to see if he's still there. I hate the feeling when I can't grab the information I want from my usually organized brain. I just need to get one more look at him, and I know I'll be able to put the pieces together.

But he's gone.

CHAPTER FOUR

Team Unity, Friday

[*Team Unity has exited the map. Queue again?*]

BobTheeQ: Nice job, team!

shineedancer: ahhhh we're gonna kill it tomorrow!!!

ElementalP: you're all welcome for the HEALS

JHoops: half of those were mine but go off I guess

BobTheeQ: Jake, P, you're both pretty.

ElementalP: pretty good HEALERS

MUDD: i wish we were up against fury tomorrow we'd destroy them

BobTheeQ: I'm feeling good, glad everyone else is feeling good. P and shinee are you both set to carpool?

shineedancer: the jersey girls are ready 2 road trip. we got pocky.

MUDD: i'm riding with my friend who got tickets

JHoops: I . . . got the bus schedule

ElementalP: ruh roh

BobTheeQ: What happened to your dad driving you?

JHoops: arghhh

JHoops: we had a fight

JHoops: my Spanish teacher sent him an email about my test scores and he thinks GLO is making me dumber

BobTheeQ: I'm sure he doesn't think that.

MUDD: you can't get any dumber

ElementalP: MUDDY I SWEAR TO GOD

shineedancer: no bby jake are you ok

JHoops: i had a pretty good week so I can take it

BobTheeQ: Good week!

ElementalP: DO TELL

JHoops: KOD smiled at me

MUDD: so are we thinking a spring wedding or do you wanna wait for June

JHoops: i mean she kind of smiled? i was watching her play field hockey and she looked over at me like she kind of knew who i was and I was like 'omg she's looking at me' and then she fell down in a bunch of mud and I ran away

MUDD: lmaoooooo

ElementalP: she's human after all

BobTheeQ: Well, that's certainly something to talk to her about. After tomorrow.

JHoops: idk it kind of made my week

shineedancer: you're so cute I could murder you

JHoops: so cute you'll swing by Hillford and give me a ride?

shineedancer: lol no you are so out of our way

ElementalP: but we love you

shineedancer: and we think you're smart, right muddy?

MUDD: so smart

BobTheeQ: Keep your head up, man. You've been on fire, everyone's been on fire this week. Don't be late tomorrow. I'll meet you at the gate and I will be wearing the hat.

BobTheeQ: Wear the jerseys.

BobTheeQ: Bring the lint brush.

MUDD: very important ^^^

BobTheeQ: Get some sleep fam. We got winning to do in the morning.

CHAPTER FIVE

Emilia, Round I, Saturday

A FEW THINGS I'm learning at my first *GLO* tournament:

1. There are a lot more people interested in watching this than I thought there would be. The Wizzard-Claricom Arena is huge and so new it still smells like paint, but there have to be thousands of people here for the opening day of the competition. I know because I pushed through most of them to get to the front door before Byunki texted and told me teams were going through the back like *real-ass athletes*.

2. Should have expected this one, but a lot of people are surprised that I'm a girl? I tried not to get caught up in how Byunki was marketing my debut because that's a recipe for me getting crushed under pressure, but he didn't tell anyone that Fury's new DPS was a woman, and that's going to be a weird reveal

when it happens. I also learned Byunki lives for
drama. I'm going to make that point 2.a.

3. People are loud as hell at these things. Everyone
   plays with noise-cancelling headphones so we should
   only be able to hear each other, but I can hear the
   crowd even backstage, and the sound is incredible.
   I think that if my parents could see what a huge deal
   this tournament is, they might actually be impressed.
   I mean, they won't, there's no reason they'll ever see
   me play, but it's still cool as hell.

To be blunt, my parents would hit the roof if they found out
how much time I spend playing *GLO* or doing literally anything that isn't going to help get me into college. They didn't
have money growing up and sacrificed to give me every
advantage—my mom missed her own mother's funeral for a
job interview at the Monteronni school I attended when I was
a kid, because teaching there would mean free tuition at the
state's best Head Start program. My dad worked full time for
decades, taking a 5 a.m. train every morning to New York
while building his VPN company on the side before he could
quit and support his own business. Squandering an inch of
the headway they earned is like crapping on my abuela's grave
while telling the two hardest-working Puerto Ricans in Pennsylvania that they've wasted their entire lives.

Of course the risk of my parents finding out that I'm here

is fairly low. I told my mom I was heading out early to meet Penny at Starbucks for a campaign meeting and told Penny I needed her to cover for me for something "personal," which she assumed was Connor adjacent and didn't interrogate further. I hate lying to both of them and won't sleep tonight to make up the campaign work for tomorrow, but so far so good. I can totally keep this going as long as nothing unexpected happens. Right now all I have to worry about is waiting in the green room the arena assigned Fury for the tournament.

I feel like I knew empirically that green rooms aren't actually green, but it was still kind of a bummer to walk in and see that we're basically quartered in a windowless basement room. The walls are white concrete, there's some grayish bargain carpet on the floor, and the only furniture they gave teams to start is an L-shaped couch, a coffee table, a mounted TV screen to watch the live feed from the stage, and a whiteboard with a new box of markers.

I didn't expect them to roll out the red carpet for a bunch of amateur teams, but I'm sure it will be different once they start using the arena for professional matches. Maybe we get an upgrade every time we progress in the tournament like in *Animal Crossing*. Banners and little trophies and stuff. At least our jerseys look official. Wizzard sent all the teams a link on where to get them so we'd all look professional onstage, but we had to pay for them ourselves. Byunki covered ours, because he's the best.

I really wish Byunki would hurry up and get to the green room. I'm getting antsy sitting here by myself. I can hear other players and staff walking around in the hallway, and I don't want anyone else to accidentally walk in and see me. Even if they assumed I belonged here, every interaction backstage seems like another way someone can get my real name out of me or ask me questions I really don't want to answer. I'd feel better if the rest of Fury were here. They're a lot more interesting than me. If any one of them showed up, I could parry any attention right back toward them, just like Byunki promised he'd do when I told him I was worried about showing up today.

I know that seems very dramatic, but I really do have my reasons. Aside from my parents is the issue of being, you know, a girl competing in an esports tournament. I'm well aware of what just showing up here could do to Fury and my online life, which is why I need Byunki to protect me.

If the greater *GLO* community doesn't know who I really am, the worst of them won't be able to find me. When I first started playing *GLO*, I loved everything about this game. The characters, the strategy, and the players themselves too. For a while it was enough to be good. I got invited to waiting rooms with people I watched all the time on Twitch, played some matches with absolute legends, and made friends all over the server on Discord. It wasn't until I bought my first headset and got on voice that everything changed for the worse.

It was stupid. *I* was stupid. I thought they wouldn't care

that I was a girl, but the second those same players heard me speak, my inbox transformed into the online equivalent of Dante's second, fifth, and seventh circles of hell. I was four- teen, man; I didn't need to know what that many different dudes' dicks looked like. My dad's entire business is internet privacy, so my IP address was safe, but that didn't stop hun- dreds of men, boys, whoever, really, threatening to hurt me when I beat them in a round, rape me if I got ahead of them on the leaderboard, and track me down if I dared report or block them. I don't even know what they would have done if I still had an accent like my mom or if they knew I wasn't white.

It was light-years beyond anything else I'd experienced, which is saying something considering the residents of Hill- ford aren't the most enlightened Philly-adjacent suburbanites in America. When I created a new account and started over, I stayed off voice entirely and didn't say anything that hinted I was a girl. Some of the same guys who harassed me even tried to play with me again, not knowing the person whupping their butts was the girl they tried to drown in hardcore porn GIFs a month earlier. Nobody suspected anything, I kept hav- ing fun, and one day Byunki DMed me with an offer to try out for Team Fury's new DPS slot.

Showing my face at the tournament is dangerous, but Byunki promised he'd never leak my real gamertag or name to anyone, not even press who wanted to cover Fury. He made everyone else promise too. The rest of the team uses some form of their real name in their competition titles—JOON, YUNG, VANE, RIKK—but I came up with something that had nothing to do with Emilia Romero. KNOX. Like Fort Knox, where no one gets inside and everything important is under guard.

I need my guards here now. Why aren't they here yet? Is it really hot in here, or is it just me? Why don't they put these green rooms on the ground level so we can have a window to open? I bet this is a fire hazard. Oh my god, I'm sitting on a polyester couch in a fire hazard.

No you're not, I think. *You're panicking. It's different. This is something you can control.*

Under normal circumstances, meeting the most impressive *GLO* player in the game who also is giving you the chance of a lifetime at the expense of his own reputation would not be a thing that calms me down, but the sudden sound of Byunki's voice outside the door snaps me out of my budding panic spiral.

"Are you sure this is right?" He sounds different without the distortion of voice chat, but I'd recognize his tone anywhere. Even when Byunki asks a question, it's phrased like a military order. "This room is too far from the stage. Do you know who I am? Who this team is?"

I can't hear what the arena aide tells him next, but it doesn't make him sound any happier.

"It's fine, man," says another voice I recognize. Ivan, the

other Fury DPS. I stepped in as his new partner on damage after Byunki kicked a guy he'd been playing with for years off the team. I thought he might be salty about it, but honestly Ivan's been nicer to me than anyone else on the team. It totally tracks that he'd be trying to smooth this situation over. He's known Byunki the longest out of all of us.

I instinctively stand up when Byunki and Ivan finally enter. Byunki gives me a quick up-and-down look and nods. Ivan, sweet Ivan, is generous enough to smile.

"Emilia!" Ivan says, and walks over to give me a hug.

"KNOX," Byunki corrects. "She's our little secret, remember?"

"Right. Duh!" Ivan peels off a leather jacket and tosses it over the back of the couch. He strikes me as the kind of person who could be comfortable anywhere. He looks good in our Fury jersey (competition name: VANE), like one of the quidditch world cup players from *Harry Potter*. Dark hair, massive eyebrows. Yeah, Ivan's our Krum. "I forgot you're, like, super paranoid."

"I'm not—" I try to defend myself even though I know he's just teasing me. Byunki cuts me off before I can.

"She's got reasons," he says brusquely. He's out of his jacket now too and looks authoritative in Fury red as well. Byunki's smaller than I thought he would be. His usually black hair is blond on top, a change from his streaming look that I'm sure he intends to debut onstage today, and the new look suits him well. He looks severe, deadly even. And short. Napoleon by way of South Korea.

"I do," I answer in agreement with Byunki. "I'm down for this as long as no one knows anything about me."

"No, I like it," Ivan answers. "It's mysterious. It'll play well, right, B?"

Byunki doesn't answer.

The door to the green room swings open again to reveal the last two members of Team Fury. Han-Jun and Erik are our healers. They're a dream team that came up in *GLO* together and can team heal like actual combat medics.

"Your lifelines have arrived," Han-Jun announces before falling in to hug Ivan and salute Byunki.

"Hey, it's the new Arjun!" Erik points to me. I don't know much about Fury's old DPS. Ivan told me Byunki waited less than a week to replace him with me this summer. Am I the new Arjun? I'd rather be the first Emilia. "Can I call you Knoxy?"

Knoxy? Thanks, I hate it.

"Maybe!" I answer with a smile anyway. These guys are legends, and I'm starting at the bottom. I have to earn my way up to having an opinion on my nickname.

"Everyone's here. That's good. Shut up," Byunki barks. Han-Jun and Erik haven't even taken off their jackets yet, but he gestures for them to sit down. I glance over at Ivan to see if that's a normal way to start our first team meeting. He rolls his eyes and moves over to give me a place on the couch next to him. Okay, so this is normal. That's cool. Just wanted to know. Byunki takes his place at the whiteboard and rips open the marker box to start scribbling on the board.

"We're up against a low seed in round one. Team Vulcan. They're morons. That means Wizzard expects us to win. If this competition was online, I'd tell us to sandbag to keep some of our big moves under wraps for Round Two, but we're not doing that. We are going big. There's no point in keeping our profile low anymore. This is going online. Could mean sponsorships, could mean global attention."

I mean, yes, but also please keep *my* profile low. I'm here to win, not to plot a sponcon pivot.

Byunki writes a series of *GLO* character names on the board and draws a question mark next to the list. "The meta jacked a lot of rosters up, so we can't count on knowing which characters Vulcan will play." I genuinely can't tell if this is a motivational speech or marching orders. Thrilled to find out, though. The panic I was feeling before is transmuting into excitement. I'm really here! In a green room with the rest of Team Fury! Ivan just passed me a little plastic beanbag, and I don't know what that's about, but I'm excited about that too!

"They won't have a Pharaoh," Ivan says. He seems to be the only one with enough authority to interrupt Byunki. "Their whole team is a bunch of PVE streamers who play popular characters. They didn't make time to get good on him."

Vulcan was one of the teams I had to study going into the first round, so it might not be terrible if I drop some knowledge on our pregame chat.

"They're good on cooldowns," I say with all the courage I can muster. It strikes me that I don't have to feel brave. I'm right, and that's better than being brave. "But their cooperation is garbage. Everyone on Vulcan plays like the spotlight is only on them. I've never seen them pull off a sophisticated combo, so we should pick out a few of our best to scare them straight out the gate. If they see us doing something they can't do, they'll get insecure. You know, because they're streamers."

Han-Jun and Erik turn to look at me like I'm a toy they forgot made noise. Ivan, however, is smirking.

"She's right," Ivan says. He reaches into my lap to pull out the plastic beanbag he gave me and smacks it between his palms with a loud popping noise. "It's a hand warmer. You have to break it first. Keeps the fingers limber? You're doing great."

"Speaking as a streamer," Byunki begins. My eyes go wide. Did I just totally insult him? He has to know I wasn't calling him insecure. He's the most secure person I think I've ever encountered. He's a shield of a person, a tank in every sense of the word. "KNOX is right. Let's do that parachute move to give her a look at the map to see if she can spot the payload first. We'd need Pharaoh, which we have, and one of the healers would have to play Jenkins. Erik, you wanna play Jenkins?"

Erik looks as surprised as I do that Byunki agreed with me. He stammers when he lets Byunki know that he's good to play as Jenkins this round.

"Dope. I'm playing Klio, obviously, fire tank has the best loadout. Ivan, you're on Morrigan. Han-Jun, you're Glace. I need that ice protection."

"On it," Han-Jun replies. Now that Ivan's popped my hand warmer, it does feel pretty good on my fingers. I sneak a peek over at how he's using it to do some hand stretches and start copying his movements. An arena staff member knocks on our green room door to let us know we're playing next. Byunki starts talking faster.

"We're aiming for a checkmate, so taking down their tank is the name of the game. I have a feeling they're going to play Lucafont in the tank position. His health is high, but we can whittle it down. He's a ghost and Pharaoh is magic, so he'll be weak to KNOX." He turns to address me directly, which feels very cool now that I'm sure he's not mad. "You're on debuffs. If one of their healers tries to boost team health, focus on Lucafont and strip his armor. Charge up your Special Attack, but only use Pharaoh's Shatter on my signal, got it? Don't aim early, don't aim late."

"Got it." That's me! I'm on debuffs! I'm here and I'm helping!

"VANE: damage, Bend Time, damage," he continues. "JOON stays with me, and I need RIKK moving fast around the map to heal the rest of you. Use Shadow Step and poof if you see a red dot."

"Fury, you're up!" The people running the tournament are really on top of the timing here. Wizzard's reputation rides on this competition going well. No mistakes allowed.

Byunki was only kind of whining about our green room being far from the stage. We're down a long, awkward ramp that leads up to the backstage holding area, which my field hockey–trained calves can handle but sets Erik and Han-Jun complaining.

"One more thing," Byunki notes when we're lined up. "We're changing our order walking out. Wizzard already knows. Usually the DPS would follow the healers, but I'm going out after Ivan."

That doesn't make any sense. This is the first time I'm competing as Ivan's new partner; why wouldn't we walk out together? Byunki sees the confusion on my face and pats my shoulder.

"Trust me," he says. I guess I do?

The announcers call Vulcan out first—all five of their players get a decent amount of applause from people who know them from Twitch. After that, it's our turn, starting with Han-Jun and Erik. The crowd recognizes them and cheers, but they get louder when Ivan follows them out onto the stage.

Ivan was the better DPS of the two who played for Fury before they recruited me, and I had hoped that walking out alongside him would lend me a little goodwill. Without Ivan by my side, I'm walking out a total stranger.

When Byunki appears, the cheers stop for a half second before resuming—they're exactly as surprised as he wanted them to be.

I'm either going to ride the wave of enthusiasm the audience has for Byunki or be a crushing disappointment, so I give him a few more seconds to soak up his welcome before walking out from the side of the stage. The walk from the wings to my PC setup can't be more than a few yards, but my vision tunnels and makes it seem like I have to make my way across the entire arena in a matter of seconds.

Byunki and I briefly bounced around the idea that I would play in a mask as a gimmicky way to hide my identity, but I'm glad we didn't go with that. Stepping out onstage and being about to see everyone in the audience wouldn't be nearly as exciting if my peripherals were shielded. Even though no one knows who I am, the feeling that I'm about to be cheered by a crowd of strangers who want to see me play *GLO* is a huge rush—finally, I can show people that I belong here, that I'm good at this game and can keep up with Fury on my own merit. I take a deep breath. This is it. No going back now.

The stage lights hit me, and I think for a moment that I've gone deaf. There's no sound, just light and the rest of my team waiting for me to move. Why can't I hear? Penny told me about all the ways she's had stage fright over the years, and she never mentioned not being able to hear.

Wait, no, my ears are fine. It's the arena that's silent. I can't stop myself from shading my eyes and staring out at them, a crowd of thousands all holding their cell phones in front of their faces to record my entrance. I look away from them and toward the back of the stage, where my just-revealed Fury portrait is lit up in massive LED perfection and my new, four-letter competition name written right below it.

#4. KNOX. DPS.

CHAPTER SIX

Team Unity, Saturday

MUDD: where'd you guys go? fury is about to play

JHoops: i lost everyone i'm in the players box

BobTheeQ: I'm backstage, S and P were hungry and we have another hour so I told them to fuel up.

MUDD: didn't pack enough pocky eh

BobTheeQ: I got a screen back here, Fury's rolling out.

JHoops: JOON and RIKK are out.

MUDD: I'm way in the back, is that VANE?

BobTheeQ: Yup VANE. The new DPS should be out next. I couldn't get anything on him. Really curious to see who they got after Fury kicked Arjun out. Arjun and Ivan were legendary together.

BobTheeQ: Wait no that's Byunki.

[Languagebot: language.]

JHoops: did you seriously add his name to languagebot

BobTheeQ: I forgot I did but I did lol.

JHoops: cmon cmon show us the new guy

MUDD: WHAAAA

BobTheeQ: Didn't expect that!

MUDD: what the hell is a KNOX

BobTheeQ: I never thought Fury would play with a girl, anyone heard of her?

BobTheeQ: Anyone?

JHoops: i have

MUDD: you played with her?

JHoops: not GLO

BobTheeQ: You know her???

JHoops: kinda

JHoops: guys KNOX is KOD

MUDD: no

ElementalP: KNOX IS KOD??? Sorry I'm backreading.

shineedancer: oh my god???

ElementalP: Jake where are you we're coming over we have fries

ElementalP: I got Ki we're on our way to the box

JHoops: i'm leaving the box i need a minute

BobTheeQ: Do you want to come backstage? You want to talk?

MUDD: I got to the box he's not here. Q is he with you?

BobTheeQ: He's not here. Jake is MIA.

CHAPTER SEVEN

Emilia, Saturday

BYUNKI WANTED ME to be a surprise, but I wasn't prepared to stun everyone into silence. Other teams have girls. One other team, I think. They have two. It's not that weird for me to be here, is it? Is it because it's Fury?

I hear a couple of girls start it. I can't tell exactly where they are in the arena, maybe up in the players' box, but their chant punches through the quiet that's frozen me to my spot on the stage. "KNOX. KNOX. KNOX. KNOX."

Yeah, wow. I don't have anything to say as the chant catches on. Compared to the silence before, this is louder than anything I've ever heard in my life. I feel my feet vibrating as the stage shakes; they're stomping and yelling—in a good way!—and chanting my name. They're shouting for KNOX, and that means they're shouting for *me*.

What happens now? I smile and wave, I guess? Moving my arm makes moving my legs easier, and I can finally start walking again. Behind me is my own face blown up to the size of a brownstone, and I'm seized with a cheesy impulse to point to it like "Yo, would you look at that? That's a lady up there!" and when I do the crowd amps up to absolutely wild sonic proportions. By the time I get to my seat, I'm beaming, and Ivan is here to clap me on the shoulder. We are the New New. Fury DPS: ready to rock.

Byunki gives the signal, and we lift our headphones up to our ears—in an instant, the roar of the crowd is gone and replaced with the hum of noise cancellation and team chatter.

"Back in, focus, we have a countdown"—that's Byunki calling us in. The screens around the arenas light up with a digital clock ticking down to the start of the match. On the other side of the stage, Team Vulcan, I'm happy to say, looks shook. Who's trending now, Twitchbois?

Each time a number clicks away, I can feel myself sliding further into the place in my mind I go whenever I log into *GLO*. I'm hyperaware of my fingers tracing over the ball of my gaming mouse, feeling it roll in a beautifully familiar way. The monitor zooms in to fill my line of sight, locking out the glow of cell phones and the bright arena screens. The headphones help, but the way I drop into the world onscreen is something I've always been able to do with games. There are just the buttons, my eyes, my hands, and the instantaneous connections firing between them all. The clock hits zero. Showtime.

We land on the Frye Island map, a tropical location that's meant to look like a post-apocalyptic Hawaii, if Hawaii were populated by space warriors and alien wizards. I know this map like the back of my hand and feel good about being able to pilot Pharaoh around it.

Byunki gives us our first orders. "Luca tank. KNOX is up."

YES, the other team went with Lucafont. I can't see where he is, and since we're both trying to capture a wandering payload, I'll need a better look to see where he might be going.

Pharaoh isn't the most mobile character, but he piggybacks well with other people's abilities. I whistle for Erik, and he obliges, using his healer Jenkins's cannon to send me up and over the map. Pan down, two-second aerial view before I land. Lucafont spotted on the Celestial Beach.

"Beach, coming east," I report.

I let Pharaoh deploy his parachute beyond their Lucafont and cast a three-second fog that keeps me from his line of sight. I get two hits in—not enough to fill my meter but enough to claim first blood of the match, which starts Fury's Special Attack counter before Vulcan's. The team that hits first always gets a boost, and the more damage we deal, the faster we earn more points toward deploying our best abilities. Now the rest of the game can start.

I dip out from the beach and start darting around the map according to Byunki's instructions, counting down the milliseconds until I can pop my stealth fog ability and hack away at Vulcan's other members. I mistime it once and take a few shots, but Erik is doing a great job keeping Ivan and me alive. Byunki clicks his tongue into the mic, telling us his Klio tank has the payload in sight.

Both Fury and Vulcan race to the center of the map, a weird, little island made of crystals surrounded by a doughnut-shaped lake. Han-Jun uses some of his Special Attack bar to generate a heal/harm barrier, which tops up our health but will damage anyone from Vulcan who tries to cross it—like this guy is right now.

The Vulcan DPS loses control of his character and slides into Han-Jun's wall, earning himself a nice hot cup of murder. One down, four to go. Or one, if we get their Lucafont in a tank kill. That's an instant checkmate in *GLO*, which is why all of their tank characters are crazy overpowered in the health department.

Lucafont's a ghost character, which means he's weak to Pharaoh's necromagic. He's going to do everything he can to take me out first, and I have zero intention of letting him. He spots me through the wall and pauses for a second, probably timing the cooldown from Han-Jun's deployment, and nails his lunge perfectly. He'd have taken me out if Erik didn't Shadow Step my Pharaoh away like a dad shoving a stroller out from in front of a speeding car; he takes a huge hit in the process. Han-Jun is busy keeping Byunki alive closer to the payload, and Erik's self-heal isn't ready yet. He'll go down if I don't strip Luca.

Without waiting for Byunki's signal, I start hammering at the tank's armor with Pharaoh's relatively weak dagger attack. My special isn't charged yet, but Ivan gets a kill on one of the Vulcan healers and bumps up all of our bars. Ivan, I love you. Thanks for the hand warmers.

"KNOX, stop. Let Erik get his timer back," Byunki grunts through the exertion of manning Klio.

I can't do that. A quick glance up at my team health shows Han-Jun has used too many heals in the last minute and has depleted his mana. Byunki is babysitting the payload, which is transferring ownership to Fury way too slowly. One of Vulcan's DPSes is trying to take him down, but Byunki has his shields up every fraction of a second, parrying his attacks. We're going to lose Han-Jun, and a red flash on the side of my screen tells me Erik is next in line for a drop. Without healers, we're toast.

I fog one more time and slide over to Byunki's attacker, spiking him with a death magic spell that paralyzes him for just enough time to fog back and face Lucafont. Erik dies, but the length of my spell charges me one more tick toward my Special.

Han-Jun throws his last heal at Byunki and drops. With no more heals available, Ivan goes nuts around the perimeter of the payload, hitting his Bend Time Special and cutting down both a Vulcan DPS and a healer—an incredible play, but Lucafont turns from the payload and takes him out with *his* Special, Ectoplasmic Chains.

I really, really hate ghost characters, and we're running out of time. With me and Byunki up against the two remaining Vulcans, it's not looking great. Fury isn't going to lose this match. I won't let Fury lose in the first round.

Time for a Hail Mary. I ping a ranged shot at Lucafont, which doesn't do much damage but certainly gets his attention; he whirls on me like a cat that just felt a toddler yank his tail. Oh, did you think I meant to hurt you with that? Look again, a-hole. My Shatter is *charged*.

So I hit it. Purple magic explodes from my crossbow, and the charged bolt turns Luca's silvery armor to glitter. Byunki swings for the final blow but misses by a millimeter, so I take the kill shot. Lucafont goes down.

In the absence of their tank, Vulcan auto-surrenders the payload to Fury and we win the match. Ivan leaps up next to me and yanks his headphones off to strike a victory pose. I can't hear a word he's saying, but he's grabbing my arm and pulling me up to a standing position. Han-Jun and Erik are up too, making gestures around their ears and looking at me expectantly. Noise cancellation! I don't need that anymore.

When I lift my headset off, the noise from the arena almost knocks me back into my seat. Every one of the dozens of gigantic screens is alternating between showing Fury's logo and the three coolest words I've ever read in my life. TANK KILL: KNOX.

That's what the crowd is still shouting when Fury heads backstage, "Tank Kill: KNOX." We basically clamor all over each other as we follow Byunki through the arena's staging area, just an absolute conga line of arm rubs, high fives, and shaking each other by the shoulders while jumping around (I thought that only happened in sports movies, but nope; it's happening IRL). This feels like love. It's teamwork! We are Fury, and I'm a part of this. I could either vomit or fly, whichever one feels more plausible.

Han-Jun, Erik, Ivan, and I have not calmed down by the time we get back to the green room, which makes sense because we just showed everyone why Fury belongs on top.

"Ivan, you got two with one Special!" Han exclaims.

"Not gonna lie; I thought we were going down." Ivan's looking at me like I'm made of solid gold.

"A checkmate on her first match! KNOX got a checkmate on her *first match*." I could do without Erik's disbelieving tone, but I'll take the accolades where I can get them. "How did you even know to pull the Shatter right then?"

"I didn't even think before I did it! I was just like 'he gotta *go*' and then WHAM." That's me, talking somehow even though my mouth feels like it belongs to someone else. My usual level of articulation has been substantially reduced by the sheer volume of adrenaline swishing through my bloodstream.

"Well, you killed it," Ivan admits. "KNOX for the win."

"KNOX didn't listen to instructions."

Byunki's voice slices through the chatter as he marches his tiny, imposing body up to me in the room. He has his finger pointed at my chest, like he's actually Klio jabbing me in the heart with his segmented sword.

"I told you not to Shatter until my signal. You didn't listen. And you took the last shot before I could hit my Special. You stole *my* tank kill."

I, um. Don't do great when I'm being yelled at. Chalk it up to my parents having forceful personalities and my need for everyone who isn't Audra Hastings to like me. There's just this feeling I get when people sound mad, even if they're not mad at me, that makes my whole midsection seize up like I'm expecting a punch. When someone actually is mad at me, it's worse because my problem-solving brain bisects into the half that wants to throw down a handful of smoke powder and disappear and the half that wants to burst into tears.

It just doesn't make any sense. I won the match for Fury, but Byunki still hates me. All that time I spent drilling Pharaoh's Shatter and every possible move to help Fury win this match and he still doesn't like me. At all. The other guys in Fury are staring at me now. Not even Ivan, who I thought was my boy, has anything to say in my defense.

I really don't want to cry in front of these guys. Please don't let me cry in front of Fury.

"Byunki, I'm sorry. I saw Ivan go down, and I had my Special ready. I didn't see another way."

"It's not your job to see another way; it's your job to take directions! Next time, don't think. You're not good at it. Just do whatever I tell you to do. This isn't the KNOX show. It's Fury, forever."

Yup, there will be tears. Real tears. I need to get out of this green room now. There's nothing left for me to say, and everyone is still quiet, so I run out and take whichever lefts and rights will get me farthest away from Fury and from him. Byunki hates me. I just got here, and I love it so much, and he's going to take it away forever. Is this what completely fucked feels like?

I'm so deep in the backstage of the Wizzard-Claricom Arena I'm not sure I can find my way back without help. This far back there's catering staff and event people passing by every so often, but if any player was looking for a place to be alone, this would be an ideal spot. As I turn another corner, I see a competitor sitting on a folding chair in an empty hallway. I should have guessed I'm not the only one who wants to be alone.

I try to backtrack before he notices, but my sad girl stompy feet give me away. He looks up, sees me . . . and reacts like I just pulled a gun on him. Seriously, he kind of puts his hands up and looks shocked. Relax, nerd, I'm—

"Emilia? Wh-what are you doing back here?"

Wait, what? There's no way a random player should know my name, but something clicks for me when I hear the way he says it. I take a second look at his face and notice his big eyes refracted behind thick glasses, half-remembering his dark hair and imagining it spiked up like a fourth grader instead of falling in shaggy waves. He's taller now, and I haven't seen him in years, but I'd bet my ass that's—

"I'm Jake," he says through what still sounds like panic to me. Now that he sees I'm not going to shoot him with my invisible nothing gun, he repositions one of his raised arms to mess with his hair. That was definitely his plan the whole time, to do that with his hands. It's very convincing.

"Jake Hooper from . . . Todd? Or Emmett's birthday, if you remember." He looks over his shoulder, like he's worried someone else is going to find him talking to me. "I go to Hillford West now. I didn't know you played *GLO*, though."

He goes *where*? It takes a second look for me to put the final pieces of the puzzle together, something I missed in my surprise at finding Jake backstage. His tournament shirt has a blue cross and a black shield. It's the shirt I saw on the guy on the bleachers before I wiped out in practice a couple of days ago. He goes to my high school. Which means he knows me. He knows both of me.

I was wrong. *This* is what completely fucked feels like.

PART II

Jake again, Saturday

SORRY, JAKE NEEDED a minute.

Pretty much the only good thing about being Jake Hooper was that his brain could do this thing where one second stretched out way longer than it was supposed to. Part of it was his thoughts speeding up so he went over a million things at once, and the other part was this super terrible slow-motion perception that reminded him of making a choice at the end of a Telltale game chapter, one of the big choices that changed the ending or forced him to kill off a main character he'd really have preferred to keep alive. Those choices always stressed him out, but Jake refused to cheat by pausing the game and looking up what happened in either case.

That turned out to be a good habit to get into. Slow as these moments stretched, he hadn't figured out how to pause real life yet. Also, there were no helpful Reddit spoiler threads for making story choices like the one he was presented with right now.

On one side of the Telltale decision matrix was Emilia Romero, the exact person whose two-story image he'd fled the players' box to avoid. His surprise at seeing her had made words tumble out of him before he even had a chance to think, and now that he had a moment to recoup, the idea of saying anything else to her seemed ill-advised and entirely terrifying. Jake's vision snagged on Emilia as one possible focus, which seemed indulgent and made him feel as if his rib cage had swapped functions with a beehive. Jake had tried so hard not to look at her when he found out he'd transferred to her school. Just looking made him feel like he was bothering her somehow. Here in the back hallways of the Wizzard Claricom Arena, he couldn't stop himself.

Unless! There was always the other choice. Shut down, tune out, run. There were so many things in the universe that were not Emilia Romero—there were doorways and hiding places, people, ducks, mushrooms, boats maybe—all he had to do was think about literally anything else, and he could postpone this conversation for never, completely sidestepping the part where he tripped over his own dangling heartstrings and whiffed the *GLO* match he had coming up in thirty minutes.

What made it worse was that up until he saw Emilia walk out onstage with Team Fury, of all the evil *GLO* teams in Pennsylvania, Jake had been having a nice day. He'd gotten up early, stopped at Dunkin', took that nasty bus into the city, and finally met his best friends in the world. Team Unity was more of a family than his actual family was, and seeing Bob with his bald head and silly hat, Ki and Penelope completing each other's sentences IRL, and even Matty (who was kind of a jerk but, like, *their* jerk) had Jake absolutely floating with joy.

Jake hoped that by the end of the day, he'd be able to write a list in his head of the most important things that happened to him at the competition, and the thing that was happening to him right now wouldn't even crack the top ten. Best case scenario, Unity won the match and moved on to compete next week, and that would be number one on his list. Worst case scenario, they crashed and burned, and the one thing he took away from this day was running into the girl he baby-duck imprinted on in the fourth grade, the one who didn't even remember his name and made him feel physically and emotionally microwaved.

It was pathetic. Nobody else had to tell Jake this was pathetic. He was incredible at producing that assessment from both himself and apparently everyone he'd ever met in his entire life. It was not very cool to have met someone once and been like "yup, we should be best friends," and then hit puberty and have that morph into "help, I want kiss" and proceed to go absolutely nowhere with that. If his dad knew he was flipping out over a girl at school, he'd give Jake some awful Boomer lecture about how Hoopers don't think, they just do, and no son of his was going to stand by while the girl of his dreams ignored him, blah-blah-blah . . .

Jake's dad had clearly never met Emilia Romero. Just "doing" wouldn't work on someone as smart as her. Also Jake's parents' marriage exploded when his mom cheated on his dad and left his entire family in this dust, so Jake assumed he'd learned more about talking to women from *Mass Effect*.

No, sorry. That was a lie. Jake played fem Shepard. He learned more about talking to gay aliens from *Mass Effect*. To be fair, Emilia may as well have been from another planet.

What was she even doing here? Jake had assumed Emilia didn't even game anymore. She'd become something else in the years since he last saw her, something Jake couldn't touch: a cool person. She played field hockey, made the honors list every quarter, and hung out with people who'd never give Jake a second glance. Just last week four girls in his grade showed up wearing the exact same outfit Emilia wore on the first day of school and hashtagged their group photo #RomeroStyle. The Romero in RomeroStyle couldn't possibly care about regional esports.

"Jake Hooper from the birthdays, right? And the arcade." Jake's minute was up, and Emilia was talking to him. "You're tall now."

The Telltale engine of life had made Jake's choice. That always happened when he stalled. With nowhere to go and a heart full of bees, he accepted his fate.

Sort of. He was still gearing up to actually talking.

"Yo. Buddy. You okay?" Emilia was looking at him the same way she had when they were kids, like she wasn't sure if a puppy she found on the sidewalk was dead or just sleeping.

Not enough time. Default mode activated. "Sorry." Jake's brain-moment collapsed around him. "Sorry!" He already said that! *Help*, he thought.

"You really have to stop saying sorry."

Jake wondered if that was the first time a girl had said that to a boy in the history of civilization, then realized he was still obligated to reply. If this were *Mass Effect*, fem Shepard would use the conversation choice that pointed out the obvious, so that's what he decided to do.

"So—Okay. Hi. You remember me?" Now that he'd said something, every function in Jake's body switched to manual control. His breathing took effort, and he had to remind himself to blink. He became aware of how weird tongues were and the weight of his own against his teeth.

"I remember you. It's been, what, five years? I didn't know you went to Hillford or played *GLO*. I didn't think I'd run into anyone I know here." She checked over her shoulder, as if she was worried someone would come up behind her and see them talking. As far as Jake knew, there weren't any rules against players mingling between matches, but it would make sense if Fury held themselves to a higher standard. They were the old testament, fire-and-brimstone gods of the Philly server.

"That works out then. Because you don't really know me!" Jake intended for that to sound reassuring and was certain he did not achieve his goal.

"You know me," Emilia pointed out. "That kind of counts." Ow? Yikes. How was he supposed to take that? Guided by his experience with alien conversation trees, Jake changed the subject.

"I just know your team because Fury's amazing. Makes total sense that you're playing with them; if you were going to be on any team, of course it would be Fury. Like, legends only, you know? Not that I think you're a legend. Well I mean if I would have guessed anyone I kind of know was a legend, it would probably be you, but not in a bad way? Just, like, given the context of how I know you. Which I really don't. I just see you at school sometimes."

From the way Emilia's face fell, Jake guessed that he had once again managed to say the wrong thing entirely. Even though every neuron in his brain zoomed toward whichever hemisphere controlled his shut-the-hell-up valve, he felt badly enough to at least try to fix whatever he just did. Once he figured out what it was.

"I mean you've always been good. You've been kicking my butt since we were in the fourth grade, and Byunki—wow, it just hit me that you're actually playing with *the* YUNG, wow—would only bring the best to this tournament. He's not going to call in the sandbag squad, you know? I'm not even going to ask if you just won, because I know you did."

Finally, a smile. All it took was a monologue.

"We did win. I got a checkmate."

"Of course you did! Jesus, on your first match? You are . . ." Oof, Jake struggled for a word. ". . . terrifying." It was true, in more ways than one. Emilia seemed to take it as a compliment.

"That's the vibe. And what about you? You're Team Unity?"

Jake looked down at his own jersey. Right, he was also here to compete. Very soon.

"Yeah, we're kind of up next."

"Right! Don't let me keep you. You were probably getting in the zone down here, sorry."

That was a liberal interpretation of what Jake was doing before Emilia showed up, but he was more than happy to let Emilia keep thinking that. On the whole, he'd give this whole incident a B minus, with points subtracted for awkward silences and the fact that he still had not managed to regulate his breathing despite earning one (1) smile and had blinked maybe four (4) times since Emilia started talking. And he'd stopped thinking about his tongue. Well, he had stopped thinking about it until he just thought about thinking about it. Tongues. So freaky.

"The zone. Yup. I should probably head to a green room or something." Something about that B minus emboldened Jake beyond anything he felt capable of before, even though failing the charisma check he was about to attempt would have catastrophic emotional consequences:

"I'll see you Monday at school, though. We shouldn't, like, spy on each other, but maybe we can get lunch and talk about the tournament?"

"That's not a good idea." Just like that, Emilia disappeared and in her place was KNOX. Jake, ever perceptive to the exact moment anything went south, felt his chest bees drop dead and hit whichever part of his body was the floor.

"Cool. That's fine too, very cool. I'm gonna . . ." He would have moved around her and booked it down the hallway to save face, but his feet suddenly weighed three tons each. He was also by his own estimation two inches tall, which meant it would take him an hour just to jog around Emilia's titanic figure.

"No, this is your spot. I'll go. Just don't . . ." Emilia trailed off and checked behind her again. It was the second time she'd done that. This time Jake was sure she didn't want to be seen with him and reaffirmed his assumption that he was a humiliating conversation partner at both the arena and at school.

"Don't tell anyone you saw me here. Not even Todd. And if you could also not tell your team that you know me, that would be great."

All of that buildup wondering if Emilia remembered him, and Jake finally had his answer. It was a terrible answer, and he got it because he was an idiot, but it was still an answer and a lesson. Just because Jake thought about someone didn't mean they were thinking about him too. In fact, they probably never were.

"Yeah. Of course. Lips sealed."

That seemed to satisfy her, at least. She waved a quick goodbye and turned around the corridor. Despite his crumbling, dead-bee insides, Jake admired the way she walked away from him. Emilia Romero had never second-guessed a walk away once in her entire life. He could just tell.

When Emilia was out of sight, Jake suddenly remembered that he had a body that felt things. He was painfully tense in his shoulders, which he would have to roll out before the match, and the back of his neck felt boiling hot. His pants were even buzzing a little, which was crazy but not surpr—No. Phone. Someone was calling him.

He didn't expect his palms to be as sweaty as they were and nearly dropped his phone when he whipped it out of his pocket, but in a feat of coordination he would surely never repeat, he managed to get it out, unlocked, and close to his ear before the call went to voice mail. Two voices yelled his name in near unison.

"Jake!"

It was Ki and Penelope. The Ladies of Unity.

"Hey, sorry I dipped. I'm coming back to the players' box now."

"It's okay!" "It's totally okay. Are you okay?" Ki and P were weirdly in sync because they knew each other before they started playing *GLO*, and after two months Jake still had trouble telling them apart on Discord and, by extension, the phone.

"Fine, yeah. Just sat alone for a bit back here. Had to clear my head."

"Come to the green room!" "We're in the green room!" "We still have the fries."

"Yup, see you in a few." Those fries were definitely cold by now, but the idea of putting something in his mouth that used to be delicious and was now extremely sad felt right. Jake ended the call before the girls asked any more questions and picked up his marginally less heavy feet to begin moving down the hallway.

It was too late for Jake to un-confess to Unity that he knew Emilia, but the silly sense of loyalty he still felt for her meant he would keep his promise. There was no way he was telling anyone what just happened.

CHAPTER EIGHT

Emilia, Saturday

THERE'S NO WAY I'm telling anyone what just happened. I'm a master of planning ahead, but my long-lost arcade friend from fourth grade showing up at my top secret *GLO* tournament and telling me he goes to my school is not something anyone could have predicted, much less covered in a contingency plan. God, I bombed that whole conversation. If Jake didn't rat me out to every gamer at Hillford West the second he saw me onstage, he's definitely spite ratting now after the way I just treated him.

Would he do that, though? I remember Jake Hooper being a lot of things—a giant nerd, a serial apologizer, the only guy who didn't think I was weird for liking games—but he was never mean. I haven't had time to think about him much in the past few years, but when I did, I always remembered him being sweet. Not nice, like some people are just "nice," and that's barely a personality, but genuinely sweet. He tried to give me a whole roll of arcade tokens once when he messed up my game because he's the kind of guy who would do anything to make things right. Or at least he used to be.

Then again, he used to be short too, and those days are clearly over. People change all the time, and it's terrible. Even if he has told a gamer or two, I can probably still contain it. Containing means I can plan, and planning means I still have control over the situation. Well, over half of the situation. The other half is standing on the other side of the door to Team Fury's green room, which I have somehow reached without thinking too hard about where exactly I was going. Nice job backtracking, feet. I'm glad you know what to do in these trying times.

I can hear Byunki talking through the door. He doesn't sound as mad as he did when I left, but he has the kind of voice where he always sounds a little mad, even when he's not. At the beginning of the day, I thought that made him authoritative, but now I'm starting to consider that he does it on purpose to intimidate people. I'll admit I let it get to me after our match, but talking to Jake reminded me of something. I *am* on Team Fury, and I earned my spot here.

Byunki may have been the one to bring me into the fold, but he can't argue with a checkmate in my first competition or the fact that Fury wouldn't be coming back next week without me. Fury is about winning, and if I win, then Byunki being mad at me is 100 percent his problem. Also, I look really good today, and my shoes are cool.

That's right. Positive self-talk. Penny would be so proud of me right now. I almost wish she was here or that it was even remotely possible for her to be. Jake did a pretty good job taking over in the pep talk department, though. I don't think he meant to, which kind of makes it better.

Now might be a good time to stop thinking about Jake. He's a problem, not a solution.

Team Unity is probably starting their match, and they're the last round of the day, so all I have to do is survive the Fury regroup and drive back to Hillford in time to maintain my alibi back home. Under these circumstances, I pull the same move I do every morning before school and shove everything Byunki said earlier (and everything relating to Jake) to the back of my mind. Poof. It's gone. I have bigger things to focus on.

Ivan, Erik, and Han-Jun are all sitting on the couch when I pull the door to the green room open, and Byunki looks like he was in the middle of lecturing them but lost his train of thought. They're all staring at one of the TVs mounted on the wall, where the Unity match is playing out in real time. It's nuts that one of the little figures zipping around up there is Jake, but I'm not close enough to read any of the comp names, and Byunki has the volume too low to hear the commentary.

"KNOX, you're back," Byunki says without turning away from the screen. He was absolutely waiting for the door to open just to pull off that supervillain move. All he needs is a swivel chair, a fluffy cat, and more flattering lighting to complete the picture. "Have you calmed down after your little outburst?"

I can't tell if he genuinely thinks that me leaving the room after he yelled at me for no reason is classifiable as a "little outburst" or if he's rewriting history on purpose, but either way I'm not taking the bait.

"I was hungry, but I couldn't find craft services," I half lie. I'm actually very hungry.

Byunki finally turns toward me and rolls his eyes. If he expects me to react to that, he's dead wrong. I am a tree undisturbed by the wind. My thoughts are the surface of a placid mountain lake. I am absolutely not visualizing what Byunki's lower half would look like sticking out of the drywall after I physically pick him up and yeet him across the room.

"Fine, sit down." Byunki steps aside to let me walk past him to the couch. "Those Unity noobs are ripping Team Herald a new one, so we need to re-strategize for next week."

It looks like Jake's mystery team is better than I expected. Team Herald has an amazing roster, and Unity was seeded so low they weren't expected to beat them. I do a very good job of hiding my smile while Ivan scooches over to make a spot for me on the cushions. Thank you for treating me like I'm supposed to be here, Mr. VANE.

"Even if they win this one they're up against Beast Mode or Tempest," Erik says, waving at the Unity match on-screen. "Either of them will crush Unity in Round Two."

"That would put us up against Beast in the finals," Han-Jun adds.

I realize that I completely missed the match after us while I was talking to Jake. It was Chronic versus Solar, one of which we're going up against next weekend. If Chronic won, I have my work cut out for me since they have an excellent Pharaoh, but if Solar won, we're gold. Their healers have no rhythm and couldn't time a cooldown if their lives depended on it—and they do.

As much as it sucks to admit I wasn't fully checked in for the last round of competition, I have to ask. "Who are we playing next week? The signal by . . . craft was garbage, so I didn't see."

Byunki gives me a look that says I ought to be ashamed of myself, but whatever, I'm already lying to him. I can only feel shame about so many things at once. "Chronic, obviously. You thought Solar was going to beat them?"

That strikes me as cocky coming from the tank who didn't have his Special Attack ready when it mattered, and considering he *just* said we're here to regroup in case an underdog takes down a team that should be one of our closest competitors. It ticks me off that Byunki learned nothing from today when I spend every second calculating what might happen next. His algorithm for life blows, and if I keep allowing him to think he knows better than me, we're not going to make it past the next round.

"Byunki, I don't think we should count anyone out. We're front runners, and we would have lost today if it wasn't for me." Sing it with me: it's true, and I should say it. Unfortunately, no one else seems to think so. Ivan and Erik are frozen next to me, with only their eyes moving between my traitorous face and Byunki's increasingly red one.

Before our fearless leader can blow up at me, Han-Jun shouts from the other end of the couch. I look over, and he's scrambling with the remote, turning up the volume so we can hear the commentators.

"They did it! Unity just beat Herald with a payload win."

"Not even a checkmate?" That's Ivan, suddenly interested in the match wrapping up on-screen as opposed to the one going down in front of him.

"Payload. They didn't lose anyone the whole match."

Holy crap. Unity getting a payload win is huge. Who knew that Jake's little team actually kicks ass? I know he's my competition and the number one threat to my personal and professional equilibrium, but I still have room to be impressed. I'm vast like that and also worried about what it means for the next round.

"Shit," Byunki mutters under his breath, then repeats it louder. "Shit!" The arena TV zooms in on Unity onstage, where Jake and four other people I don't recognize are jumping around and hugging each other. Aside from Jake, there's a tall bald guy who must be their tank because everyone's

crowding him like a bunch of kids trying to tackle their favorite uncle. Unity also has two girls—were they the ones cheering me on before?—one of whom has a truly remarkable afro
and the other clearly stans LOONA from the Vivi Pink shade
of her hair. The only one not going in for hugs is the other
white guy who isn't Jake. He's more interested in mugging for
the cameras, angling for a sponsorship that just might come
considering he's one of this competition's better-looking players. Get your paper, man.

For a second I get lost seeing Jake celebrate his win, but
Byunki brings me back to the green room when he picks up a
water bottle from the coffee table and chucks it across the
room, not unlike what I imagined doing to him earlier.

"God damn it! Fucking *Bob*."

The bottle is sadly closed and bounces off the wall without
the big climactic splash I'm assuming he wanted. I look over
at Ivan, then Erik, and they both shake their heads at me. Got
it, not asking.

"Just go," Byunki finally says after the world's most awkward silence. He's still glaring at the TV like it's his next target
for an anticlimactic Dasani assault.

Don't need to tell me twice. I'd say goodbye to the rest of
Fury, but Byunki's deep in his drama, and as much as I don't
love his behavior today, I respect his commitment to brooding.
Everyone else seems content to slip out quietly as well.

My first order of business is to take out the hoodie I stuffed in my tote bag and zip it up over my Fury uniform. The second order is to get out of here unnoticed.

I put my hood up before I leave the green room in case the back halls are flooded with people, and it turns out to have been a good choice. Now that the last match of the day is over, players from every team have their phones out, and the last thing I need is to show up in the background of a Vulcan streamer's Instagram live. I always thought it was silly how the characters in *Assassin's Creed* could blend into crowds when they're the only people walking around Victorian London or wherever wearing a big-ass hood, but my sweatshirt gambit actually seems to be working. Nobody would expect me to avoid the spotlight after my grand entrance onstage this afternoon, so moving through the crowd is as easy as looking like I'm someone who doesn't want anyone paying attention to her. I think this is what Penny calls method acting.

Once I'm away from the hallway that leads to most of the team green rooms, I'm pretty much in the clear. Following the exit signs takes me past a bunch of craft tables stripped of everything that isn't mini bottles of water and a sad veggie spread sans ranch (the dressing bowl looks so clean I suspect a streamer licked up its contents for content), and in the name of hydration I grab a water and shove a few extra in my sweatshirt pockets. Full-time gamers might be able to survive on a diet of Monster and Doritos, but I have to be a well-hydrated athlete for field hockey tomorrow. From craft it's just a short hallway to one of the arena's many confusing back doors, which I quietly push open to find it's pouring outside. Like, zero visibility, sheets and sheets of freezing rain pouring. And I parked my car as far from the arena doors as I possibly could to avoid anyone catching my license plate in a backdoor selfie.

Some would call that paranoid. I say prepared. Both parties would agree in this moment that it was a mistake.

I cram my tote bag under my arm to avoid getting my phone wet and start sprinting across the parking lot. Most of the cars back here are team vans or arena staff, so there isn't a huge risk that I get hit by a rogue Honda, but if I did I'd be more concerned about someone telling my parents I died outside an esports tournament than I would about sustaining any grievous bodily harm. In the interest of not having my mother resurrect my ghost just to ground my spirit for eternity, I run to the right along a median that leads past a shiny new Wizzard-branded bus stop. One of the posters on the side shows Pharaoh in his original skin (I have his Platinum-tier robes on because his launch costume looked dumb as hell), and as I get closer, I see the other side has a character I don't recognize. Some sad-looking tall guy in a blue jersey. In the rain, it almost looks like he's shivering.

Upon closer inspection, he is shivering. I'm not seeing another character through the rain; I'm seeing someone standing in front of where the other poster should be. It's Jake Hooper, standing at the bus stop in a T-shirt, looking sixteen seconds from hypothermic collapse. God, he looks awful. I don't know the bus schedule here, but the tournament still has at least forty-five minutes of wind-down time to get through. He could be stuck out here in the freezing rain for an hour if not more.

Welp, sucks to suck. I'm sure Jake can't hear me over the rain, so I jog past the back of the bus stop and keep on moving toward my car. It's another few minutes before I reach it, and by the time I do, my entire sweatshirt is soaked through. Once I'm in, I crank the heat up, check my bag to make sure I didn't forget anything, and see my phone screen glowing through the wet fabric. Two missed calls from Connor. One voicemail from Connor. Seven unread texts, all of which are some variation of "What's up" from, I just guessed it, Connor.

The phrase "Why are boys?" runs through my mind as I tap through to listen to—ugh—the voicemail he's left me. I have a few minutes before my car heats up anyway.

"Hey, Lia, it's me. Connor D. I was going to ask if you wanted to hang out tonight and Penny told me you were busy." Yikes. I need to come up with something else to tell Penny about today since she'll know I wasn't with Connor. Also, is it just me or is it weird of him to ask my friends if I'm free? Penny's not my assistant, bro. If anything, I'm hers. Or I will be once I start being a better VP.

"So whatever you're doing, I definitely think you should ditch it so we can have another date. Just kidding. Kind of."

He is not kidding at all. The audacity of this—"Seriously, let's hang out soon. Some of the guys are coming over to play *Madden* tomorrow if you want to watch or something, I think Ben's new girlfriend will be there so you won't be the only one. Let me know. Bye."

In the immortal words of John Mulaney, we don't have time to unpack all *that*. First of all, I'd smoke any one of Connor's friends at *Madden*, though it's not his fault he doesn't know that. Second of all, girlfriend? I need to clear some stuff up with this boy, like, yesterday.

But first: getting home. Connor's voicemail disappears when I swipe through my phone and connect my map app to the car's Bluetooth. Everyone else is still inside watching the day's final *GLO* rounds, so there's no one in the parking lot to slow me down when I pull out of my spot and make my way toward the side exit. Almost no one.

Jake's still there, looking wet and miserable in my rearview mirror with no bus in sight across the entire abandoned lot. I glance at my map. Thirty-five minutes back to Hillford without traffic, forty given traffic and the current total downpour. I have time. I could help if I wanted to.

Why should I, though? The easiest thing to do would be to have faith in his niceness and ignore him at school and for the rest of the tournament. Being seen with him at either place could lead anyone to make the connection between KNOX and Emilia Romero, student at Hillford West. I've been on

Tumblr, and I follow the Philly *GLO* subreddit. I know what kind of investigation even a blurry picture of two people talking can spark. He's the only link anyone on both sides of this horrible divide could use to out me, not only to my family and friends in Hillford but also to the entire *GLO* gaming community.

Now that I think about it, Jake was the reason I thought it would be fine if I went on voice chat in *GLO* in the first place. I think I'd assumed every gamer was like Jake, who only cared about how well I could play and always treated me like an equal he could learn from. Naive assumption, I know, but I don't want to be angry at my younger self for not knowing how shitty things are.

Jake doesn't know it yet, but he holds the key to Fort Knox, and one word from him could burn it to the ground. Jake Hooper, who is shivering in the rain at a bus stop a few minutes away while I sit here in a warm car knowing that being seen with him is the worst thing I can do for myself right now. Jake who was once so nice to me it made me have faith in gamers as a whole. *Gamers.*

God damn it.

CHAPTER NINE

Team Unity, Saturday

ElementalP: WEEEEEEE

shineedancer: ARE THE CHAMPIONS

MUDD: jesus christ stop

ElementalP: boo

BobTheeQ: I promise if we make it to the finals I'll tell muddy to let you finish.

shineedancer: but that was one of the greatest GLO matches of all time?

JHoops: OF. ALL. TIME.

BobTheeQ: There you are! You've been running and hiding from us all day, I thought you'd want to stay for some pictures.

MUDD: seriously i know you're always like 'where's muddy' but today the name of the game was where the hell is jake

LanguageBot: language, MATTHEW

MUDD: really Bob?

BobTheeQ: Don't worry I customized LBot for everyone while we were waiting for Jake today.

shineedancer: really? Hell! Damn! Byunki!

LanguageBot: language, KI

ElementalP: omg I love it even more now???

JHoops: that's neat

JHoops: and sorry, I was in a weird place n wanted to get home asap. at the bus stop and it's so cold i hate this

BobTheeQ: You played well today in spite of everything. Proud of you and the whole team. I'm getting in my car so I'm off chat. We'll talk tomorrow and see you buddies next weeeeeek for round 2!

JHoops: bye bob

BobTheeQ: Love you bye.

[BobTheeQ has left the chat]

MUDD: anyway we need to dangle a picture of jake's long lost love in front of him before every match because he was way on top of those heals today

JHoops: please do not do that

ElementalP: leave him alone Muddy

ElementalP: hold on K is about to start driving so I'm typing for both of us now

ElementalP: how are you feeling bby jake?

ElementalP: about all of it

JHoops: wait was that you or Ki?

MUDD: does it matter they're the same person

JHoops: fair

JHoops: it's all cool, I didn't see her or anything so it was fine

MUDD: i stuck around backstage to see fury leave and she wasn't with them

ElementalP: that is weird, you think they'd want to show her off after the checkmate

ElementalP: Ki says we stan an intentionally mysterious queen

JHoops: yeah i think she's doing it on purpose and i don't want to make fury mad so can you guys not kjfblhreg

MUDD: . . .

MUDD: is he dead

ElementalP: I KNEW WE SHOULD HAVE DRIVEN HIM BACK TO HILLFORD

JHoops: sorry dropped me phone

JHoops: i gotta go my

JHoops: bus is here

MUDD: i'm not staying online if its just me and the girls

ElementalP: get home safe baby Jake!

ElementalP: Ki says muddy can choke

[MUDD has left the chat]

JHoops: oh don't tell anyone that I know KNOX from before that's what i was going to say

JHoops: Fury might try to take me out idk theyre scary

ElementalP: good idea. have fun on the bus!

[JHoops has left the chat]

ElementalP: hell yeah i'm gonna spam the chat with song lyrics and there's nothing anyone can do about it until they log back in

LanguageBot: language, PENELOPE

CHAPTER TEN

Emilia, Saturday

TO BE CLEAR, I did think this through, but something about the ten straight minutes of complete silence that followed the moment I pulled up to the arena bus stop and told Jake Hooper to get in my car makes me think that I didn't think it through enough. Do I want him to talk? Talking would mean we're being cordial, which is too far down the path to friendly, and friendly is not the goal here. I'm literally, in the actual definition of the word, not here to make friends. Jake is in my car because if I didn't offer him a ride, he'd get a cold or something, and I didn't see anyone wipe down the tournament stage's keyboards between matches. He could get everyone sick. That would be terrible. This is actually so selfish of me, driving Jake back to Hillford. And because I'm doing this for selfish reasons, we absolutely do not have to talk.

Except that if we don't talk, this whole decision has the air of a kidnapping instead of a rescue.

Listen, I didn't force Jake to accept the ride. He was messing around on his phone when I drove over to him; I'd hoped he was hailing a car, which would save me from having to save him, but when he looked up and saw me through the window, he dropped the phone in a puddle and held his arm out as if to stop me from driving away while he scrambled for it.

"Hey! Hi. It's me, Jake!" he said, like that wasn't the entire reason I was at the bus stop in the first place.

"I know," I shouted through my rolled-down window. "Get in."

For all his stumbling over himself earlier, I didn't have to ask him twice. He was shivering so hard it took him ages to send a final text to whoever he was talking to and dry his phone on the inside of his shirt. The heat from the car fogged up his glasses, but he didn't make a move to clear them up with his shaking hands.

"Thanks," he managed to say through chattering teeth. "J-just need to warm up."

"Nope, you'll die," I said. It would look worse if someone saw him leaving my car after idling in front of a bus stop for a few minutes. "Let me drive you home."

If he looked surprised, I couldn't tell behind his whited-out glasses. Dude looked like Kevin from *Sin City*—and while a bespectacled comic-book cannibal was not the most charming comparison I could have made for the virtual stranger I had invited into my car, the bright light coming from the bus stop's painfully white lamps made it the most apt.

"Okay," Jake said, too cold to argue. He gave me his address and leaned back to let the blowing heat bring him back to life.

That was those ten minutes ago, and now we're here on the highway. The rain has lessened up, but there's still something creepy about driving quietly in a straight line when someone else is in the car not talking to you. If I start playing music right now, would it be too obvious that the silence is killing me?

Out of nowhere, Jake turns to me like he'd been gearing himself up to say something for the past few minutes. Maybe the silence was killing him too.

"You know, I didn't get to see your match with the check-mate. Was it cool?"

I can't tell if he's asking in his capacity as my competition or my hostage, but it can't hurt to tell him something he could easily look up on YouTube when he got home. Obviously, I have no business telling him what happened after my match, but I haven't really had a chance to flex about my win since Byunki rained on my parade. It might be nice to put the fear of Fury in someone who could actually come up against us in competition.

"It was cool," I begin. How much should I tell him? "I played Pharaoh since Vulcan came out with Lucafont. Used

Erik's Special to get eyes on the payload, and I got first blood. It was a slap fight at the end, but our healers double sacrificed to give me a shot at the tank." That wasn't exactly what happened, but the video wouldn't include audio of Byunki's warnings to me, and that's a much better narrative to lay over the facts of the match.

"Smart." Jake nodded. "Do you always play DPS?"

"What am I supposed to be, a healer?" Healers are stereotyped as the caretakers of the team, so any girl in gaming gets asked if she heals. I wouldn't have had as hard a time as a girl in *GLO* if I had played a cute little field nurse, but it's not my thing and never will be. Nothing against them, but I just resent the assumption. "Are you asking if I'm a healer because I'm a girl?"

"No! Come on." Jake throws his hands up, offended that I was offended. "I'm a healer; I was just wondering if Fury lets you switch roles. We switch sometimes."

I'm not talking Fury's strategy with a competing team, but if Jake's team is as cohesive as they are while still switching their placements, they're better than I thought. It's hard enough to master more than one character in *GLO*, let alone a completely different mechanic.

"I'm DPS. I'm always DPS."

"You hit 'em where it hurts."

"That's the vibe."

And . . . more silence. I'm so good at talking about stuff

when it comes to my real life—dances, classes, whatever Connor and his friends are into—but why am I so bad at this when the topic is something I actually like?

Jake surprises me again by speaking up. He's either one of those people who has to fill a silence or he's determined to get some Fury secrets out of me. I glance over at his face—his glasses have defogged on their own, revealing his huge, dark eyes, and I make a mental note to watch what I say around him: *Sure, he looks cute when he's wet and helpless, but there might be a devious mind lurking under all that hair. Engage but do not trust.*

"You used Pharaoh's special on Lucafont? The Shatter thing? We don't play him, so I don't know his loadout."

This topic is fine. Pharaoh's loadout is a fact, not a secret.

"Yeah, it's this crossbow bolt that Pharaoh traps a soul in before shooting. The animation is really cool. You can only do it if at least one opposing player has died in a certain radius because the implication is he's, like, harvesting their spirit as a weapon, which is dark but also kind of sick?"

Jake's eyes widen. None of *GLO*'s healer characters have powers like that. "Wait, that's horrible. I love it."

"It's really horrible and awesome," I reply, because it is. I wasn't nuts about Pharaoh when I first started playing him, but after a few months that little necro-rogue has grown on me. "And against a ghost character, it's like *ping* and their spectral armor totally collapses."

"They must have thought you wouldn't come out with Pharaoh if they played Lucafont. Luca's only useful if—"

"—if you're playing Envy, which is hilarious because—"

"They nerfed her in the new meta."

"Exactly! Ugh, I'd never play Envy now. Her support is garbage."

Jake goes quiet for a moment. I sneak a look away from the road and see him staring sadly out the window.

"Jake?"

"I play Envy," he says softly with a hint of hurt in his voice.

"Oh, buddy, I'm sorry." Now I feel awful. I really didn't mean to tease him; I just got excited for a second! I didn't realize how easy it would be to get carried away joking about *GLO* because I never talk to anyone about it. Every meme, in-joke, and fandom quirk exists solely online for me, so actually speaking about it face-to-face is something I only started to do this afternoon with Fury and now with Jake, who I've just insulted. Again. "Envy's great for a mech build, I guess? Is she your main? Wait, are you really an Envy main?"

On cue, Jake turns back toward me with a huge grin. Once he sees the confused look on my face, the grin turns into a very un-Jake-like giggle.

"I'm messing with you, Em. Envy sucks! Literally don't trust an Envy main; they're all monsters."

Oh my god, no one's called me Em since I was little. The last time I talked to Jake, it was probably still my nickname.

Once I started playing field hockey, the girls on my team started calling me "Lia," which I sort of hate, but it was better than hearing them mess up the vowels and call me "Amelia" forever. Aw, I miss being called Em. It's sweet that he remembered. I make another mental note, underneath the first one: *Subject is still nice (probably). Adjust trust expectations accordingly.*

"I deserved that for the healer thing. And Envy mains really are the worst. Who's your main healer? Castor?"

"Penelope mains Castor. I play Pythia."

I snort. Pythia is a good healer, but she's also the subject of more than one downright filthy piece of *GLO* fanart. Something about a half-snake, half-woman priestess with a big staff and a forked tongue drives the hornier segment of the gaming population absolutely bonkers, and every new skin Wizzard releases for her only fuels their fire. You ever see a scaly, murderous Medusa with triple-D boobs dressed up in a rubber Mrs. Claus dress? Check out last year's *GLO*'s holiday skin pack. Merry Chrissstmasss.

"What?" Jake sees straight through my snorting. "Pythia has good defense, and her Prophesy attack negates future damage! Why are you laughing?"

"Because you have to spend seven hours a day looking at a thotty lizard!"

"Well *you* spend all your time looking at what would happen if the Mummy had a baby with Kylo Ren."

Oof. He's spot on about Pharaoh; he's canonically four

thousand years old, kind of a space lich, and loves wearing capes. Before I can shoot back at Jake's accurate but not entirely kind comment about my dangerous son, Jake speaks up again.

"How do you even find the time to play at Fury's level and still, like, be you? I don't do anything else besides *GLO*, my grades are garbage, and I don't—no, can't—play a sport. Do you have a twin; are there two of you?" Jake leans across the car and jokingly examines my face while I'm trying to keep my eyes on the road. "Are you the good twin or the evil twin?"

Great question. I'd have a much easier time if there were two of me. We could do that thing from that movie about the magicians and be two people living the same life. She could take the math SAT, and I'd take the reading section; she'd dominate field hockey while I climb the *GLO* leaderboards. Imagining that *Illusionist* lifestyle feels almost too good, so I yank myself away from the fantasy and shift my eyes over to Jake, who is still squinting at me like he's trying to find the telltale birthmark that proves I'm not actually Emilia.

"It's just me. I don't sleep a lot, I guess. Kinda sucks, actually." Shouldn't have said that. Is it too late to backtrack?

Jake shifts back into his seat now that I've obviously bummed myself out.

"So why do you do it?"

Great question number two. Why do I do this? I take a minute to change lanes so I can get to the exit that leads toward Hillford, but this time the silence isn't awkward. After I get in the right lane, I peek over at Jake again, and he's calmly looking out the windshield, listening to me say nothing. It's the first time in a while that any conversational silence I've had hasn't been awkward. Everyone always expects me to have a quick answer to everything, and he's just waiting to pay attention to whatever I say next, whenever it comes. *Space*, I think. *This is what it's like when someone gives me space.*

"I think . . . ," I begin, but don't know how to end the sentence. "What if I told you that *GLO* is the only thing I'm good at?"

"I'd say . . . *lying.*"

"Okay, *Saga* cat, fine. I'm good at a lot of things. What if I told you *GLO* is the only thing I'm good at that I actually like? And everything else is just doing what everyone expects me to do. Like, I'm proud of my grades and field hockey; I know I'm on a great, shiny path or whatever, but none of it feels like I do it for me."

"Oh," Jake says, nodding, "is it because you picked this? Like even if it wasn't exactly *GLO*, you'd like whatever it was that you picked because you got to choose it for yourself."

Wait, yeah. Exactly that. Out of everything in my life these days, *GLO* is the one thing I do that no one else told me to do. I don't pick my classes, my extracurriculars, my schedule, and I definitely didn't pick Connor. I didn't even realize that was why I did this, and he clocked me in seconds. Mental note number three: *Subject might be a genius. Trust or distrust, he's on his own thing.*

"Kind of? Actually yeah, no that's it. I don't get to choose a lot, and I chose this. Is it like that for you too?"

"Nope," he says with a shrug, "but I get where you're coming from. I just don't, like, uh. Um." He rubs at the back of his neck. I remember that habit from when we were younger. "I'm better at being Pythia than I am at being Jake. I'm not good at a lot of stuff, and I don't want to be this dumb, awkward guy all the time, so Unity and all of them are, like, they know the best me, and it feels nice? To know there are people who know the best me even if that's not, like, *me* me."

"You're not dumb," I say reflexively. I don't know what his report card looks like, but hearing him talk like this makes it abundantly clear that Jake Hooper is not dumb at all. "You are hella awkward, though."

Jake groans and slides his fingers under his glasses to cover his eyes. "Urgh, I know. I'm the worst."

"That's not what I meant! Everyone's awkward."

"You're not awkward. You're a fricking Targaryen. Whenever I see you in school, it's like 'Make way for the queen!'"

"First of all, rude. I'm a Martell. They're racially ambiguous in the show, but they're the only Latinos in Westeros and I identify with them very strongly. Second of all, that whole queen bee thing is, like, seven years of me trying really hard to show people what they want to see. Nobody wants to see all of me; they just want the parts that make sense to them. Stereo-types are easier for people to understand."

"I get that," Jake replies, then backtracks. "Not for you, I don't get that about you, all of you seems pretty gr—fine. But the general idea."

"And where did you get that general idea?"

"Ki and P talk about it a lot. I didn't really get what it was like to be, like, queer or not white, and they're both, so they schooled me good. They're two of my best friends, and I'd die for both of them. Pushy Tumblr girls, you know."

"Those two girls on your team?"

"Ki and Penelope." He affects a sports announcer voice and repeats their competition names: "KIKI and LMNO." He pronounced it like the alphabet song, el-em-en-oh.

"Are they . . . together?"

"Ki and P? No, dude." Jake shoots me a look that says I really ought to know better. "They're gay, not pandas."

He's right. I should have known better. There just aren't that many gay girls in *GLO* as far as I know—then again, I don't play with any other women, so I wouldn't have an idea either way. That's the other hard part of keeping myself iso-lated on the Philly servers; I can't get to know anyone else beyond the realm of *GLO*, let alone make friends with other players and find my people like Jake has. He's luckier than he thinks he is, having a team like Unity.

"I was just wondering. They seemed close."

He's quick with his answer. "We all are. Ki and P knew each other before we formed Unity, but Ki didn't transition until we had already been playing for a year or so. We all stuck with her when stuff was really hard at home, and then Bob brought Muddy onto the team—"

Bob. That's the name Byunki freaked out over. I wonder if Jake knows anything about that.

"Bob's your captain?"

Jake laughs and pulls out his phone. "Bob's basically our dad."

Now that we're on more local roads, there are stop lights, and he waits until I pull up to one to show me a selfie he must have taken earlier at the tournament. Jake, Ki, Penelope, and that good-looking dude from earlier are bear-hugging the tall guy I saw on-screen at the end of Jake's match.

"We literally call him dad because he's older than us and using his gap year to hustle for Unity. You know how they keep hinting that *GLO* is going to put a league together? If it does, Bob has sponsorships and stuff lined up."

Those rumors have been around since launch, but Wizzard's press team straight up said they planned to test out renting the space to other tournaments before they commit to a real esports division. If other teams are taking the pro league rumors seriously, I'd be very surprised if Byunki wasn't as well. He just didn't tell us anything about that—or maybe he just didn't tell me. Byunki planning out a big reveal for Fury's first female player, him hiding my spot on the team until it was guaranteed to get the most attention, and then getting angry that I was stealing his spotlight in our debut match all makes a lot more sense now. He's building a narrative in case Fury goes pro. Problem is, *GLO* doesn't have any plans to develop a league.

I've gone quiet again, but Jake snaps me back. "Vibe check? Did I say something wrong?"

"No, you're good. I was just thinking about your team. You guys are so close, it's really cute. Dad-Bob and all that."

"Yeah, we're a family. Even Muddy." Jake looks like he wants to say something else but decides against it. "Muddy's a great DPS."

"Should I be worried?"

"Dunno. Haven't seen your Pharaoh."

A little spicy, but I'll take it.

"You better hope you never see my Pharaoh."

"Should *I* be worried?"

"I'm Fury. We'll end you."

"We're Unity. We'll hug you to death."

At the same time, Jake and I both agree, "I want that on a T-shirt." Jinx. We look at each other and smile like we did in fourth grade, and fifth and seventh, every time we happened to be at the same party or arcade. We didn't even have to say anything back then; every time we saw each other, we'd pick up where we left off and dip out to play whatever game was around. Once I started hiding all of that, I didn't think I'd feel this open with anyone ever again. Funny how all it took was Jake being the same Jake. Again, he's way taller now, but the part of him that makes me feel okay showing this side of me hasn't budged after all these years.

By sheer coincidence, I drive right past Hillford West while we jinx each other. The school lights are still on at this hour, but the parking lot is completely empty. There's so much dissonance between how I feel looking at the school where I bust my butt for whatever combination of letters will make my parents happy and the lot where Connor force-feeds me matcha lattes, and how I feel laughing in my car with Jake, whose entire life is *GLO*.

These two paths I walk aren't meant to touch at all. I drew them parallel to keep them mathematically apart. Jake is telling me another story now, something about how Penelope threw a fit when the new meta launched, and listening to him while the streets around us get more familiar makes me feel nervous inside. Jake's house—apartment, actually, now that I'm driving up to the building—is only a minute away from school, and even that proximity is stressing me out.

"This is me," he reminds me, even though the GPS on my phone had already loudly informed me of that fact through my car speakers when we arrived at our destination. I slow in front of the building and realize that I'm lost in my head again.

I don't know what to say or if any further silences will be the awkward kind or the nice, Jake kind.

"Thanks for the ride," he says without making a move to get out of the car. "It was, uh. Pretty wet out there."

"Rain's stopped, though. That's good." Doubling back to talk about the weather is probably the smart thing to do. If I could ask anyone else I know what to do in this situation, ignoring the part where I have to give context for everything that happened today, they would expect me to do the smart thing and reestablish the barrier I need to keep between myself and Jake.

"Hey, at the tournament," Jake says, still not having unbuckled his seat belt, "you said not to tell anyone I know you."

"Yup. Nothing personal, I—"

"But you could have just driven out of the parking lot."

Oh boy. Come on, Emilia. Just do the thing. Tell him again, and none of this will matter tomorrow.

"You looked cold. I'm not a monster."

Jake takes that in for a moment, then nods to himself. He sounds resolved, like that was exactly the answer he expected, and he can now leave happy that his expectations were correct when he replies.

"Right, you're not an Envy main. You're just Fury." He unbuckles his seat belt and opens the passenger door, then stops himself. He closes the door again and turns in his seat to look at me. I don't want to look at him when I'm feeling like this, but I also don't want him to think my choices are his fault, so I do the absolute least I can and meet his eyes.

"Jake, I—"

"I just gotta say that I don't get why you're keeping this"—he gestures with his hands to his uniform and vaguely waves toward mine, still hidden under my sweatshirt—"a secret, but I think I'm the only one who knows. Am I?"

My mental notes are scrambled together in my brain now. The bullet points I made while Jake and I talked are either entirely wrong or completely right, and I don't know what he wants from me. In my experience, that feeling usually comes before someone starts a transaction. Just like everyone else, Jake wants something in exchange for keeping my secret, and I'll pile whatever it is on top of every other obligation I fulfill to maintain this tiny piece of personal freedom. I steel myself for whatever it is and nod to let him know he's right.

"Okay, that's good, Em. That's perfect."

Wait, what?

"If it's just you and me, we can make sure no one else finds out. If, like, your other friends knew or your parents, then it would be hard, but I'm not gonna tell and you're def not gonna tell, so we're good."

If my brain activity had a scent, my entire car would smell like an electrical fire.

"That's what you were worried about, right? That I'd tell people you're in the tournament?"

"That I, um. All of it. That I play games at all, everything about *GLO*. Everything."

He nods again and looks off to the side. He's thinking. That makes one of us.

"Cool, cool, cool. Yeah, if anyone sees you talking to me, that's a dead giveaway. Do you want to just not talk forever? I can do not talking forever after right now."

"Don't you want to know why?" I sputter. *I* want to know why he's saying this; it would make sense that he would want an explanation. Nobody just does things for me without wanting to know why.

"It's probably complicated, and I'm really dumb, so no, I'll just trust you on it."

"Stop saying you're dumb."

"Sorry."

"Stop saying sorry."

"Sorry." And this time he says it with a cheeky smile. He can do not talking forever after now, but I don't think that's what I want. It's what they all would expect, but it's not what I want at all.

"I almost got doxxed a while back." If the only way to get Jake to know I don't think he's dumb is to trust him, then I'll trust him with this tiny bit of truth. "Well, not doxxed . . . just. I was really young and being a girl playing *GLO*. There were some bad people. My milkshake brought all the trolls to the yard, you know?" Does he know? There's only so much Ki and Penelope could have told him about what it's like for us. Even if they did, there's no guarantee he'd understand.

"Right. No, I get it. Was it really bad?"

"Some of it was definitely illegal if that's what you're asking. Considering I'm a minor."

"Jesus." Jake exhales loudly. "I'm sorry that happened to you. So the tournament . . ."

"Fury has my back. No personal information, no leaks. They're protecting me even though I have to show my face."

"That's surprising. I mean, it's good. That's really good. Just surprising."

"They're not bad guys. We just like to win."

I suddenly remember Byunki's reaction to seeing Unity win their match and feel terrible for telling Jake about any of my interactions with the team. I bet if I asked him right now what the deal was with that, he'd tell me, but I don't want to ask. Sharing a car ride is one thing, but sharing the inner workings of our teams is another.

"Anyway, that's the deal. You might have jammed the lock when you closed your door right after opening it, so let me get the thingy here." I lean over to pop the lock open with my fingernail . . .

And find I am very, very close to Jake Hooper's face. I still have my seat belt on, and the resistance against my chest feels like it's the only thing holding me back from leaning too far over the edge of a cliff. We're close enough to fog up his glasses, but Jake is frozen in place. He looks just as confused as I am as he leans back in his seat to give me the space I need to move away if I want to. If I think he wants me to.

Oh no, this is easy. It's never felt this easy before.

My phone, which had so helpfully shouted directions at me through my car's Bluetooth connection, chooses that moment to blast the chorus from "Funkytown." Jake and I leap apart like we've just been accosted by the ghost of 1979. On my phone, Connor's shirtless Palm Springs picture takes up the whole screen. Connor did that, not me. Just put it in my contacts one day when I wasn't looking.

"That's my cue," Jake says in the same panicky voice he used when he first saw me at the arena. I'm scrambling at the dashboard controls of my car, trying to lower "Funkytown" to a reasonable volume level before I wake up his entire apartment building.

Come on, phone! I knock my phone from its dashboard dock and decline the call as Jake springs from my car and makes for the lobby door.

"Okay, Em, see you next week and also never, and that's fine by the way!"

"Jake, wait! Wait. Hold on for one—Jesus. Hold on." I'm tangled up in my seat belt and have that awful ringtone stuck in my head. Once free (of the seat belt, not the aggressive disco stylings of Lipps Inc.), I hop out the driver's side and run up to Jake as he's opening the lobby door.

"We can't talk at school," I say, out of breath more from stress than from physical exertion. "It's too obvious."

"Right." Even behind his heavily refracted lenses, Jake's dark eyes are wide.

"But if you meet me at the east side Dunkin' next Saturday, I'll drive you to the tournament again. No one goes there because the west side Starbucks has doughnuts now."

"Really? Starbucks doughnuts are chalky, though."

"Not the point. But you're right."

"Why do they—"

"It's a status thing. Do you want the ride or not?"

"I want the ride. And a doughnut now that you brought it up."

"I'll buy you a doughnut on Saturday. Seven o'clock?"

"Seven o'clock. And I'll buy *you* the doughnut. I'm sorry, I'm so hungry and I just realized it."

"Same. See you Saturday."

"See you Saturday."

I'm hyperaware of what almost happened in the car, and from the way Jake is purposefully keeping room for the Holy Ghost between us, I feel safe assuming he's aware too. We both lean forward in a weird, shoulder-only hug and part ways. My driver's side door is still dangling open, and my lights are on when I get back to the car. I'm about to reconnect the Bluetooth and steel myself to text Connor when I see Jake hanging halfway out the lobby door.

"Hey, Em," he stage-whispers. The sidewalk is narrow enough that I can still hear him. "It's super cool not being friends with you again."

I command myself not to smile, and my mouth rebels spectacularly. I'm still smiling two streets over when my phone lights up again. Jesus, is Connor secretly fifty years old? I was getting to you, enough with the phone calls already.

I answer before the ringtone can start and hear something that completely wipes the grin off my face: not Connor's voice, but Penny's.

"Hey, Lia. Just got a weird text from Matt Pearson? I have some questions. First question: who the hell is KNOX?"

CHAPTER ELEVEN

Team Unity Chat, Sunday

BobTheeQ: Ch-ch-checking in with Round One Winners Team Unity!

BobTheeQ: Especially and including Our Ladies, how was everything after we parted ways last night?

JHoops: i haven't been online but yes how are you both

shineedancer: not great, bob

ElementalP: I've had worse

BobTheeQ: My bots are at your service. BlockBot, WipeBot, PrivacyBot . . .

ElementalP: How about MurderBot?

JHoops: ThatsAFelonyBot

JHoops: but Bob would probably build one for you anyway

ElementalP: ok i'll take a BlockBot pls there's only so much racism I can take before noon

BobTheeQ: DMing you the code, Sweet P.

JHoops: anything you want us to handle?

JHoops: if you give me your pw I can go through your TL and only show you the nice tweets starting from yesterday

shineedancer: don't you have enough on your plate Jake? aren't you still hyperventilating and/or recovering from the bus

JHoops: why would i hyperventilate

shineedancer: oh idk. she plays with fury. looks like elena of avalor. rhymes with box.

ElementalP: or maybe rhymes with shmay-oh-shmee idk what we're going with now that she's a known entity

shineedancer: this would be a lot easier if you just told us her NAME

JHoops: oh that's all fine.

JHoops: fine fine fine. I don't want to like take space rn

JHoops: also nothing happened and I took the bus

BobTheeQ: Consider me convinced!

shineedancer: gonna butt in, can yall report this one guy? I'll link to his profile he's some blue check transphobe and all his followers are calling me a dude

JHoops: on it

BobTheeQ: I'm on it too.

BobTheeQ: Let me know if any of this creeps into *GLO*, by the way. The tournament officials told me all of our tags would remain confidential but if anyone gets froggy I can talk to Wizzard about it. There are a lot more available account protections because the company wants this tournament to go well.

ElementalP: obviously they want it to go well

BobTheeQ: No, they want it to go *really* well.

JHoops: like "pleasantly surprised by the Kotaku comment section for once" well or . . .

shineedancer: is there something you're not telling us bob

BobTheeQ: Not sure! Stay the course and when I can tell you, I'll tell you.

ElementalP: ominous. exciting. I like it

JHoops: more surprises, perfect i hate it

BobTheeQ: I'm more concerned about making sure you four are all right. We all need space to decompress after yesterday's win. Jake had a weird surprise, Ki and P put themselves out there in front of a lot of not-so-nice people, and Muddy

BobTheeQ: Wait, where's Muddy?

JHoops: probably asleep

ElementalP: It's 2pm?? how???

shineedancer: oh come on i thought we agreed to do these postmortems as a team

shineedancer: i had to explain terfs to my little sister this morning and muddy's getting his beauty sleep?

BobTheeQ: If you need to vent, we're here. I can disable LanguageBot if you need to use all of your words.

shineedancer: it doesn't matter, i know this isn't really muddy's thing

JHoops: you deserve to feel supported tho

JHoops: that's the point of Unity. blue cross. black shield.

shineedancer: ur right

shineedancer: just . . . it matters that we won though, right? even if we don't get past the next round tell me that being there and winning one match matters.

JHoops: it matters

BobTheeQ: You should be really proud of yourself, Ki. I can talk to Muddy if you want.

JHoops: is there anything else we can do?

ElementalP: not really for me

shineedancer: just having yinz around to listen helps

shineedancer: idk what i'd do without unity backing me up

BobTheeQ: It's what we do, Kiki.

JHoops: we got u

CHAPTER TWELVE
Emilia, Sunday

THIS IS THE worst fake campaign meeting I have ever had the misfortune to host. For all my field hockey squats, I don't think I'm going to have an ass after Penny finishes tearing me a new one.

"You know," Penny says through her clenched jaw, "when you ask someone to lie for you, it's nice to actually tell them why."

"I know and I'm *sorry*," I reply for the millionth time today. "I totally should have told you. That's it, though, I promise. The whole truth."

For all the time I've spent building up the lie of my double life in my head, it took a surprisingly short time to explain it. At first I thought it would be smart to hold some parts back—the part about getting bullied off the game a few years ago and everything Jake-adjacent were the two things I considered keeping to myself—but the moment I brought Penny upstairs and sat down on my bed, I couldn't stop myself from word vomiting absolutely everything I had experienced with *GLO*. The harassment, Fury, the tournament, the money, my mom, Jake, all of it became fair game.

No pun intended.

"This is nuts," Matt Pearson chimes in from the desk chair across my room. "You are the last person I would ever expect to do this. Wow."

I still can't 100 percent compute that he's in on this too. Penny was right to bring Matt along today, considering he's the one who found the video of me on the Wizzard-Claricom Arena's Instagram last night, but it's really the cherry on top of the WTF sundae that one of Connor's soccer teammates is in my bedroom listening to me spill everything I've been hiding for years.

When they both showed up this morning, Penny smoothed over my mom's confusion by introducing Matt as our new campaign manager. It gave him just enough clout to be allowed in my room as long as we keep the door open and Matt's butt never touches the bed.

"Thanks, Matt!" Penny snaps. "Valuable contribution, as always."

"Don't be mad at him," I say. I owe more to Matt than I've ever owed anyone in my life. If he had sent that video to Connor or posted it anywhere else, even as a joke, everything would have gone up in flames overnight.

"Matt, is the live still up?" I ask.

He pulls his phone out of his varsity jacket pocket to check. "It's got, like, two more hours."

"I can't believe this is happening." I bury my face in my hands. "I told you my side; can you just tell me how you found it?"

"Hold on. I have screenshots." He taps at his screen while he talks.

"Can you not have screenshots?"

"Give me a minute. I wasn't sure it was you at first. I was just clicking through the location tag for the new arena, and they had your intro on there." He wordlessly holds his camera roll up to show he has every screenshot he took highlighted and deletes them all in one fell swoop. "I was going to send it to Connor like 'yo, this looks just like your girlfriend,' but something told me to, like, stop and verify before I did anything, so I DMed Penny instead."

"You're lucky I was clearing out my DMs last night or I would have missed it. I don't even follow Matt on Insta."

Matt looks up from his phone to make a wounded face. Sorry, man, Penny's follow/follower ratio is flawless, and very few people make the cut.

"Yeah, and then I was like," Penny says, picking up the story, "that's def her, but what the hell is she doing there, and I looked up the company and the team and saw what a big deal it was and like 'whoa she's been doing this for a while and didn't tell anyone, so let's chill out and find out what's going on.'"

"And that's when you called me," I clarify.

"To find out why you were lying to me about why I was lying for you. Because that's what friends do to each other, for sure."

"Yeah, Penny, no offense, but . . ." Matt starts scrolling back through Instagram to show her the original video. He leans forward in the chair so Penny can grab his phone. "You don't know gamers. *Guardians League Online* is better than most because Wizzard takes that Gamergate stuff seriously, but look at what these guys said in the live comments. They don't even know who Lia is."

My stomach drops. I'd been avoiding social media except for a few quick checks of my private accounts to keep up appearances all weekend. I definitely didn't think to check what the comments on the arena's live video looked like.

Penny glances at the screen, then grabs the phone from Matt's hand. "Holy shit," she mutters as she scrolls, "you didn't show me this on Saturday. Lia, have you seen this?"

"No, and I don't want to. Please don't show me."

"Are you sure?"

My curiosity gets the better of me. "Is it . . . really bad?"

Matt takes his phone from Penny, far more gently than she snatched it from him in the first place. "Some of it is good. It kind of starts out with a bunch of assholes being like 'I bet she's awful, fuckin' SJWs, Fury just has her on there for a diversity slot.' This one guy was being loud in there. You can see his comments popping up a lot."

Penny grabs the phone back to see who Matt is talking about. He surrenders it willingly.

"Anyway, the comments kept going through the rest of your match, so right after it ended, that guy kind of had to, uh . . ."

The live video must have shown my checkmate! I poke at the screen in Penny's hands to scrub forward, and sure enough, the guy who was being a jerk before got completely dunked on after Fury's win.

Okay, that tastes good. That tastes really, really good. It sucks that it took winning to shut that guy up, since it only proves what I've known since the first time I played *GLO*—I have to be unassailably great to prove I belong in the same room as guys who are half as good. That's something I'm used to, though. It's the same fight I have at school, or in my extra-curriculars, or literally anywhere else I occupy space in Hill-ford. It's why my parents are so hard on me, I think. They *really* can't find out about any of this.

"Some of the comments before you won are bad, bad," Matt explains. "But after the checkmate, it was like"—he makes a brain-exploding motion around his head—"goddess mode, who is KNOX, yada yada yass queen, and now everyone wants to find out who you are."

"But the bad ones were still commenting!" Penny adds, gesturing to the phone again. "What is wrong with these people? She's just playing a stupid game, and they're acting like Lia broke into their house and cut their dicks off!"

Matt and I explain at the same time:

"Yeah, they're kind of—" "That's the vibe." "Guys are bad. I'm a guy and, like, it's bad."

I really do envy Penny's confused expression. Bless anyone who's never ventured into the gaming underbelly of the culture war.

"That's why I keep it all separate," I say once Matt and I stop talking over each other. "It's the internet, Pen. They love figuring stuff out, and it's honestly a toss-up. Some of them want to find me to tell me I'm awesome; some of them want to send a SWAT team to execute me on my couch. If they get my name, it's easy to find out where I go to school"—I look pointedly at Penny and Matt—"and who my friends are. It's better for everyone if nobody else knows I'm KNOX."

"And what about Jake? Will they do that to him too?" Penny asks.

Matt snorts. "He's literally a nerdy white guy."

I hold my hand up. "Actually, he needs to be a secret too. My team wouldn't be thrilled if they knew I was friends with anyone else competing in the tournament."

"Since when are you friends with him? I have no idea who

'Jake' is," Penny says. She still has Matt's Instagram open and doesn't ask before typing in his search bar.

"No, that's fine, you can use my phone for that," Matt mutters under his breath.

I lock eyes with Matt across the room while Penny searches. He looks more amused than ticked that Penny's taken over his phone, and I try to give him a thank-you smile while she's distracted. He shrugs in response.

"It's Jake what?" Penny asks.

"Hooper," I reply.

"Ugh, private profile. I can't get a look at him."

"Let me see." I lean over her shoulder. The profile she's looking at has Team Unity's logo as its thumbnail. "That's him. But again—I'm not really friends with him. We knew each other when we were kids, and he recognized me at the tournament, so I had to say hi and, like, bring him up to speed. It's nothing."

Penny raises an eyebrow. "I didn't say it was anything. You said you were friends, and now it's nothing. Do you trust him?"

"I do. He's cool. I mean, he's not, like, at all. He's fine." It feels weird to be talking about Jake with Penny. The world-smashing tectonic crunch of discussing *GLO* with Penny was hard enough. With one of Connor's friends here, I can't tell her about what happened with Jake. Does that mean I'm lying?

It's not like I can omit a negative. Nothing happened when

we were in my car after the tournament. Something almost did, but the almost means it didn't happen. I didn't kiss Jake Hooper. See, truth! Lawful good all the way down.

"Yo, is this your setup? This is sick." While I've been watching Penny cycle through Matt's social media in an attempt to find Jake, Matt apparently got bored and started opening the drawers in my desk. He's found where I keep my gaming PC, rigged inside a cabinet I made from taking the desk drawers out and gluing the fronts together to make a false door. You'd think I need a better hiding place, but the desk was a hand-me-down from my dad, and those drawers had been stuck for ages. My parents don't think I have the skills to fix a stuck drawer, let alone build and hide an entire PC.

"Yep. That's Florence," I say nervously. I don't like Matt having my secret cabinet open while my bedroom door isn't closed.

"You built a computer and named it *Florence*?" Penny snorts. I know she still loves me, but she's not going to let me live a single second of my newly discovered nerdhood down, potentially ever.

"Of course, 'cause she's the machine," Matt says matter-of-factly. "That's dope."

For the second time since Saturday, I realize I've massively underestimated a boy in my orbit. Matt Pearson couldn't pass a history quiz without a TARDIS, but he's no dummy. I'd never tell him how little I thought of him before, but I am about to throw a rare compliment in Matt's direction when my mom calls us down for lunch.

"Oh, I'm not really that hungry," Matt says. Penny tilts her head at him like she's looking at a picture of a puppy in a hat.

"Sweet summer child. You can't turn down food in this house," she explains.

I take Matt's phone from Penny's hands and haul myself off the bed to hand it back to him. "Just eat and don't say anything about anything."

Halfway to the door, Penny taps my arm and waves Matt on to go downstairs. "I need to talk to Lia for a second," she says. Matt eyes both of us, Penny smiling and me looking gently terrified, and takes the out he is given. Once we hear my parents greet him in the kitchen, Penny pushes the door to my bedroom closed with the tip of her finger.

"I'm still mad," she says. "When you asked me to cover for you, I thought you wanted to hang out with Connor or do something, I don't know, normal?"

"Penny, I—"

She grabs a pen from my desk and holds it up. "I have the talking stick. This tournament is a big deal for you. I get that. I mean, the money alone is huge, but there are going to be weekends where I need my VP available for real campaign meetings. And after-school stuff too. How often do you practice with your team . . . Angry?" She hands me the pen.

"Fury. Every night, pretty much. Even after field hockey

I'm up till midnight or sometimes later." I don't have much else to say beyond that, so I pass the pen back.

"That's not going to work," she sighs. "I'm dropping you from the ticket."

I try to yank the pen back to respond, but Penny holds it tight. Can she just let me explain?

"No, nuh-uh. You don't hide a huge part of your life from your best friend unless it's something really important, but *come on*. You signed up for this tournament knowing you'd be half-assing my campaign. What am I supposed to do with that?"

I've been so focused on getting Penny to seem less angry that I wasn't really paying attention to her feelings until now. She's not mad, I don't think, but she's hurt. If I were her, I'd be hurt too. I've blown her off so many times for *GLO*-related stuff, and she's smart enough to put those skipped diner nights and sorry-I-can't-sleepovers together now that she knows the whole story.

"I . . ." I look at the pen in Penny's hands. She places it slowly back on my desk. "I wanted to be a good candidate, you know."

"You're the perfect candidate, actually. Well, you were." She punctuates that with a sarcastic toss of her braids. "I thought you were, at least."

"Will you let me fix it?" There has to be something I can do. I can draw up a list, convince anyone to be on her ticket, do cartwheels in the cafeteria on election day, anything to help get Penny out of the mess I put her in.

"Let you? You're gonna fix it," Penny replies. "And if you pull this off, I'll do you one better."

Pull what off? What am I pulling off?

"I want Connor on my ticket," she says simply. "He can get me the soccer team, and, like, half the school is in love with him, so that will make up for losing the athlete loyalty I'd earn with you."

"You want to run with Connor?" I mean, cool strategy, but that's a way bigger get for Penny than asking me, her . . . objectively shitty best friend. I'm going to have to work this out for her. It's the least I can do.

"Yup. He was my second choice, and you're going to convince him for me. While you do that, I'll cover for you with your parents on tournament days. If you lose . . . we'll explain that you dropped out to focus on Model UN or something."

"And if I win?"

Penny wraps me in a hug. Wait, I thought she was mad at me. Is Penny inventing a new, angry hug? "If you win, you'll have new problems and even God can't save you." Well when you put it that way, damn. "This whole thing is just so you."

"You think so?" I gasp when she releases me.

"I mean, yeah. Only you would be Olympic-level good at something and never tell anyone about it. You're, like, obsessed with making everything so much harder than it needs to be.

I'm your friend, Lia! It really sucks that you didn't trust me. I don't know. It hurts that I had to find out through Matt."

I think back to Matt deleting the screenshots without me asking and letting Penny use his phone mid-warpath. "He's actually not that bad."

"Right? Go figure. He might make a half-decent campaign manager for real." She opens the door to start going downstairs. "Imma go hire him."

"Wait!" I say. I kneel down and close my PC's false cabinet. Penny watches me line up the hinges and shakes her head in disbelief.

"Florence," she mutters, "my god."

I'm impressed with how much restraint my parents have shown with lunch knowing we have guests over. Penny's here all the time, but Matt is New People, so I thought there'd be a spread of enormous proportions—instead it is merely massive. My dad grilled some chicken and chopped it up for salad in a bowl big enough to bathe a spaniel, and Mom threw together a cheese board that takes up half of our kitchen island. When the two of us get to the kitchen, Matt is thoroughly entranced by my dad, who is using a pair of chopsticks to flip thin medallions of plantain in a pan of bubbling oil.

"Yo, Lia, can I come here for lunch all the time?" Matt asks. "The plantain chips in the vending machine at school suck compared to these."

"It's all in the timing, young Padawan," my dad explains.

"Here, that one's almost ready to flip." He hands the chopsticks to Matt, who holds them like Obi-Wan just trusted him with a lightsaber.

Dad smiles and points to Matt's first frying attempt. "I like this kid. Matt, are you into computers at all?"

Matt nods robotically, focused entirely on his chips. I think he's actually breaking a sweat from sheer concentration. "Yeah, my brother builds 'em."

"After lunch I'll show you what I have in my office. No one else around here is a techie. I might have some components your brother would be interested in."

Matt breaks focus to look over his shoulder at me. Yeah, I know, dude. Telling my dad I picked up more computer skills than he knows would be mad suspicious. He doesn't know about Florence, and that's exactly how I like it.

"How's the campaign planning going, Madam President?" my mom asks while she tosses the grilled chicken salad.

"Going good, Mrs. Romero," she says sweetly. "Much better now that we have Matt as our campaign manager."

"That's good to hear." My mom eyes Matt standing at attention next to her double-size kitchen range and appears to make up her mind about him. "Every campaign needs a good manager. Have you done student government before, Matt?"

"Heck no," Matt replies. Penny coughs loudly, and he changes his tune. "*But,* I am . . . really interested in civics.

Because"—he looks over my mom's shoulder at Penny and me for a hint at what to say next, but I got nothin'—"we . . . are —"

"The future, Mrs. Romero," Penny finishes for him. "We are the future of America, and it's our job to learn how to be good citizens. Matt understands that, right, Matt?"

"I do." He flips the last plantain out of the pan and admires its golden texture. "Hundred percent, I totally—that's my whole thing."

My mom nods solemnly, more amused than confused.

"I think that's admirable," my dad adds happily. "You're all a few short years from college, and that's when you can get really involved in the process. You know, when I was at UPenn—"

I groan. My dad has exhausted every single possible story about his time at UPenn. I hear them at the dinner table, at parties, doing yard work, in the car, through the door of the bathroom when I'm getting ready for school . . .

"Everyone knows you went to UPenn, dear," my mom says, not unkindly. "Emilia, grab some forks and knives from the drawer. Everyone else can take a plate and come around the island. Someone has to feed the future of America."

"Thanks, Mrs. Romero." Penny walks over to take her plate. "So it's fine if Emilia comes to my place next Saturday? The debate is the Monday after and I need an audience to really nail my delivery."

"That's fine." Mom nods. My dad gives a thumbs-up over

her shoulder. I shoot Penny the most grateful, wide-eyed expression I can manage and feel marginally less terrible when she sticks her tongue out in response. Penny has my back. I guess Matt does too. Last night may have been on the bizarre side of interesting, but everything is coming up Emilia.

PART III

Jake, Sunday Night

JAKE HAD DONE the math, and there was a 28.6 percent chance of his dad being in the kitchen at the exact time Jake was hungry for dinner. He was aware of developmental research that suggested eating meals as a family was conducive to stronger parent-child attachment and a lowered chance of psychological problems, but as far as Jake was concerned, that ship had sailed a long time ago. He was here, his relationship with his dad was meh, and whatever his parents were going to do to him complex-wise was pretty much in the bag at this point.

Still, he was very hungry. Bob gave Unity a break from practice today so they could cool off from yesterday's tournament, but Jake spent most of his afternoon checking up with Ki and Penelope and trying to noodle his way through homework assignments that felt cosmically unimportant in the scheme of Jake's suddenly remarkable life. Somewhere between another chapter of *Beowulf* and some absolutely incomprehensible bullshit about triangles, he felt his stomach rumble.

Jake rose from his desk chair with every muscle in his leg tensed to stop the chair's old springs from squeaking. He poked his head out his bedroom door and squinted to see if his dad's bedroom light was on. It wasn't, which didn't tell him much. His dad slept a lot lately. Sometimes Jake would be chilling in the apartment for hours without realizing his dad had been asleep in his room the whole time. Jake crept a little farther down the hallway and peeked around the corner to check the kitchen light. It was on: 28.6, your number is up.

He tried to look nonchalant as he strode into the kitchen on bare feet and saw Jacob Hooper the Elder eating a plate of reheated ziti at the table.

"Dad!" he said. *Too high key, tone it down.* "You are awake."

"Haven't seen you all weekend, son. Where did you go yesterday?"

There wasn't any special reason Jake didn't talk to his dad about the tournament. Not a reason like Emilia had anyway. When he was in the car with her, which by the way was freaking incredible, Jake understood her issue as being one of systematically detrimental attention. By no fault of her own, her existence in the world of *GLO* was a beacon for other people's opinions and garbage commentary. Jake didn't talk about the tournament for the exact opposite reason: no one gave a shit what he did.

"I met some friends," he said. The inside of the fridge was packed with leftovers. He pulled the rest of the ziti his dad was eating out from underneath something steaky-looking and a tub of mixed greens. *When did I make this?* Jake thought, looking at the marker date on the bottom of the Tupperware. *Thursday. Still edible.*

"You're already making friends at school. That's good."

Jake shut the fridge and grabbed a plate from the cabinet. "Not from school, Dad. My friends from that game thing."

His sudden need to be honest wasn't an attempt to connect with his dad. Jake knew enough about himself to realize that. It was guilt, manifesting in a regurgitative urge to say something true after lying to Unity all afternoon.

He really, really hated lying to his team about Emilia. Lying by omission counted, and he'd cringed when Ki reminded him he hadn't even told them her name. Unity had a right to know that he'd gotten a ride home with Em, and they *definitely* should know that she was driving him to Round 2 . . . but telling them would break Emilia's trust. What kind of choice was that? A smarter person could have figured it out to some grand moral satisfaction. Jake figured he'd just do what he always did and kept his mouth shut, like he promised.

"Your internet friends?" Jake's dad had perked up for a

moment when he imagined his son hanging out with "real" people, but hearing that Jake had instead been palling around with a group of weirdos from the world wide web deflated him once again.

"Yup." Jake noted the change in his dad's voice and responded as dispassionately as possible. He concentrated on the microwave buttons and punched them in one by one to stay calm. "The internet friends. We actually—"

That niggling feeling that he should tell the truth crawled up Jake's spine again. Just because he was good at secrets didn't mean he liked them. "We had a tournament. The game we play is doing a thing at that new arena. My team got past the first round. If we w—"

The sound of a fork dropping onto an empty plate stopped Jake from saying anything else. When he was younger, knowing his dad was angry with him made him want to crawl somewhere and hide, but after what happened last year, Jake found he could bear his father's toothless disappointment better. What was he going to do, honestly? Blind Jake with his own projected expectations?

"So you played video games. You snuck out all Saturday and didn't tell me where you were going because you went to play video games."

Something Emilia said echoed in Jake's head. "That's the vibe."

"When I was your age, I snuck out too, you know."

There was no way to avoid the rest of the conversation, so Jake pulled his dinner out of the microwave and sat down across from his dad. *Lay it on me,* he thought. *Nothing I haven't heard before.*

"We'd get into trouble. We'd hang out in someone's backyard. This time of year, there were bonfires and girls. We played *real* sports."

"Girls play video games too," Jake said quietly. No way was he going to say anything else, though. Not about that girl.

"Those two on your 'team' you used to talk about? One of them isn—"

"Don't. Stop it. You don't know what you're talking about!" Jake was surprised by the ferocity in his own voice. He'd spent enough time talking to Kiki today to want to punch the next person who misgendered her, but he'd never raised his voice to his dad about it before.

Jake wasn't the kind of person who defended himself even when he knew in the back of his mind he was right. There was always that voice telling him that he might be wrong or was too stuttery to say what he was thinking and should probably shut up for the sake of everyone who had to listen to him. It was the voice that made him preemptively call himself stupid before anyone else had the chance to lob it at him as an insult. When someone called him dumb, Jake had long ago realized it was easier to say "I know" than "I'm not."

Emilia didn't let him say that last night. She would have

kicked him out of the car the next time he said he was stupid; he got that sort of energy from her. Maybe that was why he felt okay telling his dad to stand down.

After a tense silence, his dad spoke up again. "Fine. I'm . . . Two years ago h—she was different, right? I can't keep up with all that."

Jake had touched the metaphorical stove once and wondered what would happen if he tried it again.

"Try," he said simply.

"Try a sport," his dad replied, half joking. Jake did not get his tension-diffusing skills from that side of the family. "I would be more comfortable with this game thing if you were also putting yourself out there more. You can't spend the rest of your life stuck behind a desk pressing buttons."

Mr. Hooper's job was literally sitting behind a desk pressing buttons. Jake was feeling brave tonight. Bringing that up was a level beyond brave. He decided, however, to avoid that option on the conversation tree.

"It's different now, Dad," he said. He could tell he was getting whiny, which his father never tolerated. "Lots of people play *GLO*. This tournament is a really big deal."

"Will it bring your grades up? Will it get you into college so you can do something with your life? Jesus, will it get you a girl's phone number so you can take her out?"

"Honestly, debatable."

"What's gotten into you?" his dad asked. He rose from the

table to rinse his plate, not even looking at his son. "I'm just telling you the facts. Last year was hard. We both had to adjust. By now you should be . . ."

Jake got up then and dropped his plate in the sink. He knew what his dad was going to say, and it would be the end of the conversation. Be normal. Be a man. Be the kind of guy who crushed beer cans against his head at bonfires and married his high school sweetheart, only to have that marriage end in fire and flames when—

". . . happier."

Unexpected. Jake stood by the kitchen door quietly, still hoping he had time to slip away if this whole situation got any weirder. It didn't seem like his dad had anything else to say. He was standing over the sink rinsing plates to put in the dishwasher. He looked the same as he'd looked ever since they moved to the apartment, since he started sleeping all weekend and relying on Jake to batch-cook meals for the week. Jake's dad looked defeated. Checkmate: life.

"Okay, I'm gonna go," Jake said. *Be happy in my room* was the unspoken retort he decided to keep to himself.

Jake tiptoed around the corner and down the hallway toward his room, not relaxing until the door was shut behind him and he settled back into his squeaky, creaky desk chair.

So that was terrible, he thought. *What else did you expect?*

Being an all-powerful healer in *GLO* was Jake's dearest fantasy. Pythia was venomous, sure, but when Jake played her character, he could fix anything. He could make people stronger whenever he wanted, and his friends depended on him to do just that. He was good at it. Jake could do that math. Whenever he unplugged his brain from the game, the reality of his tiny bedroom in the apartment he had no choice in moving to washed over him in a lukewarm wave that felt like absolutely nothing. His dad was depressed. His mom was far away. This was his life. He was an idiot.

Stop saying you're an idiot.

Jake felt his lips jerk up in an involuntary smile. That was what Emilia would say to him right now. He could feel as bad as he wanted, but he couldn't call himself stupid. Everything about yesterday was the opposite of a lukewarm wave. It was a . . . red-hot . . . beach? A very cold pier. This metaphor was getting away from him. The point was, it was different. Emilia had pulled up next to him in the parking lot, and every moment with her was pure energy. He felt smarter and funnier; she was surprising and honest. By the time Jake got home, it was dark outside, but the world had never looked so colorful.

Especially the part when Jake thought she wanted to kiss him. He was wrong, obviously; she'd never want that when she was dating Connor Dimeo, but as far as mistakes go—whew. A whole thrill ride in the space of a few awkward milliseconds.

Jake let the energy of the impossible propel him to sit up straighter in his chair and turn his computer back on. He reached a leg out from underneath his desk and flipped the switch of his white noise machine with his bare toe. The *GLO* log-in screen glowed before him as he typed in his username and password. He didn't have to practice with Unity tonight, but he wanted to hang out in one of the freestyle maps for a bit.

The first thing he noticed when he logged in was that his friend list showed no one online. Unity was asleep. Jake should soon be too. The second thing he noticed was that two seconds after he logged in, a DM request appeared on his screen. *GLO* was good about knocking out spam, so random messages weren't common on his competition account. He checked his list again to make sure no one was awake and clicked the request with trepidation.

Message from: beloveandabow. Accept?

Who the hell was beloveandabow? Something about the name seemed familiar albeit unplaceable in Jake's memory. He accepted the message and almost fell straight out of his chair.

Jake! It's Em. Found your account. Penny and Matt know & they're cool but there was a video today. Need to keep tabs on it. If you hear anything from the gaming club, text me?

The following line of text would have frustrated Jake's dad immensely. His son got a girl's number from a video game.

CHAPTER THIRTEEN

Emilia, Monday

JAKE IS BETTER at this "secret friend" thing than I am. I gave him my phone number fourteen hours ago, and he hasn't sent me so much as an emoji, but he's managed to stay in contact all day without me even seeing him. First came the note on the library chair Penny always saves for me during our free period: *Todd knows nothing.* Then, after English, a scrap of notebook paper was shoved in my locker vents: *Jaime and Evan, nope.* I think my favorite one this morning was in biology, when I got to class and noticed that someone with terrible handwriting had scribbled a cypher only I would understand in the corner of the whiteboard: *ENJ: All Clear.*

How did he even get into the bio lab? I think Jake might be a ninja.

I don't even know who the names are. I'm guessing they're the students most likely to have watched the Instagram live before it disappeared. All that matters is that Jake Hooper is somewhere on the Hillford West campus going full rogue on the entire gaming club, and he's doing it for me. I mean, he's also clearly a drama queen and could just text me the damn updates, but even his reluctance to leave a digital trail that could connect us is . . . sweet? I'll go with thoughtful. He's careful, and I appreciate that.

Now that I'm at lunch, I half expect to find a sticky note with coordinates for a clandestine debrief in my cafeteria burger. I take a bite, and nope, just mystery meat and soggy tomato.

"Check your six." Matt tilts his head up to get my attention from across the table. "He's coming."

I whip around to see if it's true. Oh. He meant Connor, not Jake. I have a plan to convince him to join Penny's ticket today at lunch, so of course he meant Connor. There's no reason I should be disappointed about that. None at all.

"He's late. Lunch is almost over," Penny adds, annoyed. "You did tell him we had to talk to him, right?"

"I did," I confirm. "And I asked him to come early, so I don't know what that's about."

While I'm talking, a pair of chilly hands wrap around my face from behind.

"Hey, girl," Connor's familiar voice whispers in my ear. I'm sure it's supposed to be sexy, but the deep weirdness of Connor's growing expectations after only two dates is starting to grate on me. Also, if he presses his fingers on my face any longer, he's going to smudge my makeup.

"Hey," I answer and peel his fingers away from my hard-won lash volume. "It's halfway through lunch; where were you?"

"You said you wanted to hang out, so I drove out and got you something," he explains grandly, then drops a crumpled paper bag on the lunch table in front of me.

I dig into the bag and pull out—joy of joys—a plastic tub with two half-melted scoops of bright green matcha ice cream. That explains the cold hands. Penny has the decency to hide her smirk by looking down and letting her braids make curtains over her face. Connor slides onto the bench next to me and looks beyond happy with himself. How am I supposed to eat like this? Serious question, I don't have a spoon.

"Thank you." I feign all the enthusiasm I can for two green, sludgy lumps. "I'll wait until it's all melty and drink it like a milkshake." Penny likes ice cream like that because she's an alien.

"So what's the group meeting about? What's the tea?" Connor asks.

Penny recovers from behind her hair and raises an eyebrow at me. I nudge Matt with my foot under the table since I planned on him easing Connor into the idea.

"We're talking about the election, man," Matt begins cheerily. "I'm Penny's new campaign manager."

"That's great!" Connor reaches across the table and claps

Matt on the shoulder. "Making headway with the theater girls, that's dope."

Penny locks eyes with me across the table. I know, girl, I know. He's still a good choice for VP.

"Is that, like, it, though?" Connor looks at all three of us. "That's kind of a 'text me' thing, no offense."

"There's another thing," I pipe up. "I'm dropping out of the race."

Connor's brow scrunches up. "Wait, why? I thought you wanted to be VP."

"I did, but with field hockey and some . . . other stuff, I don't think I can do it. We"—I gesture to Penny and Matt— "wanted to offer the slot to you instead."

"Me?" The scrunch intensifies. "I don't get it."

"So," I begin slowly, "since I can't do it, I thought about who I could trust to take my place on the ticket, and you were the first person I thought of. We've all been friends for so long. I thought of who would support Penny like I would support Penny. And that's you."

"I'm not surprised you thought of me," Connor says, perhaps too ready to believe the pile of garbage I just told him. "I'm very supportive." He nudges my arm expectantly. What is he even talking about? Is that a bra joke? Happy to clarify; Connor has never seen my bra. Why is he so weird these days? It was only two dates, and if I'm being honest, I had more fun in a thirty-minute car ride on Saturday than I ever . . .

Out of the corner of my eye, I spot the table where Jake is sitting with some boys in his class. He catches me looking and betrays nothing with his eyes. Damn, he really is better at being a secret friend than I am.

"So what do you think?" Penny poses the question to Connor directly. "Darwin and Dimeo?"

"Double Ds?" Matt suggests. "Could be a campaign slogan."

"Well." Connor squeezes my shoulder. "I don't love that, but if we get to do this together, I'm in. I think Lia would like that." He looks down at me fondly, like a farmer showing off a pig that won first prize at the county fair.

"I think you should definitely take my place," I try to say diplomatically, "but I'm still dropping out. I don't know how much I specifically can contribute to this alliance," I add quickly.

"I can think of a few ways you can contribute." Connor grins. "Emotional support, for one thing"—he pecks me on the cheek—"eye candy, for another."

Okay, first of all, gross. Second of all, what? I don't know what forums Connor's been browsing, but this rapid escalation of maybe-dating to him talking about me like I'm his own personal motivational poster is not what I expected to get out of this conversation. The personal is political for sure, but not that personal. Christ.

To Connor's credit, he senses my discomfort and tries to

backtrack. "And your brain. Because I respect you. Actually, since we're talking, I was kind of wondering . . ."

"Guys! Connor! Matt!" The only person who could make this lunch more terrible waves at our table from across the cafeteria. Connor waves back, which Audra Hastings takes as permission to strut directly toward us. Not like Audra needs permission to do anything.

"Does Audra just magically teleport to the exact place nobody wants her?" Penny wonders aloud. "Is that what the mean witch cursed her with when her parents stole beans from the garden?"

Audra's been behaving herself since the field hockey incident last week, which means she's overdue for some kind of scene. Most of the time she doesn't bother me, but her crush on Connor and her subsequent decision to brand me as her rival is annoying on principle. As far as enemies go, she's virtually toothless; Penny and I have privately speculated that if you pull on her hair hard enough, her mask will come off and reveal a spooky old groundskeeper cursing us meddling kids for foiling her plan to do hand stuff with Connor in the bathroom at prom.

"Hey all, big news." Audra wedges herself between me and Connor on the bench. I cede the territory without a fight. If Connor's disappointed, he doesn't show it. It strikes me that Connor could be just as happy with Audra as he thinks he is with me, if only he stopped subscribing to the idea that only things worth having must first lead you on a merry, infuriating chase.

"What's the news?" Matt asks. Unlike Penny and me, he's fairly Audra-neutral. No one in our social circle has a problem with Matt, so he never has problems with anybody. After witnessing his odd strain of loyalty in action, I think I'm beginning to understand why.

"Is this from the sushi place?" Audra asks, picking up the plastic tub of rapidly liquifying ice cream.

"Yup," I answer curtly. "Connor brought me matcha ice cream. What's the news?" Lunch is almost over, and I'd love it if Audra went away to save me a little time.

I'm out of luck. She leans toward Connor with zero subtlety and all but purrs, "I looove matcha. Why didn't I get anything?"

Something dawns on Connor's face. His smirk makes me think he enjoys feeling like the payload on this incredibly boring game map. If he thinks I'm going to beat Audra's ass for flirting with him, he's going to have to live with disappointment. "I can get you one next time. Lia's a matcha girl too."

Sure. We'll go with that. "Yes, I love it. Love leaves, love eating them on purpose. Are you going to tell us the news or what?"

"Oh, right!" Audra giggles like she completely forgot the reason she sat down and wasn't stalling to keep us in suspense. "I'm running for class president."

Across the table, Penny's eyebrows shoot up toward her hairline. "You're what?"

"I just got back from Principal Klein's office. I'm running!"

Instinctively, I scoot a few inches away on the bench like Audra is about to spontaneously combust. She can't run for president. It's already one week into the campaign period.

Matt says what I'm thinking and asks, "Hasn't the deadline passed? How did you swing that?"

"I told Klein there wasn't enough diversity in the tickets. He saw reason," Audra says smugly. "Since there are two guys running against Penny, I made him see the light of feminism. He gave me the permission slip and said my parents could sign it tonight. Connor"—she pivots on the bench to put her back to me—"do you want to be my vice president?"

You have to be kidding me. Audra couldn't have known that we were just recruiting Connor for our ticket, but her timing couldn't be more awful. Penny hasn't had a chance to file the VP change with the student gov office.

"Oh, Audra, I, um . . ." Connor trails off and leans around her to look at me. "That's nice of you, but I just told Penny I'd be her vice president. Lia's dropping out."

Audra is not fazed by this news at all. "Wait, she just asked you? So she hasn't filed the change with the office yet? You could still join my ticket!"

Penny looks as if she'd really like to try the hair-pulling

thing on Audra. Not to see if she's wearing a mask, but just to tear out a bald patch.

"What the hell, Audra?" she asks sharply. "Those campaign rules are there for a reason. You should have put your paperwork in with the rest of us, and you can't just come here and steal my VP."

"Girl, why you so mad?" Audra leans back like Penny's completely normal reaction is something she ought to be afraid of.

"I'm not your girl, *girl*," Penny replies, "and I'm not mad, I'm right. There's a difference."

"Penny, calm down," Connor says. I know he's just trying to diffuse the situation, but he could not have chosen two worse words. "I'm not ditching you. Don't be mean."

"Yeah, calm down," Audra echoes.

"I am calm," Penny says. "I just think it's funny that I had to work for weeks on my campaign, write *and* submit my speech, mock-up my posters, and give Klein a two-page summary of my platform before he even allowed me to take the permission slip home, but you just walked right in and bypassed all of that. Why'd he do that, do you think? And why do you think you can barge in on our candidate meeting like that's going to get you anywhere?"

Oh, I know this one! The answer is raging entitlement. Pick me for this one, Penny. Pick me.

"I don't know," Audra replies defensively. "You probably

would have done the same thing. I didn't even know Emilia dropped out, and it's not my fault you did a bunch of extra work you didn't have to."

Penny closes her eyes and takes a deep breath. When she opens them again, she looks surprisingly chipper.

"Nope," she chimes. "Not doing this. Emilia, you're up." She taps her hands on the table with an air of finality and hauls her leg over the cafeteria bench to leave. Matt almost dislocates his kneecap rushing to stand up with her.

"Same. I gotta . . ." He trails off, trying to formulate an excuse. He comes up with nothing. Before Matt heads off with Penny, he looks back at me and gives me a thumbs-up. I take it to mean either "good luck" or "you got yourself into this so have fun getting out."

Definitely one of those two interpretations. Either way, he's right; I'm going to need all the luck I can get to knock Audra out of the ring, and it's my fault there's even a ring in the first place. Penny deserves a drama-free campaign, and it's the least I can do to give one to her after what happened on Sunday. I put my dreams before hers and didn't even give her a choice. That was wrong of me, I get that now. I wish it felt more likely that Connor might understand that.

"Honestly I don't even know how you're friends with her," Audra says stiffly once Penny is gone.

"It's easy, she's dope as hell, and she works hard for what she has," I snap. I'm really regretting the moment I let

Audra squeeze in between Connor and me. There's a lot I'd like to say to him right now without having to lean over her; Connor has no such reservations.

"And what about you, Connor?" Audra says sarcastically. "Are you cool with her?"

"Yeah, I guess," he says, shrugging. "She's passionate? I don't get why she's mad, though."

My patience for Connor is wearing way thin, way fast. I can't lose him in the final stretch. "Penny did everything right," I try to explain. "How would you feel if a random new kid was picked to be soccer captain over you and asked for your jersey number?"

I don't know, man. Sports analogies aren't my strong suit.

"That's different," Connor argues. "This is just paperwork."

Audra looks caught between wanting to cheer for the fact that I'm fighting with Connor and wanting to speak to my manager.

"Audra, you mind giving Connor and me a minute?" I ask as sweetly as I can given the circumstances.

"Actually, I do," she says primly.

"I don't care."

Audra stands up in a huff and nudges me so hard I almost slip off the end of the bench. "I'm actually happy because now Connor sees who he's running with. Penny's literally the thought police."

There is, and I cannot stress this enough, a zero percent chance Audra finished that book.

"It's like *1985* with her."

Yeah, bingo. I don't have time for this. If I had a month I might be able to explain it to her. No, a year. I have about three minutes, so I need to choose a different tack.

"I'm going to go too," Connor says and pushes away from the table. Behind him, Audra aims a smile directly at my distraught face. She thinks she's winning. For the first time since she's gotten in my face about Connor, I'm worried that she's winning too. Connor wouldn't move to Audra's ticket because he's mad at me, right? I'm the only reason Penny's in a situation where she needs him. I can't let him go with Audra now.

"Are you even going to eat that?" Connor asks, pointing down at the soupy ice cream container.

I sigh. Salvaging this situation means swallowing my pride, even if I don't swallow the matcha. "Probably not," I say. "Thanks, though. It was really sweet of you."

"Fine," Connor says. He picks up the tub and looks genuinely hurt. "If you don't want it, whatever. It's garbage." He attempts an overhand throw at a garbage can near the cafeteria doors, but—as a reminder—Connor plays soccer. He misses the can by a mile, and the ice cream tub bounces off a nearby table.

There's a thump, a splash, and then—

"Ouch!" someone yells from behind us.

There aren't that many people still sitting at tables, but there's enough left to make the complete halt in all conversations noticeable. Some of them are staring at Connor, some are staring at me, but most of them are staring two tables behind us where the tub of matcha ice cream landed, splattering the people sitting there with bright green goo. Someone has a splotch of it all over his shirt, and two other gamers I don't know knocked over their drinks trying to duck away from the mess.

Jake has it the worst, though. It's everywhere on him. Coating his glasses, dripping down from his hair, and I hope he didn't love the shirt he's wearing today, because it's the matcha's shirt now. In the enduring silence, I see one guy press a napkin into Jake's hands so he can at least wipe off his glasses, and when he puts them back on, he looks at me first with confusion, then shock.

Connor is still standing in front of me with his arm crooked over his shoulder like a remarkably stupid topper on a javelin trophy. He slowly turns around, sees Jake's table covered in goo, and doubles over with laughter.

They say laughter is contagious, but as it spreads around the cafeteria, I find I'm immune. Jake isn't laughing either. I know because even though I told myself I wouldn't, I can't take my eyes off him.

"Connor, what the hell?" I say under my breath. I don't have to be quiet; the laughter is loud enough to drown me out even if I shouted.

"Oh my god," he wheezes. "Hey, kid, are you okay? All good?" He makes a thumbs-up motion in Jake's direction and clearly expects Jake to make one back. There are no consequences for soccer stars at Hillford West.

"Can you at least get him a towel?" I try to yell. My throat feels too tight to get the air I need to speak.

"What, do you know him?" Connor asks.

I glance back at Jake, who says nothing. The laughter has died down. He and everyone else in the caf can definitely hear us now. "No," I reply.

"Look, he's fine." He cups his hands around his mouth and makes a condescending show of shouting, "Sorry, whoever you are!"

"That's hilarious," Audra snorts. "Let's go." She tries to playfully pull him toward the door. I have to stop her and him both.

I can't lose Connor to Audra. I can't lose Penny her VP. I can't go to Jake, even though he's miserable and it's all my idiot almost-boyfriend's fault. *Parallel*, I think. *I can't let my paths touch.* It's time for a Hail Mary.

"And where do you think you're going"—I borrow Audra's tone of smug self-righteousness and throw it back in her face—"with my *boyfriend*?"

Connor's face lights up while Audra's falls. "Boyfriend," he says warily. "You mean it?"

I've been sitting on the payload long enough; it's time to capture the damn thing and get this stupid match over with.

"Of course." I smile. "Now can *we* go?"

"Hell yeah." Connor shoulders Audra's hand off his arm and leans down to kiss me on the lips in front of the entire cafeteria. He closes his eyes, but I keep mine open long enough to catch a glimpse of Jake leaving through another door. He doesn't give my traitor ass a second look. I am officially the worst secret friend ever.

CHAPTER FOURTEEN

Team Unity Chat, Monday Night

MUDD: no offense but can we focus

BobTheeQ: Give us a minute, we'll stay on longer
tonight to make up for it. Jake, are you OK?

JHoops: relatively

MUDD: it's monday. round 2 is this saturday.

ElementalP: and you said you don't even know this
guy? like at all?

JHoops: don't know him at all. never met him. no
friends in common

JHoops: not even a passing acquaintance

ElementalP: it's just so weird???

shineedancer: It's a total Glee move I'll tell
you that

BobTheeQ: That was slushies, this was ice cream.

ElementalP: somehow the dairy element makes it all
the more sinister

shineedancer: it DOES

MUDD: what? how?

ElementalP: i'm lactose intolerant ok milk is scary

shineedancer: omg jake are you lactose intolerant was this attempted murder

shineedancer: je telephone a la police

ElementalP: you're going to jail, random guy

BobTheeQ: Yeah, I'm Team Jail.

JHoops: i'm actually kind of worried

BobTheeQ: Why are you worried? Do you think he's going to bully you again?

JHoops: it wasn't a bullying thing. it was kind of an accident but also maybe don't throw ice cream

ElementalP: so why worry? random is random. anyone can die at any time

shineedancer: you're cheery tonight P

JHoops: im not worried about me. It was kind of between him and someone else.

BobTheeQ: Someone you know?

JHoops: no

MUDD: then why do you care? you showered right? got the ice cream out of your hair? got your feelings out bro? can we get on a map now?

BobTheeQ: Matty. It's OK. We will be ready for the tournament. We will practice tonight.

shineedancer: just want to make sure bby jake is ok

ElementalP: so he can make sure -we're- ok. gotta support our support

MUDD: as long as we don't forget to support our DPS too. we're still not vibing with the new meta

BobTheeQ: OK, where do you want to start tonight?

MUDD: i get to pick the map?

BobTheeQ: Tonight is special. Just for you. Jake, are you OK to start?

JHoops: yeah

MUDD: see, he's FINE. can we please focus on beating Fury?

JHoops: you think they're going to make it past the next round?

shineedancer: with KNOX on their team imma say yes

shineedancer: women in the sequel and all that

MUDD: I spent all weekend crunching the numbers and yeah, fury's gonna smoke chronic

ElementalP: anyone. can. die. at. any. time.

BobTheeQ: Please be careful around Fury next week. That payload win put us on B's radar. Don't forget he plays dirty.

ElementalP: is that what put us on B's radar

shineedancer: like are you sure

BobTheeQ: Not funny.

JHoops: ?

MUDD: sounds like a story

MUDD: and I DON'T CARE

MUDD: let's start on the pygon fortress map. it didn't turn up at all in round 1 so Wiz is probably saving it for round 2

shineedancer: ugh i hate pygon fortress it has so many fricking environmental hazards

ElementalP: Muddy's right tho

MUDD: i'm always right, you people don't listen

BobTheeQ: Good thinking ahead. I'll queue it. Mics down, we're going to voice.

ElementalP: can i sing you guys a song while we queue

JHoops: no

MUDD: no

BobTheeQ: Abstain.

shineedancer: yes please <3

[Team Unity is queued for battle.]

CHAPTER FIFTEEN

Emilia, Wednesday

"YOU'RE JUMPING TOO early, KNOX! Erik can't get the heal up in time. Coordinate, for god's sake; we only have a few more minutes."

I am, or rather Pharaoh is, jumping exactly when I need to jump. Erik is slow on his heals tonight, and Byunki is either too distracted or too annoyed to notice. The combo we're putting together is hard enough without our tank lumbering around shouting at us like a drill sergeant.

"Reset the combo; we're trying again. Ivan, take her health down."

On a real *GLO* map, players can't hurt people from their own team. Friendly fire would make *GLO* a total mess, considering all the elemental magic and circumstantial damage a team can deal in some relatively enclosed spaces. Team Fury is working on a freestyle map tonight, a closed clone of real maps that turn up in competition with different rules. On this map, Ivan can whack my Pharaoh around all he wants and I'll actually take damage. It's what I've been doing all night, basically: standing still and letting Team Fury beat the crap out of me to nail this combo. Every once in a while, I get to jump off a building.

I watch as Ivan's character slashes at Pharaoh until my health is critical.

"Sorry, Knoxy," he jokes. "I know I'm not supposed to hit a girl."

How does he feel about getting slapped by one? Ugh, I need to calm down. None of this is personal. Still, I'm getting tired of watching my little necrobuddy take everyone's shit tonight.

"That's enough," Byunki notes over voice chat. "KNOX, get back on the roof. Take your place, Erik."

I mechanically tap the sequence of moves that brings Pharaoh up from the ground level of this map to the top of a ruined bell tower. We've run this so many times I could do it in my sleep. It's late enough that I might actually have to if this practice goes on any longer. Byunki said he had to break early to do something else tonight, which was the first time I ever heard him indicate he might have a life outside of *GLO*, but early for Byunki still won't give me enough time to finish my calculus homework, refresh my bio reading, or proofread the sample position paper I need to submit ahead of Model UN tryouts.

"Everyone ready?" Byunki asks. The rest of Fury takes their places for the combo. "KNOX, jump."

With Pharaoh's health already down, I leap from the tower and aim for an area just behind Erik's Jenkins character. *Please get this right*, I think as Pharaoh plummets. *I'm tired, and my head hurts, and I'm having a bad week already.* If Erik doesn't get his heal/harm wall up in time, I'll take enough fall damage to drop and we'll have to load this map all over again.

Byunki clicks his tongue as a signal, and Erik slams a horizontal heal/harm right below where Pharaoh will land. I see it bloom underneath him, and—thank god—it's fully operational when he hits the ground. Instead of taking fall damage, Pharaoh is powered all the way up. For my part of the combo, I use the surge to whip off three successive crossbow bolts that hit Byunki, Ivan, and Han-Jun square in the chest. Easy peasy, once Erik got his shit together.

"Gorgeous," Ivan moans. "Seriously, can a combo be sexy? I'm feeling something over here. Something adult."

"No one cares, Ivan," Han-Jun comments. He and Erik are the quietest during these practices. I can never tell if they're concentrating or if they have a separate healer chat where they talk about the rest of us.

"Good job," Byunki says begrudgingly. "I'd tell you to run it again, but I have to go. Keep that in the bank for Round Two, Erik. It's a good combo. Your strategy is getting better."

"Oh, actually," I chime in, "it was my idea. Remember?" *I* told Byunki I thought we could do something cool with Jenkins's horizontal heal just a few hours ago. *I* told him Pharaoh's near-death surge ability could piggyback on it with a triple bolt. We've spent half our time tonight practicing it; how could he forget that it was my combo in the first place?

Byunki's tone shifts from impatience to annoyance. "Whatever, it's not about credit, KNOX."

I DM Ivan on the side: is he srsly doing this again

Ivan types back quickly: its not a big deal, let it go

Fine. Ivan's right. Byunki's been better with me in the first half of the week, and I don't want to mess it up by throwing a tantrum three days before competition. Then again, asking to be credited for my strategy shouldn't constitute a tantrum in anyone's book.

"Tomorrow we'll try it again and see how it works with the rest of our playbook. KNOX, since you're on a strategy kick, I want you to analyze Chronic's tank choices for Saturday. I really gotta go. Stay sharp. Same time tomorrow."

Great, more homework. All I have to do now is watch all of Chronic's matches, find out their elemental weaknesses, and do a statistical breakdown of who they're likely to play in their swap spot within a margin of error Byunki feels is adequate. At least it's more fun than bio.

Ivan DMs me a goodbye before signing off while Han-Jun

and Erik drop offline. The freestyle map times out and kicks me back into the *GLO* main screen.

"Emilia?" Mom taps at my closed bedroom door. "Can I come in?"

"Just a second!" I shout back and quickly switch my monitor cords from those that connect to Florence to those attached to the laptop I use for school. As far as my parents know, that's the only computer I own. Sliding Florence's cabinet closed takes a little longer.

"Is everything okay?" Mom asks.

In the last moments I have before she gets suspicious, I pull my arms into my pajama shirt and spin it around so I have it on backwards.

"All good, I was just changing! You can come in."

Mom opens the door and finds me posed over my bed going through my homework papers.

"Were you just getting changed? Your shirt's on backwards."

I look down at my shirt and force a laugh. "I was, and yeah. Look at that. I've been so deep in"—I check the worksheet on my bed—"the Krebs system I didn't even notice when I put it on wrong."

"You've been busy lately," she remarks. "I'm checking to make sure you're staying on top of things."

"I am, Mom." My grades aren't dipping any, thanks to my one-woman summer school program, but I'd be lying if the pressure from the tournament hasn't been throwing me off with school, Connor, and my upcoming extracurriculars.

"What's the rest of your week look like?" she asks. This is more than a check-in; this is a full status report. I clear my throat.

"Bio quiz tomorrow, and we're wrapping *Gatsby* in English, so the test on that is next week. Calc is still basically going over precalc since it's early. AP US History is still precolonial."

Mom nods. "You have field hockey tomorrow too. And how's the campaign going? I talked to Dad, and he said he'd be happy to make you two a website."

"That's okay," I say too quickly. "Uh, Penny has our socials covered. Websites are a little millennial, you know? We're doing a lot to keep the support up."

"Sometimes a lot isn't enough, Emilia," Mom says. "You need to be the best, not just better if you're going to stand out." She pauses. "I don't mind you dating Connor Dimeo as long as he doesn't distract you from what's important."

"Oh, he won't," I snort before I remember who I'm talking to. "I mean, he gets it. He's in most of my classes, so he knows the workload."

"Are you still going to Penny's for the campaign meeting on Saturday? Will he be there?"

Right, that's this week's excuse for the tournament. "I don't think so. It's kind of a whole-day thing, and he has other stuff to do."

"Next week you should have Penny over here and invite Connor. I think your father wants to meet him."

God, that would be a scene. I don't think my dad ever needs to meet Connor for any reason. I may have told Connor I'd be his girlfriend to checkmate Audra, but I've been trying to backtrack on that since the ice cream incident on Monday. Just thinking about Jake's face, knowing he heard me call Connor my boyfriend right after he humiliated him . . . it makes my chest clench up badly.

"Maybe!" I reply. "I should get back to my bio, though. Once I finish that and my position paper, I'll head to bed."

"Stay up as late as you need," Mom agrees. "It's a big year for you."

I know. I know, I know, I know. "'Night, Mom."

"Good night, Emilia."

No rhythm is more familiar to me than the sound of my mom walking from my bedroom to hers at night. Down the hallway, up a small landing, the sound of the door to the master suite opening, a pause, and the same door closing with a muffled knocking noise. It's the rhythm of my parents fully retreating into their world and leaving me a scant few hours to spend some time in mine.

The bio can wait, the position paper is basically done, and it's not even midnight yet. I wait another few minutes to make sure neither of my parents feel like emerging for a glass of water and hold my pose next to my bed in case they do. It takes another few minutes until I'm fully in the clear.

Florence is still on in her cabinet, so all I have to do is switch the monitor cords and the *GLO* main screen appears again. A green dot by my recent contacts list indicates that someone on my contacts is online. Is Ivan still practicing after Byunki let us go for the night? If he was, I can't blame him. I'm about to do the same thing.

I click the list to see if he wants to play together but see his username logged off. The only person on my list currently playing is Jake. JHoops. Maybe, if I was careful . . .

Nah. Don't do it. He probably thinks I'm a monster for the ice cream thing.

This is useless, I think to myself as I hover over his name in my *GLO* mailbox. *I told him to leave me alone, and now I'm bothering him. The way he looked at me doesn't matter. What he thinks of me is irrelevant.*

He didn't leave me any more notes after lunch on Monday. He didn't have to, since his recon mission was complete, but I had sort of hoped that he might keep it up through the week. The surprise of it all made for a very exciting morning. I liked the idea that he was trying something fun for me. It's exactly something I would like, and I didn't even have to tell him that. He just did it.

That day was a lot more fun than the others in this week. On Tuesday I found a bunch of floppy rose petals crammed in my locker courtesy of Connor, and they stained one of my notebooks. Today it was confetti. Now that I'm thinking about Connor, I check my phone to see if he's left me any texts while I was playing. Oh, yup. Five new messages, none of which I will check tonight. He can live with assuming I'm asleep. Or terrible. God, it would be nice if he just realized I'm the worst.

Now you sound like Jake, I think. It's something he would say. I don't want him to think he's the worst. I should talk to him, get in quick and apologize before dipping out of his life forever.

When I click on Jake's player profile I can see his most played characters (Pythia, two other healers, a DPS that got nerfed quickly after launch), his win/loss ratio, his ranking, guild association, and achievements. It's a gold mine of information on Jake the player that fits perfectly with what I know about Jake the person.

I have to stop myself from scrolling down to look at more of his stats. After Unity's healer-heavy performance in the first round, I know Byunki would kill to get a look at these numbers, but I'd have to be a jerk of titanic proportions to bring Jake into my inner circle one moment and betray him to Fury in the next.

Not handing it over is technically betraying Fury, I think. For the moment, Fury can suffer.

Hey, it's Em, I tap into a DM.

A long pause from Jake's side of the screen.

I wish *GLO* chat did the three-dot text thing. I never feel more alive than I do when those ellipses appear, then disappear, then appear again. It's watching someone else's mind work in real time. This message window gives me no such pleasure. After a minute, I peek up at Jake's name on the profile window to make sure the green dot hasn't gone anywhere. He's there, just out of reach.

Gatsby, my brain volunteers. God, no. That guy sucked.

Who? he finally replies.

Oh no. I check the previous message in our DMs and see that whoever JHoops is never responded to my initial message. Did I send my phone number to a complete rando? How did Jake know to leave the notes then, if it wasn't his account?

sry wrong person, I type quickly and exit out of the message window. Well, that was humiliating. That's enough *GLO* for tonight. I slide my cursor up toward the log-out button and am about to dip when a new message window pops up. It's JHoops.

messing with you em

Really? I wish that didn't make me smile, but it does. The guy has one move, and he's gotten me with it twice in five days. Before I can come up with a response, the message window unexpectedly glows greener with an invitation to voice chat.

The green window pulses to the tune of the *GLO* ringtone, and the hypnotic gradient washes everything on my desk the bright verdant color of . . . matcha, unfortunately. I take it as a sign.

"Hey. Again," I say once I answer the call. I'm sitting up straighter in my desk chair now, like I've been sent to the principal's office and Klein's just walked in with disappointment on his face.

"Oh, wow," he says, and from the crackle on his microphone, I think he's letting out a breath he was holding for as long as it took for me to answer, "it's you."

"Yes, I just told you."

"Sorry, yeah. It's just weird communicating."

"I gave you my number!"

"Right. I didn't want to . . . I didn't want to intrude. Figured there was an easier way of letting you know you were okay without leaving a digital trail."

He thought a morning of deep espionage was easier than sending me a text message? High drama Jake Hooper strikes again. Can't say I hate it.

"The notes were . . ." I stop myself to think of a more neutral word than the first one that comes to mind. Amazing? Delightful? The only thing that made my day this week? ". . . cool. Nice touch with the bio whiteboard."

"After I did it I was like, 'Aah, that was corny, like way too corny.' "

"Jake." I have to stop him before he talks himself into another self-effacing spiral. "It was dope. Thank you. And thank you for checking in the first place, obviously. Def helped me sleep easier this week."

I hear Jake chuckle into the mic. "No it didn't! You're awake now."

"Touché. So are you, though."

"I'm kind of in a waiting room and don't want to get out. Do you want the ID?"

Right. People who are logged into *GLO* at midnight are usually there to play the game. That's fine. Playing through the conversation I actually want to have with Jake might make it easier for me to get through it.

"Sure, yeah. DM it to me. I'll meet you in there."

The message window blips again with a room code from Jake. It's for another freestyle map, but this one is a beta, which makes it perfect for role-playing or just hanging out on the server with friends. Back when I first played, freestyles were where I met some of the guys who turned out to be total assholes. Before they found out I was a girl, they were pretty cool to hang out with.

Some of the more popular beta builds get overloaded, hence the waiting room, and the one he's invited me to is Crystal Cathedral, an unreleased map for Diamond-tier players to beta test before Wizzard releases it to the rest of the game. It's a flex that Jake is even in the waiting room and a compliment that he knows I'd be able to get in alongside him. There's still a bit of a wait (the hottest club on the internet is this beta map), so we have a few minutes to talk before we're in.

"Who are you playing?" I ask as I sort through the many, many Pharaoh skins I've collected over the years. Should I go for his extra-dead-looking Halloween outfit or the rare gold robes I got before *GLO* nuked their loot boxes?

"I am Pythia and Pythia is me," Jake replies. I don't ask what skin he's putting on his poison prophetess.

"Cool." I settle on the gold robes. I feel like a sleep-deprived turd, so Pharaoh will have to look fresh for both of us. "Hey, before we go in, can I talk to you?"

"Mhm," Jake answers sleepily. If I keep him up any longer, I'm going to have more than one thing to apologize for, and that will surely be the thing that kills me.

"I, um. I want to say sorry about Monday. With the ice cream." It's a good start. I don't want this to come across as one of those crappy non-apologies, though, so I keep going after Jake leaves me hanging in deserved silence.

"I'm so, so, so sorry I didn't help you, or stick up for you. Or get you a paper towel; you definitely could have used a paper towel. I saw you, and it was my fault he threw the ice cream, and I feel horrible. Are you okay? Were you okay?"

"Em, that was two days ago." He seems surprised I brought it up.

Dilemma: how do I explain that I'm a massive coward who was scared of admitting that I did a bad, mean thing without sounding like a massive coward who does bad, mean things?

"Yeah, I'm fine," he says. "I mean, no, I wasn't right then because it was really sticky and stuff, but I'm fine now.

I showered." He pauses, more to catch his breath than to think about what he's actually saying. "I didn't, like, only shower then; that wasn't my only shower. I shower every day, so it's not like that was my one shower and I'm done for the week."

From the cadence of his speech, Jake's in ramble mode. I'd stop him, but I find it oddly charming. He talks the way I think, nonstop and always trying to cover every possible interpretation of whatever he's going to say.

"I was more asking if you were okay, like, emotionally."

"Oh. Yeah. Once it was over, nobody really noticed. Perks of being invisible."

"That's not—"

A trumpet interrupts whatever dumb thing I was about to say. We're up for the freestyle map. I hadn't planned on playing much longer tonight, but now that I'm in, I can't help but feel the same flutter in my chest I get whenever I'm up in *GLO*. Right as Pharaoh spawns in front of the cathedral—and, look, it really is all made of crystal—I flag him for combat, just in case I want a little target practice while I try to get through to Jake.

"Hold that thought. Where did you spawn?" I ask.

"West side, in the gardens."

"Coming to you."

The late-night crowd is mostly role-players with very few people toggled for combat, so it's a piece of cake to keep Pharaoh moving through clouds of fog and remain unharmed as I make my way toward Jake's Pythia. The map is dominated by the cathedral in the center—like most things in *GLO*, it's a bizarre architectural combination of gothic spires and glowing alien tech, with buzzing blue screens in the place of stained glass windows and suspicious surveillance droids instead of gargoyles. In front of the church is a stone plaza where a few players are mingling—Lucafonts and Envys dressed in last year's spring fever skins, Munes and Hyves wielding the Diamond-tier editions of their standard weapons—but Jake's coordinates place him to the west, in what looks like a hedge maze when I zoom out on my minimap. Pharaoh fits right in as I half run, half hop down the stairs and move toward the coordinates on my map.

When I finally see "[JHOOPS]" hovering above a player, I can't contain my laugh to a volume-controlled snort. His Pythia is wearing a cross between a nurse's outfit and a clown suit, complete with a big red nose and a jaunty candy striper's uniform. It's an exclusive from way back in the game's day-one patch, when all the healers got silly *Patch Adams* outfits to celebrate the launch.

"Sweet Christmas. You look ridiculous," I say as our characters link up. A reddish tint on the side of my screen indicates an enemy nearby who's probably confused as to why two combat-flagged players aren't tearing each other to pieces, but I spin my camera and slam a crossbow bolt into their shield as a warning. Not now, twerp.

"Nice shot. Your mummy looks like an Oscar," Jake says as the other player turns tail.

"Thank you. It's fashion."

"You were going to say something before?" he says.

Was I? Playing around with Jake for a few minutes put me in an entirely different headspace to the stressed-out, anxious garbage brain I've toted around all week. Wait, I remember. "Why do you think you're invisible?"

I hear a creak, like Jake is closing a squeaky door or moving around in a seriously dilapidated chair. I can almost picture him rubbing his neck out of habit, messing up the way his hair falls in the back.

"There's this cool maze thing here; want to check it out?"

Sure, I'll walk the maze. I follow Pythia's lead around the fountain and toggle my character to slow-walk alongside Jake as the purple alien hedgerows rustle with animated life. This is a good map. The maze will make PVP even more interesting, especially if the devs hide the payload somewhere in the middle.

"The invisible thing is nothing," Jake says after a long pause. "I mean, *you* know. It's part of your thing. And it's fine, by the way. The thing is totally cool with me."

"My thing?"

"The thing. You don't notice me, I don't talk to you, nobody at school finds out you're a Diamond-tier necromummy, and sometimes you *GLO* chat me in the middle of the night. Your very normal thing."

When you put it like that, it does sound cold and one-sided, which makes me feel a little defensive. I don't *want* to ignore Jake; I *have* to ignore him. Even if it's functionally the same thing, I would hope that my intent matters a little bit. Then again, if I look at what happened on Monday from his perspective, I don't think any intention could have excused it. Of course Jake thinks I don't think about him—how was he supposed to assume anything else?

"Jake, you know I notice you, right?"

"Mm?"

"You said you don't talk to me and I don't notice you. That's not . . . that's not the thing."

He makes a "hm" noise, and I don't know if it's a skeptical "hm" or a thoughtful "hm." My deep, irritating need to clarify—to have him understand exactly where I'm coming from—brushes up against the fact that I have absolutely no idea where I'm coming from.

"Just because we can't talk doesn't mean I pretend you're invisible."

"Okay," Jake says quietly, then lifts Pythia's hand to cast a bolt of magic almost directly at my Pharaoh's face. "Almost" is the operative word, because when I spin to avoid it, I see another player, whose level is way too low to be in this server turned to stone behind me. It's probably some Diamond player's alt. They must have forgotten they're outmatched by almost everyone else in the map. That attack has a seven-second countdown, so Jake and I re-toggle our sprint and move out of range before they crack out of their casing.

"Thanks," I say. "Where were we?"

"We were talking about me," Jake says, "which is weird for me."

"I wish you were nicer to yourself," I reply.

"Hey, Em?" he asks, changing the subject while stifling another yawn. The yawn snaps me out of the fallen-in feeling I'd had on the exploration map and reminds me that I'm not standing at the edge of the world with Jake Hooper; I'm slouching in my pajamas with a cold mug of Café Bustelo and six hours until I have to be up for school. "Can I ask you a question?"

"Sure."

"I saw you on my first day at Hillford. I wanted to say hi to you, but I didn't know if you would have wanted me to."

That's not really a question, but I know what he's asking. At this hour of the night, our last four combined brain cells have definitely fallen in sync.

"I wanted you to. Or I would have wanted—Okay, maybe not fully in context because then the whole tournament thing would have been even weirder to deal with, but in a vacuum, and speaking solely on the *concept* of you saying hi on the first day of school—"

"You really wouldn't have minded?"

I honestly don't know the answer to that. Now that Jake's here being sleepy and delightful on voice chat, it seems like it should be obvious, but realistically I don't know how I would have reacted to seeing him at school before the tournament. Half of me would have liked it very much. If he talked to me then the same way he's talking to me now, I don't think I would have had any other option.

Then again, if Jake had just rolled up to me and started talking about games, I would have had to shut him down fast. I'd never be able to talk to him like this if I pegged him as a threat from the start. Knowing that I would have done that makes me hate myself a little more.

When I started building up these walls around my gaming life and my real life, I told myself I was doing it so I could have everything I wanted. I hadn't considered that the separation meant there were other things, better things, that I'd miss out on. Penny is one thing; she understands one half and is trying to learn a new language to decode the other, but Jake doesn't have to translate. He gets all of it, straight out the gate. That's why everything with him feels so easy.

I was missing Jake before I even met him at the tournament.

"Actually it could have blown everything up if you did," I answer honestly and surprise myself by staying honest: "But I wouldn't mind."

"I won't blow anything up."

The red highlight appears again, this time on the bottom of my screen. That player who we turned to stone earlier is back; I just can't see where. I know Jake sees the danger glow too, because his Pythia blesses me with a defense boost and whirls around to face the maze we both emerged from.

"I know you won't. Thank you," I say as I navigate Pharaoh in front of Pythia. She's a great healer, but Wizzard tempered her powers by giving her a smaller amount of health compared to other characters. If Jake drops, he'll be kicked back to the waiting room, and what can I say? I like exploring this map with him.

"Wait, I want to try something. I don't play with Pharaohs a lot," Jake says quickly. "Shoot into the maze to draw him out; make sure you miss."

Sir, KNOX does not miss. "Why? I could paralyze him with a clean shot." Our hidden enemy is playing Nero, an alien character weak to Jake's poisonous Pythia.

"Trust me," Jake says. I can hear his smile through the audio.

"Fine, but don't go telling your team I have a bad eye," I mutter and level a shot into the bushes. Nero emerges and comes straight for us brandishing a shiny galactic sword that is, in the words of Wizzard's legal team, definitely not a lightsaber.

"Keep shooting and missing. He's going to come for you."

"Are you sacrificing me?" I almost yell. "I thought we were cool!"

"We are cool, hold your ground," Jake says quietly. When Nero is two steps away from me, Jake calls out another attack: "Boost my magic, go!"

I still think he's being a little bossy, but let's see what his thotty snake can do. I hit my key for Pharaoh to buff Jake and watch as Pythia slams her staff into the ground to generate a bubble of sickly green magic around us both. The other player charges right into it and loses a quarter of their health with a stun on top. How do you like that poison damage multiplier, bro?

I'm impressed. The timing on that was absolutely perfect.

"Nice ability!" I observe. I'm too tired to bother with this Nero any further, so I take advantage of the stun to open a portal back to the spawn point. "Hop in here. This guy's annoying me."

"Sure."

One purpley swoosh of magic later, Jake and I are back on the plaza. Some of the players from before are still around, but they're all crowded in smaller groups and dropping emotes in a pattern I recognize as some elaborate RP argument. Jake and I may as well be computer-generated nonplayer characters, total NPCs in the backdrop of whatever scene they're playing out.

"Why are we even toggled for player-versus-player

combat?" I ask. It's too late to undo the PVP choice now, but I'm seriously regretting thinking I would need any further distraction when I have Jake on the mic.

"I dunno. I figured you would, and if you needed a healer I wanted to be there."

That's exactly what I thought he'd say. I don't understand where Jake gets that selfless impulse from.

"See, that's nice. I can't see you blow anything up when you're that nice."

"Don't think that," Jake says so quietly I almost don't hear him on the mic. "I've ruined things for people before. A while ago I told someone something I shouldn't have, and I learned not to do that anymore."

That's not a great sign. Not a bad sign, either, if he really learned his lesson the hard way. "What did you tell? Was it about *GLO*?"

"Nah, something else. I don't want to talk about it. I keep my mouth shut now, so it's kind of better that no one listens to me."

"I'm listening."

Jake sighs again into his mic. "You are. Which, by the way, is totally nuts. Just from a personal standpoint, for me."

"Me too." Wait, that didn't come out right. "Not nuts that I'm listening, just nuts that we're, like, talking like this. I don't get to talk to anyone like this."

"You don't have heart-to-hearts with random guys in front of towering monuments to Space Catholicism?" Jake jokes.

"No, I do that all the time, obviously. Totally normal Wednesday. Don't let me keep you up, though," I say. "See you on Saturday?"

"You still want to risk it? It's okay if you don't."

"I do." Of course I do.

"Okay, tell you what. You bring the car; I buy you a matcha latte. Just the biggest . . . grande-est . . . green tea thing you've ever seen. I'll dump half of it all over myself, just how you like it."

"Jake!" If I laugh any harder, I *will* wake up my parents no matter how far their bedroom is from mine. "I have to get to bed. I'm delirious. Sorry."

I can almost hear his smile through the microphone, the same smile he gave me in front of his apartment when he said it was super cool not being my friend again. It makes me smile too.

"Em, you gotta stop saying sorry."

CHAPTER SIXTEEN

Team Unity Chat, Friday

BobTheeQ: I'm going to keep it real with you. That was balls.

shineedancer: I messed up the countdown, my bad

MUDD: and their Klaudio burned me out

BobTheeQ: Jake, you stayed alive. Where were you?

JHoops: I whipped their carrigan into the lake to short out his mech special

JHoops: by the time he was in ki and muddy blinked out

BobTheeQ: We can't let this happen tomorrow. We were on fire last week, what happened?

JHoops: muddy's balor was literally on fire just now if that helps

MUDD: can you not

BobTheeQ: In less than twenty-four hours, we play Beast Mode. If we beat them, we get a shot at Fury.

With the way we're playing tonight Beast is going to eat us alive.

ElementalP: idk maybe we're TIRED and if you let us sleep we'll be fine

BobTheeQ: Fine isn't going to give us a win over Beast Mode.

JHoops: isn't there a thing like "bad dress rehearsal, good show"?

MUDD: if it turns out you've been a theater kid this whole time i will physically hurt you with my hands

BobTheeQ: We're running Pygon Fortress again. If we can't get our timing right with the environment, we'll run it again. And again.

shineedancer: bob r u ok

shineedancer: i know you really want a shot at Byunki but you don't even sound like you right now

[LanguageBot]: *language, KI*

BobTheeQ: I'll be OK when I know we're tight enough to not embarrass ourselves tomorrow. Trust me when I say it's vital that we get to the next round.

MUDD: i'm with bob

MUDD: like it was fun and games going into round 1 but we're one match away from taking fury down. it's not cute anymore we need to focus.

shineedancer: what, like you focused on our postmortem last week?

ElementalP: THERE it is

shineedancer: which was mandatory

shineedancer: because you can just show up and play
and not have to worry about everyone's fucking son
coming out of the woodwork to make your life hell
because you're good at a game

[LanguageBot]: *SECOND WARNING, KI*

MUDD: sorry i couldn't make it to your therapy
session girls i was resting up so we could actually
play later

JHoops: dude that's not the point. we all said we'd
be there for Ki and P and you didn't show up. do
better next time

MUDD: says the guy who would kick us off a bridge if
KNOX said so

ElementalP: ummm?

BobTheeQ: What does that mean?

MUDD: nothing.

MUDD: jake didn't mess up that last match. he's not
the problem here

ElementalP: does that mean ki is the problem here?

shineedancer: it takes two to deal damage BRO, you
got set on fire before you could even start your
clock.

shineedancer: check your six before you come for me
booboo

BobTheeQ: Everyone is right and everyone is wrong. Muddy, show up for the postmortem on Sunday. If we don't have each other's backs we have nothing.

MUDD: if we win tomorrow i'll show up anywhere

BobTheeQ: Ki, let it go. Muddy messed up but we need our DPS in sync for tomorrow. Hash it out on DM, or don't, just get it together for tomorrow.

shineedancer: let's go with don't

BobTheeQ: Jake, I don't know what Muddy's talking about but you've been quiet on KNOX all week. Is there anything I need to know about?

JHoops: nope

BobTheeQ: Penelope . . . IDK, you good?

ElementalP: i mean i'm breathing

BobTheeQ: Mics down, we're going back in. This is important, so take a few deep breaths and get in the game. Muddy, swap from Balor to Nero so you don't get caught up with the fire weakness. Ki stay on Doctor Jack for the ice attacks.

BobTheeQ: Healers are fine on Pythia and Castor, I'm swapping Fabella for Reigh.

Shineedancer: on it

MUDD: I can def do nero

BobTheeQ: We'll only run Pygon one more time before bed. Jake has to be up early for the bus.

[Team Unity is queued for battle]

CHAPTER SEVENTEEN

Emilia, Saturday, Round 2

I'VE NEVER FELT more like a ninja than I do right now, pulling slowly into the parking lot of Hillford's second and noticeably crappier Dunkin'. It's not a bad feeling, and it's certainly not a new one relating to the tournament, but knowing I'm here to pick up Jake before engaging in further *GLO*-related subterfuge adds a little extra thrill to the usual proceedings. A thrill garnish, if I may. Thrarnish.

That thrill is of course 100 percent related to Jake's status as my competitor in this competition, naturally. The fact of it being him specifically is a nonfactor. Byunki would be furious with me if he knew I was fraternizing, and I don't know what Jake's team would do if they caught us together (knowing what I do of Team Unity, they'd probably kiss him on the forehead and give him a kitten), but I simply and purely do not care. Giving Jake a ride is the right thing to do, and surreptitiously flipping Byunki the bird might be the only thing that gets me through another day at his hypercompetitive mercy.

My phone rings through my car speakers as soon as I put the car in park. Penny's name and all-American photo from her campaign poster pops up on the screen (unlike Connor's photo, I put that one in myself). This is the second time she's called me in two weeks, and I gotta say, as much as talking on the phone is the realm of the elderly, it's actually a pretty good way to quickly communicate information. Go figure.

"Pen! It's 6:45 in the morning."

"Hi to you too." She sounds grumpy, which I read as tired. I'd sympathize if I hadn't been up past midnight every day this week.

"Sorry, hi. Good morning. What's up?"

"I"—she doesn't bother to stifle her yawn—"got up early because I'm a *fantastic* person and wanted to say break a leg. Or wish you good luck? Smash a . . . controller thing. I don't know what you people say."

Her delivery could use some work. I'm still touched.

"Thank you. I think it's good luck? No one's ever said it to me before, about this kind of stuff."

"Like I said, fantastic person."

"You really, really are."

"Are you alone?"

That's ominous. "Yeah, I'm waiting to pick up Jake at *the location*."

"Aha. Can't forget Jake. Like any of us could forget Jake," she replies. Her sarcastic tone is duly noted. I may have developed a teeny, tiny case of the mentions about Jake in the latter half of this week. Only around Penny and Matt, of course, but they were curious about the tournament and I couldn't *not* bring him up. Especially since I've been good about not looking or talking to him during school hours.

Okay, I maybe look at him a little during school hours.

And I have been talking to him after practice for the past three days.

And that might be the reason I'm even more sleep-deprived than usual because Fury stuff wraps at 11:30, but the Jake stuff wraps whenever one of us is about to fall asleep. Or whenever one of us does fall asleep, like I did Thursday night and Jake had to sing the "Funkytown" beeps over voice chat to scare me awake.

"I can't forget Jake because he doesn't have a ride without me." The defense is crappier than this Dunkin', and I know it. Penny apparently knows it too.

"I hope you know what you're doing," she says warily.

"I'm driving one of my competitors to the *GLO* tournament. It's good sportsmanship."

"Yeah, no."

"It's good sports*woman*ship?"

"Lia. I'm talking about Jake, not *GROW*."

"It's *GLO*, and it's fine. I also know what I'm doing with Jake." Nope, that didn't sound right. "I'm not doing anything with Jake. I know what I'm doing because it's nothing. Everyone knows how to do nothing."

I feel Penny's sigh reverberate in my spine.

"It's too early for this. I'm gonna do it, though: did you lock it down with Connor just to get him on my ticket? 'Cause if you did and you really like Jake, you need to break up with him."

On any other day I would appreciate, no, count on Penny's annoyingly clear-minded assessment of my actions. Any other day that is not today. Did I throw the boyfriend word at Connor to get him on the ticket? Yes, but it was more complicated than that. Maybe if I had more time and more dates with him, I would have gotten there anyway. I don't want Penny to feel guilty about my romantic choices—and it's not like Jake was an option anyway. My choices at the moment were to not date the hot guy who likes me or watch Audra drag Connor out of the cafeteria. I took the prize behind door number one. Simple as that.

"That's not even close to what's happening here. Jake is a friend, a secret nerd friend."

"With big puppy dog eyes that follow you everywhere, and who you sacrifice sleep to talk to, and who you have managed to work into every conversation with me and Matt for a week."

"Part of that was because of the ice cream thing."

"Sure. It only took two days of you flipping out about that before you could talk to him. You, who could talk to a mailbox if you felt it needed to hear you out."

"I don't need to break up with Connor."

"And you're not dating him just because of the campaign?"

I look across the parking lot and see Jake nudge the Dunkin' door open butt-first to avoid dropping the doughnut box and coffees he's carrying. I know I just saw him at school yesterday, but seeing him this early on a weekend snaps my brain back to our car ride last week, to picking him up in the rain and almost definitely not kissing him in front of his apartment building. He looks more awake than I do this morning, brighter and happier around his dark eyes than I do even with concealer. He spots my car across the lot and awkwardly shimmies his shoulders since his hands are too full to wave, and he looks so silly I kind of want to throw up? Or laugh? I don't know, man. My stomach feels weird. I slide down in my seat instinctively. Ninja mode: reactivated.

"Lia, are you there?"

Right, Penny is still on the line. "Still here, sorry. Jake's here too, though, so I gotta go. I'm definitely not dating Connor because of the campaign." Jake's *Saga* voice from last week echoes in my head. *Lying.* "Please don't worry about that."

"What do you mean he's here? Is he in your car? Hi, Jake, I'm Penny! We should talk. Vote Darwin."

"Oh my god, Penny, no. Bad! He's not in the car." But he will be soon. "Thanks for wishing me good luck. Love you, bye!"

"I'm going back to sleep." She hangs up. She can't do it on her cell, but I know Penny would want me to imagine the dramatic sound of a phone slamming down on its . . . phone-holder. No idea what that's actually called. I imagine the slamming noise anyway in her honor.

I jump when I hear the knock on the passenger side window. Jake must have sneaked around the back of my car, which is impressive considering he's balancing the coffee cups on top of the doughnut box and holding them like a fancy butler.

"Hi!" I say before realizing my windows are up and he can't hear a thing I'm saying. I reach over to pop the passenger side open. All of my height, of which there is not much, is in my legs and not my torso, so it's an incredibly awkward position for me to be in. When Jake hip checks the rest of the door open, I'm staring somewhere at the bottom of the black cross on his Unity jersey. He couldn't have covered up his team affiliation with a sweatshirt or something? Jake, you're terrible at this game.

"Good morning?" he asks, looking down at me sprawled across the car seat. It takes me more time than I wish to core strength my way into a sitting position.

"Hey," I reply when I'm finally upright. Through the door, Jake holds out one of the coffees.

"It's not matcha," he says reassuringly. "It's black, and I have sugar packets in my pocket. Unless they exploded 'cause my jeans are too tight, then I just have sugar in my pocket.

These pants are clean, though, so we can just like . . ." He mimes emptying his pocket out carefully into a cup and makes a *pshhh* sound.

"A lint latte. Sounds great."

"A lint-te."

"Get in the car." I take my coffee with a smile and set it in one of the cupholders, then hold my hand out for the doughnut box. "I thought you said you'd get me *a* doughnut."

"I did. Well, I got four. Two for you, and two for me. I'll probably still be hungry, though. These things are delicious, but is it just me, or do they barely exist?"

"Empty calories, dude. Hits your stomach like a cotton ball."

Jake snorts and climbs into my car. "I'm going to have to figure something else out for real breakfast."

"We can stop on the way; we have plenty of time before By—before our teams arrive."

For all the time Jake and I have spent talking over the past few days, we've managed to avoid the topic of competing. After that first night in freestyle mode, we moved on to playing a few five-by-fives and a battle royale or two, but even playing alongside each other in the tournament's match style didn't bring the topic up. It wasn't as if we were avoiding it, but we just had other things to talk about—*GLO* itself, his first few weeks at Hillford West, catching up on the years since we last saw each other—and it simply hadn't come up.

Sitting in a car on our way to duking it out for a shot at playing each other in the finals makes that a little harder to avoid. I put the car in gear and swivel around to make sure no one's behind me before pulling out of the lot and pointing us east toward Philly. Jake keeps busy getting the doughnut box open and taking a sip of his coffee. From the look of pain on his face, it's too hot for him to keep using it as an excuse not to talk.

"Hey, uh, how's your friend Penny? I convinced a few of the guys at my lunch table to vote for her on Friday."

"She's fine. I was just talking to her, actually. She"—kind of accused me of having a thing for you—"really wants to beat Audra Hastings. Thanks for the votes."

"Is it weird that Audra's running now? Wasn't she, like, *not* running a few days ago?"

"Don't get me started on that. It's a whole thing. Can I have a doughnut?"

Hopefully Jake doesn't mind being my breakfast concierge while I'm driving. I may be reckless enough to put on mascara at stoplights, but I don't mess around with multitasking. I've seen way too many *Grand Theft Auto* stunt compilations not to know how quickly a car can flip over, or knock down a bunch of pedestrians, or zoom off a highway ramp and knock a helicopter out of the sky in a totally awesome but definitely fatal explosion.

"Sure. You want your coffee too? How many sugars?"

"Is this packet sugar or pocket sugar?"

Jake grabs at his pants to double-check. "Packet sugar, we're good."

"Four, if you have that many."

He twists around in his seat to dig around in his sugar pocket and pulls out exactly four. "Perfect, that's what I got."

"What about your coffee?"

"I drink it black," he replies. "I don't want to like it too much or I'll start seeing it as a beverage instead of a utility. Anxiety, you know. And ADHD."

"It's definitely a utility after the week we've had."

"For sure."

Jake passes me a doughnut (chocolate frosting, good choice), and we both sit in somewhat happy silence while we eat. I pass the street that leads to Jake's apartment, which brings us closer to Hillford West. It occurs to me that I don't know how Jake got to the Dunkin' Donuts from his place; it has to be a few miles even if the drive is a relatively straight shot.

"Jake, did you walk to meet me this morning?"

He takes a few moments to answer since his mouth is full of doughnut. Connor would have just talked around it. "Yup. It's like two and a half miles."

I didn't even think about what picking him up away from his apartment would have meant. I just didn't want his parents to see me and ask questions, and didn't know if anyone else from school lived in his building.

"What! I'm so sorry. I would have picked you up closer if I knew you were going to walk. I thought your mom or dad would drop you off."

"My dad doesn't really know I'm competing either. I mean I definitely told him, but I don't think he listened to my half of that conversation. My half of any conversation, really."

Suddenly Jake's issues with feeling invisible seem like a lot more than having issues at a new high school. I've never met his dad; his mom was always the one who would pick him up from parties. She seemed like a nice lady, kind of distracted, but Jake never mentioned having any issues with her. Not like that's a normal thing a thirteen-year-old brings up between Pokémon battles with a girl he sees once a year.

"What about your mom, though? I thought maybe she'd drive you."

Instead of an answer, Jake offers me another doughnut. It's chocolate again, so I look back at the box and see he really only bought four chocolate doughnuts. That was a gamble, but his consistency impresses me again. Jake likes what he likes, and I like it too.

"My mom, uh. She's not around anymore."

I swear to god, I should eat this doughnut with a side of my own foot.

"I'm so sorry, I didn't know. Is she . . . ?"

"Jesus, your face." Jake laughs, which is a good sign. "I just realized how that sounded; my mom's not dead. She doesn't have custody. My parents divorced last year. That's why I had to transfer schools. They sold the house, and she lives in Jackson; I stayed with my dad, and we moved into the apartment in Hillford West's district."

That story, while not exactly happy, is a whole lot better than his mom dying and me bringing it up like an asshole.

"Oh, right. I was kind of wondering how you just showed up when you weren't here for freshman year."

"Yeah, that's why." Something seems off about Jake's voice. He tucks into doughnut number two. "You should drink your coffee before it gets cold. I put the sugars in."

"Thank you. Can you open it for me? Driving, hands."

"Yup." Whatever Jake's feeling, he's still down to be my breakfast concierge.

I don't taste any sugar in my first sip, which means all of it has floated to the bottom and will be waiting for me there in a gross brown sludge. I don't think I have any space to complain; it's still better than a bright green matcha monstrosity.

"Actually," Jake says after I put the coffee back in the cupholder, "that's sort of the thing I blew up. The one I was talking about on Wednesday."

I'd be lying if I said I hadn't been thinking about that since we met in Crystal Cathedral. Jake hadn't brought it up again, so I assumed it was something small that he felt outsized guilt over (I may have been projecting on that), but knowing he'd narced on someone before did bother me a little. I still trusted him with my secret—didn't have much of a choice—but I had wondered what the deal with that was. Now that he seems ready to talk about it, do I really want to know?

"You blew up something with your parents? You don't have to talk about it if you don't want to."

"Eh, may as well. We have a long ride."

"It's, like, half an hour."

"I talk fast."

"Well, I'm listening."

"Okay," Jake starts, then takes a sip of his black coffee to steel himself for the telling. "You know how you, like, never ever want to see your parents having sex?"

Sweet Christmas, where is this going? I turn to give him a frightened look, but he's deadass about this being the way he wants to start this story. I swap to a more neutral expression. I don't want to make him think that I'm laughing at something he doesn't think is funny.

"I do . . . know that."

"Yeah, so the only thing you maybe want to see less than your parents having sex is see one parent having sex with someone who is *not your dad*."

Now I see where this is going.

"I was fourteen, so this is early last year. Came home sick from school one day. And to be fair, I didn't, like, see anything, but I heard it from the front door, and when I walked into the living room there was, you know. Not Dad and Definitely Mom kind of . . ."

"You don't have to paint the whole picture."

"Yeah, you get it. She told me not to tell my dad. And I didn't want to tell him because, honestly, my dad is kind of a dick? He hates me."

"I'm sure your dad doesn't—"

"He doesn't like me. He thinks I'm weird and not smart . . . A lot of it is gaming stuff."

I pile Jake's constant self-deprecating comments about how "dumb" he is on top of his issues with being ignored. Maybe every TV therapist is right, and everything really does start with our childhoods.

There's room in the conversation for me to come out with another "you're not dumb, Jake," but at this point I think he knows it's implied.

"I sat on it for a while, like a month. It started feeling really weird and wrong in the house, though. My dad was being an asshole, and I knew she was cheating on him. I didn't even blame her for cheating, but the lies and stuff kind of messed me up."

"Keep going. I just want to say it's insanely fucked up that your mom put that on you. Like, beyond."

"I know. Anyway, long story short, I told my dad what I saw. He flipped out, threatened to bury her—"

"Whoa."

"In court. Not, like, the backyard. She lost custody on all kinds of technical stuff; I don't know. We lost the house. And my dad hates me even more now for telling him. Or maybe for keeping it from him? Probably both."

We're on the highway by now, and a siren from somewhere behind my car begins to whoop its way through to the fast lane, getting closer and louder as Jake finishes his story. That's not a metaphor, but it sure feels like one.

"So yeah, he wasn't going to give me a ride to the tournament or the parking lot. I walk everywhere."

I genuinely don't know what to say to any of that besides what I've already said (because, wow, that's fuuucked up), so instead of being smart or comforting, I just tell Jake that next time, I'll pick him up at home.

"Next time?" he asks. "There's only a next time if we win today. Both of us."

"Right, and I'll pick you up in front of your place."

"And then play me in the finals?"

Yes. No? Shit. I was so focused on Jake being Jake that I once again forgot that he's right. If we both win, we're going up against each other in the finals. Byunki seems sure that we'll beat Chronic today. Unity has as good a shot as anyone at beating Beast Mode after their payload win last week. I want to win today more than anything, but would that make it impossible to keep talking to Jake?

"Oh," I say. "That might be a bad idea."

"I bet Fury wouldn't be happy."

"If Byunki could see me now, I think he'd transform into

Klio and decapitate me, so yeah. Next week would be worse. Would Unity be mad?"

Jake breathes in deep. "Maybe. Probably. They kind of know I know you."

He had *one job.*

"Jake! I asked you not to tell anyone!"

"I'm sorry, I'm sorry. I told them I knew you before I ran into you, though. I haven't told them your name or anything, and they don't know about this." He starts gesturing something between himself and me, then seems to second-guess whatever idea he's trying to convey and not very smoothly pretends he was trying to grab his coffee from the cupholder. "We all saw you onstage when you played Vulcan and . . ."

"And what?" Jake telling his team he knew me before I asked him isn't as bad as I thought. It's not the greatest, but it's not as bad.

"And I'd already told them about you. Before we even heard about the competition or got to the tournament. I was surprised to see you and told them you were the girl I was talking about."

"Why were you talking about me before the tournament?"

Jake's hand flies to the back of his head. I find it substantially less cute than I did in our previous conversation.

"They're my best friends, Em," he begins quietly. He doesn't want to say whatever he's about to say. "When I transferred to Hillford West and I saw you on the first day, they were the first people I told. I was excited to see you, I guess. I thought we were going to be friends."

What is it about Jake that makes me feel like a huge jerk for assuming the worst of him? He's not the only person to surprise me with hidden depths in the past week, but for some reason he's the only one who makes me actually want to question what a cynic I can be.

To be clear, I feel fully justified in being a cynic. Between my first time on *GLO*, Connor, my mom, and everyone else in my life that wants a piece of everything I can give them, I haven't met that many people who won't punish me for slipping up and trusting the wrong person. Or doing the wrong thing, saying the wrong words, acting the wrong way. My walls are here for a reason. Jake just keeps popping up inside them with zero effort, which raises some serious questions about the integrity of my defenses.

"So when you told them you knew me . . ."

"They only know you as K-O-D. It was a jokey codename, really stupid."

"*Knights of Darkness*?"

Jake looks at me like I just sneezed out a tiny, nostril-sized unicorn. The look of disbelief on his face should make me feel worse, but it pleases me to know I can surprise him too sometimes.

"*Knights of Darkness*. You remember," he confirms. The

smile on his face is so beautiful it melts away any anger I felt thinking he'd already betrayed me to Unity.

You really think his smile is beautiful? a voice in my head asks. The voice sounds exactly like Penny.

"I wonder if our high score is still there. It's been, what"—I do the mental math in my head quickly—"five years?"

"It's still there. We're not number two anymore, but we're on the leaderboard. Like, eight or something."

I sputter with indignation. "Who the hell stole our spot? Jake, we *have* to—we gotta—What the hell is that noise?"

There's a beeping coming from my dashboard. When I look down to check it, an indicator light is on. I don't need to check what it is, because two seconds after the beeping starts, I have my answer. My car's trunk pops open and starts flapping in the breeze as I make a hectic turn onto a highway off-ramp.

"The trunk!" Jake exclaims. Yes, thank you. I saw it too.

"I'll get it, I'll get it," I reply. "Just give me a second to find somewhere to pull over." We're about twenty minutes from the arena, on a smaller road that still has a decently wide shoulder. I remember to put my emergency lights on before pulling over (rather smoothly, I might add).

"Let me help," Jake says and swings out of the car before I have a chance to tell him this is clearly a one-woman job. I don't remember putting anything in my trunk this morning, so I must have closed it over the strap on my field hockey bag or something equally innocuous. I hop out to join Jake, careful to walk around the side of the car that isn't flanked by the right lane.

"You have a bag or something; it kept the trunk door open," Jake says when I catch up to him.

"Let me move some stuff around so it doesn't get stuck again. You can get back in the car, it's fine."

"Nah, I'll stay out here with you. Feels weird sitting in there by myself."

Can't say I mind the company as long as it's freely offered. I start shuffling stuff around in my truck. There are a couple of five-subject notebooks, a bunch of books from sophomore year that I never took out (Jake could probably use a few of those, now that I think about it), and the offending hockey bag with its thick plastic strap. I don't like field hockey enough to forgive the bag for being annoying; if I had my way, I'd chuck the thing into the Schuylkill and be done with it. I'm still rummaging when Jake taps me on the shoulder.

"Em, someone's pulling up."

Great, a Good Samaritan. Does he want my field hockey bag? He can have it.

When I turn around to see who our would-be rescuer is, I spot a tall, good-looking black guy with a shaved head, a Volvo, and—now that he's out of his car and walking toward us—an uncomfortably familiar shirt. Blue cross. Black shield.

"Is that—"

"Bob. That's Bob," Jake says nervously.

"Bob's cool, though, right? He won't mind that I'm driving you?"

Jake looks from me to Bob and back at me. "I mean we'll find out."

I'm gonna go ahead and say that Bob minds that I'm driving Jake today. Once he gets close enough to identify both of us, his eyebrows shoot up toward a hairline that does not exist, and he stops in his tracks.

"Jake, what's going on?" Bob shouts over the roar of traffic.

Under his breath, I hear Jake mutter the word "language." Who is he, Captain America? I feel like this isn't going well already, so I step up and try to introduce myself.

"Hey, you're Bob, right? I'm Emilia." Shoot. He didn't know my name before, but he sure does now. Here's hoping Bob's as good a guy as his teammate is.

"I know who you are," he snaps. I'm not sure I deserve that tone, but if Bob is anything like Byunki, I'm not interested in taking his flavor of shit before I even get to the arena. "You're one of Byunki's. KNOX, Team Fury. Did he put you up to this?"

Jake intervenes before I can ask Bob what "this" is. "No. She's just giving me a ride so I don't have to take the bus." He waits a moment before seemingly deciding to go balls out on the truth. "She also gave me a ride back from the arena last weekend."

I admire his desire to come clean, but his timing could be a lot better. My trunk is still open, and there are cars whipping by us on the highway. I tell myself it's the setting that's making me nervous or the fact that Jake and I have been caught red-handed doing . . . nothing, honestly.

Problem is that with Jake, doing nothing has increasingly begun to feel like doing something. Something I shouldn't be doing. From the look on Bob's face, it's something Jake shouldn't be doing either.

"You neglected to mention that to the team, or to me," Bob says with fury, ironically, in his voice. I thought Bob was supposed to be nice. Wasn't Bob Unity's dad or whatever?

I steal a glance over at Jake, and the confusion on his face points instead to this kind of vitriol being massively out of character for Dad-Bob.

"I know. I'm sorry. Em was being nice, and I didn't want you guys to worry about me."

"I wasn't worried about you because I thought you were smarter than *this*," Bob says and has the gall to point to me when he says this. Excuse me, I'm right here. I'm a *her*, not a *this*.

"Hey—" I begin. I'm not going to let this bald-ass rando talk to me or Jake like that. I'm beginning to think all tanks are assholes. Thank god Jake's a healer.

Before I can get a word in, Bob cuts me off. "I'll ask again. Did Byunki put you up to this? Did he tell you to go for

Jake after Round One or before we even showed up at the tournament?"

Yo. I do not like Bob. I look over at Jake again, hoping he'll defend me, and to his credit, he tries. Whatever he wants to say is mostly a sputtering mess, but I can make out his catch-phrase. More of a catchword, really.

"S-sorry. I'm sorry I didn't tell you. But Em's not—"

"Jake, it's not your fault," Bob says, rubbing his temples. Byunki didn't tell me to mess with Unity before Round 2, but I definitely got under their skin entirely on accident. "Byunki probably—Ugh. Can you get in my car, please? I'd be more comfortable if I could talk to you alone, and we're going to be late."

One more look at Jake tells me that this battle, if I can even call it that, is lost. I'm overwhelmed, Jake looks on the verge of tears, and I think Bob might literally be the devil.

"It's okay, Jake," I say quietly. We have our answer as to whether or not this was bad. "I'll see you . . . there, I guess."

Jake slips into the passenger side of Bob's car, and anyone watching from the highway would be well within their rights to assume this is some kind of hostage trade. I'm waiting for Bob to toss me a suitcase full of hundred-dollar bills when he gets in his own car, slams the door, and glares at me through the windshield.

Fine, dude, fine. It's not fine, but I don't know what else to do. I punch my hockey bag toward the back of the trunk, hit the button to close it, and carefully stalk back to my seat. Just go, both of you.

When Bob peels out of the shoulder, I get a last glimpse of Jake through the passenger side window. "I'm sorry," he mouths. I can't blame him for saying it this time. I'm sorry too.

CHAPTER EIGHTEEN

Team Unity Chat, Saturday, Round 2

ElementalP: hellooooo is anyone here?? I'm in the parking lot and i need someone to help me carry all this stuff

MUDD: i thought ki was driving in with you

ElementalP: she is but she got *back pain*

shineedancer: it's boob pain. you can tell him it's new boob pain.

ElementalP: are you here muddy? Come help pls

MUDD: ugh i just sat down i'm in the green room. Idk why bob thinks we need to decorate. it's stupid.

[BobTheeQ has entered the chat]

MUDD: i mean yeah wow decorating the green room so helpful totally makes sense i'll be right over

BobTheeQ: stay in the parking lot we're almost there

ElementalP: uh who are you and what did you do with Bob

ElementalP: my captain always punctuates and capitalizes

BobTheeQ: it's jake i'm typing for bob he's driving

MUDD: bob gave you a ride? lookit you, prince of unity over here. Bob never offered me a ride but thats super cool

BobTheeQ: bob says he has curtains in the trunk and a bunch of other stuff he wants to know what you have

ElementalP: some posters, a footstool, christmas lights

shineedancer: my stuff is a secret you'll see

MUDD: i brought nothin but these skillz

BobTheeQ: Quelle surprise.

ElementalP: French? that's gotta be Bob. Y'all parked?

BobTheeQ: We are in parking lot C. Jake and I can bring our stuff in. Muddy, help the girls, we'll meet in the green room.

shineedancer: soon to be . . . the blue room

BobTheeQ: How are we feeling today? We're rested, we ate?

MUDD: they put free red bulls in our room. i've had three so far

MUDD: is it bad that i'm perceiving minutes as colors

ElementalP: this wouldn't happen if you behaved yourself

BobTheeQ: Ki, can you please get Muddy a croissant on your way in?

shineedancer: no i want to find out what color right now is

MUDD: kind of mustard-y

MUDD: wait now it's black

shineedancer: one croissant coming up

ElementalP: is Jake still with you?

BobTheeQ: I'm not letting him out of my sight.

ElementalP: . . . ok?

BobTheeQ: Just get to the green room as soon as Muddy shows up to help you. We need to be on time today.

BobTheeQ: There's something I have to tell you before the matches start. Today could change everything.

CHAPTER NINETEEN
Emilia, Saturday, Round 2

SOMETHING IS DIFFERENT about Byunki this morning, and I don't care. On any other day his transformation from a walking rage comic into the chipper, positively bubbly dude standing in front of the Team Fury green room's whiteboard would be a welcome and delightful mystery. Not so much today. All I can think about is Jake.

While Byunki is chattering about Team Chronic, I'm seeing Jake death marching to Bob's car with barely a backward look at me. Jake's face through the window, mouthing, "I'm sorry." Jake being in trouble with his friends because I was selfish enough to take up time he didn't have, Jake immediately changing from the funny, sleepy boy who doesn't need me to explain anything about myself into the competitor whose teammates see me as a viper waiting to strike. Jake's smile when he saw I remembered *Knights of Darkness* after all these years.

"KNOX, are you getting this?"

Byunki, Team Fury, and *Guardians League Online*. These are the things I need to be thinking about. I blink to refocus my eyes and look up at the whiteboard.

"I am," I lie, and try my hardest to match Ivan's, Han-Jun's, and Erik's contemplative expressions. Byunki must have had a double shot in his coffee this morning—he's scribbling rapid-fire notes across the bottom three quarters of the board and not even noticing that his sleeve is rubbing half of the letters off every time he moves to draw a new diagram.

Consequently, almost none of what he's writing makes sense to anyone but him, but I studied Chronic well enough to fill in the blanks with my own knowledge.

"Who do you think Ivan should prep as his secondary character in case he has to swap?" Byunki directs the question at me again. This morning may have been sheer interpersonal hell, but my heart rate picks up at the thought that Byunki is in a good enough mood to ask for my opinion on strategy. That, or the sugar bomb waiting in the bottom of the coffee Jake "stirred" has finally hit my bloodstream.

And I'm thinking about Jake again. Right when Byunki needs me to literally get my head in the game.

"Um, if Ivan gets the swap slot, and he should totally get the swap spot, he should prep, um . . ."

That thing I do every day, the clean mind-sweep that pushes my real life away when I'm playing *GLO* and vice versa, is nonoperational this morning. I'm trying to restart it by key smashing every trigger in my brain, but instead of a blissful, focused reboot, I keep seeing and hearing the human error message that is Jake.

This is my fault, I think, when I should be thinking about how Chronic is a particularly tough nut to crack. Who should get the swap spot? Come on, think.

I should have let him hate me after the ice cream. He still wouldn't have told. Why did I have to make sure he didn't hate me? Each team gets one character swap after the clock goes off. The swap slot must be preassigned before the countdown and should in most circumstances go to the most versatile DPS. That means Ivan in this case. We'll have to match his character to whatever tank Chronic is most likely to play.

Is Unity going to kick Jake off the team? Did I take all of this from him?

Byunki made me do the numbers on the likelihood of Chronic playing a tank one of Ivan's better characters has a chance against, and it's high they'll pick Reigh or Grendel— the hero or the monster. VANE's used to playing Morrigan, but Morrigan's ghost type only has an advantage over heroes.

I should have ghosted Jake after Round 1.

If they go for Grendel, Ivan needs to hulk up and play Jubilee, the only monster DPS in the game. He can handle it. I just have to keep Pharaoh steady and do my job. Once we're safely in Round 3, I have two more weeks to keep it together, and this tournament will be over. My carriage will turn back into a pumpkin, and I can go back to . . . my life, I guess. I'll keep playing *GLO* for fun and look back on this month as a brief, shining moment of glory when I got to do exactly what I wanted to do. And I do it so damn well.

"Ivan should stick Jubilee in his swap spot. Han and Erik will be fine with their main healers since Chronic focuses on strong defense around the payload, and we'll need a monster if Chronic plays Grendel," I say. With my computations complete, I feel more like Siri than Emilia or KNOX. "They'll probably go with Grendel because they know you play Klio. Fire characters are weak to monster, and they might try to turn this into a tankfight. If we were trying to catch them out, we could give *you* the swap to play as a hero tank, but I don't think that's necessary."

"Good." Byunki sounds pleased. "Exactly what I was thinking too." He takes a second look at me and nods to himself, like he's confirming the results of some assessment I didn't know I was taking. "That's really good," he says again and turns back to the board.

Great, dope. Can we play now? I've almost regained my grip on the sweet spot of concentration I need to get through today, and any further hiccups will knock it right out of my hands.

Hiccups like one of the arena handlers knocking on the door of the green room forty minutes early and letting himself in.

"Team Fury?" The handler checks his keyboard. Uh, yeah, that's us, man. Why is he coming into our green room if he's not specifically looking for us? Whatever it is, he seems happy to be interrupting us—this random guy is grinning wider than anyone should be capable of this early in the morning (okay, it's like 8:15; I've just had a long week).

"We need you onstage now."

I look over at Ivan, next to me on the couch. He was right in the middle of ripping open his first pack of hand warmers and is now frozen, mid-tear.

"Now?" Ivan asks.

"We're not up for another hour," Erik says skeptically. He peeks up at Byunki, whose smile matches the handler's tooth for tooth. I don't think I've ever seen him smile before. Can't say I love it.

"Doesn't matter. Up. Everybody up!" Byunki herds us off the couch and toward the door. Something is going on here. If I were more paranoid and self-centered, I'd think this has something to do with Jake and Team Unity, but there's no way Byunki's sense of drama extends to faking me out all morning just to humiliate me onstage . . . right?

Han-Jun, Erik, and I follow the handler backstage and up through the maze of ramps and hallways that lead up to the Wizzard-Claricom Arena's main stage. I try to catch Ivan's eye while we're walking, but he looks as worried as I do. I'm not going to get any answers from him, and hell if I'm asking

Byunki what's going on and wind up looking stupid right after I crushed our pregame meeting.

Even more worrying is the small crowd of people waiting for us in the wings. There's not a ton of space back here to funnel more than one team through at a time, but the other three teams are crammed in here as well.

In front of us are the five boys from Beast Mode whose black-and-silver jerseys have their names printed across the back in some death metal font that makes them impossible to read. One of them might be named Dave? Or Damien? I never much liked Beast Mode. We haven't played them, but their reputation out of competition is kind of smurfy. They get off on having power over other players, no matter how mismatched the game.

I'm assuming Chronic is between them, but the Beast Mode boys are tall, and I can't see much over their heads. All I can tell is that Bob is way up front with the rest of Team Unity. Jake must be with him too. I get the truly dumb notion that I should wriggle through the other teams and tap him on the shoulder just to let him know I'm here and I'm sorry, but that's literally the worst idea I've ever had, and I'm the one who told Penny it was a good idea to tap Connor for VP.

It's better if I just leave him alone forever like he offered after Round 1. Maybe when this is all over, I can hit restart with him if he wants anything to do with me, but not if it gets him into more trouble.

"And now . . . Wizzard Games invites all of our Diamond-tier semifinalists to the stage for a special announcement from *Guardians League Online*'s creative director . . . Thibault Adige!"

I'm not the only one in the wings who gasps. Thibault Adige is a god. He cofounded Wizzard with Brian Juno when they were still at Drexel and single-handedly came up with the idea for *GLO*. Every mechanic, map, and new character comes through him, and he's been the public face of the game since its inception. I'm suddenly glad to be crammed offstage with my gaming peers, because I can't imagine anyone else in my life understanding the wave of hype that washes over me.

I feel a hand grasp my shoulder and shake me in excitement; color me surprised when I turn and see it's Byunki.

"Are you ready?" he asks, still grinning from before.

"Ready for *what*?" I squeak.

"He's about to change our lives."

From the amplified roar of the crowd, I know Thibault has taken the stage. Ivan and Erik are craning their necks to try to see over the people in front of us, while Han-Jun, always the smart one, taps my arm and points to my left—there's a monitor by the mic station behind us. I've watched every *GLO* upfront since the game's inception, so seeing Thibault on a tiny screen isn't new, but knowing he's there on that screen and *also* a few short yards away from me is almost too much to handle. What did Byunki just say? Thibault is going to change my life? I have no idea why he would want to do that, or what I'm supposed to do with that information. My mouth is suddenly wetter than usual. And saltier. I have just enough presence of mind to find that particular anxiety response incredibly revolting before I swallow it out a few times.

"Welcome, everyone, to Round Two of the Wizzard-Claricom Arena's inaugural *Guardians League Online* championship!" Thibault's French-Canadian accent makes every single word sound so much cooler than it does when the regular announcer says them. Weezard Clah-ree-com Arenah. Shamp-ee-on-sheep. My sugared-up heart can't handle this.

"Brian and I have a special announcement to make. But first, let's welcome our semifinalist teams to the stage!"

Each team walks out when he calls us (Unité, Chronique, Biest Mode, and Fyu-ree), and I am absurdly proud of my absurd, sweating body for remembering how to walk. Fury and I move as if controlled by a hive mind, keeping in step with one another behind Byunki as he leads us up to some predetermined spot on the stage. His Cheshire cat grin in the green room and unholy amount of energy are beginning to make sense. He got here early and rehearsed this without us. Byunki knows what's coming.

Thibault is standing between the pairs of teams, so Bob and Chronic's captain must have also known to walk past him and hit their marks. I'd look ridiculous leaning over to get a look at how Jake is reacting to this, so I default to looking straight ahead and trying not to wildly dissociate.

"As you all know, Philadelphia is a city very close to our hearts at Wizzard. It is our home, our foundation. When we first sought a partnership to build America's first esports arena, we knew we had to start here."

Pause for applause, pause for applause . . .

"That is why we invited local teams to this first tournament, to celebrate the Guardians who rose in this city . . . who can and will defend it!"

I can't not look anymore. I lean out of line for a moment and peek over at the other side of the stage, where Jake is standing with the rest of Unity. He's staring straight ahead as well, but he must feel my eyes on him because his gaze slides left for the briefest of seconds. I snap back into position like I'm pulling away from a hot stove. Jake doesn't know what's going on either. He would have told me if he knew something was happening today.

I mean, he told me he witnessed the inciting sexual incident of his parents' divorce; he would *definitely* have told me if there was something I should look out for at the tournament. Unless he's better at keeping his barriers up. He could like me enough as Emilia and not be so attached as to reveal any information that might knock me off my game.

"This tournament has been the culmination of years of planning, with Claricom and with my team at Wizzard. One of these four teams will be victorious in two weeks' time, but that was never meant to be the end of this journey. There is a second prize for the winners of this tournament, a"—he pauses for effect—"secret coronation. One we kept from you all before meeting our final four. After seeing the turnout from last week's matches, the ink on our contract is dry! Get a good look at them now, guys, gals, nonbinary pals, and ask yourselves, what good is a championship that does not crown a champion?"

The stage lights go dark, maintaining a spotlight on Thibault. Thank god. I'm not sure I want the audience to see how I react to wherever this announcement is going.

"We *will* find our champions, and they will lead us into the next phase of *Guardians League Online* as the first team to join . . ."

Next to me, I hear Erik whisper, "No way," as the screens behind us light up with something. Every team turns around to look up at the logo projected thirty feet high. It's similar enough to the *GLO* main title, but in gold instead of gray medieval script. And there's no "Online" at the end. The logo animates to flash a series of cities—New York, Orlando, San Francisco, Chicago, Omaha for some reason, San Antonio, and a few more that whiz by too quickly—before zooming out to rearrange the letters into . . . Oh no. Oh hell no.

". . . the Guardians League! The first professional esports league sponsored by Wizzard Games, coming next year!"

This is bad.

"The winners of this tournament will not only win the $200,000 pot, but a one-year, million-dollar contract to represent Philadelphia as the only esports team in America to have a home arena! Who will it be? Will it be Unity?"

Thibault speaks Unity's name, and a series of blue spotlights rotate in the catwalk above to settle on and highlight Jake's team on the far side of the stage. The spotlight snaps off quickly as Thibault moves on to tease the next potential Guardians League champion. From where I'm standing, I can only see the lights of ten thousand phone cameras flashing in the dark and Byunki's gleeful face shining in the strobe they create.

"Will it be Beast Mode?"

Green lights shine down on Beast Mode next to me. I need to get off this stage. Winning a tournament is one thing, an easy thing. Show up, kick ass, and be home before curfew. A yearlong contract as a *professional* player, though? That's a full-time job.

"Will it be . . . Chronic?" Team colors: electric yellow. The Chronic boys look jaundiced in their spotlight. Gross. Focus.

Going pro means travel, interviews, getting *paid* to play *GLO* as a representative of the company. It's the most incredible life I could possibly imagine for myself, doing what I love and want while being recognized as one of the best players in the country, if not the world. If Fury wins this, my real life and my *GLO* life would morph into an enormous, intractable fame monster with no room for secrets or partitions. Emilia would play for the Guardians League, not KNOX. Amazing. Impossible.

"How about . . . the Philadelphia Fury?"

The red lights hit us so abruptly I sneeze. In the five quick seconds we're lit, I get a blood-tinted view of the audience on their feet, shouting and cheering at the possibility of the five of us representing Philly on a national circuit. They're nowhere near loud enough to drown out the intrusive realization that's forced every other thought out of my mind: I really can't win, can I?

I can't sign a contract to go pro in the Guardians League. I have to finish my junior year, keep my grades perfect, and spend the summer before twelfth grade preparing all of my college applications. I have field hockey in the fall, Model UN in the winter, mock trial in the spring, quiz bowl in between all of those, and the hundred million other things my parents told me were the keys to manifesting the future they dreamed up for me. I'm supposed to go to college and major in business, then the Wharton thing, and grow up to be busy and successful and adult. I was born to build on the legacy my family worked so hard to give me, not tear it down and rebrand it as—what? A *GLO* legend? That's not a success anyone in my family would understand.

My mouth is salty again, and I don't know what to do with myself. Luckily, the rest of Team Fury takes over for me now that the announcement is over. Thibault has more to say about the league and how it will work, so Byunki nudges me as a cue to leave the stage. That's fine. I fall in line behind him like a good, albeit robotic, little duckling. Now he wants me to wave to our fans while we walk out. Thank you for being here today. Before we can disappear into the wings, Ivan wants to hold my arm up for a second to show Fury's DPS squad is ready to win. My arm is his noodle to do with as he wants.

Once we get backstage, I assume Ivan, Han-Jun, and Erik are making some noise, but my thoughts are too loud and consuming to follow their conversation or contribute in any way. Thank god the expression of shock I'm sure is on my face is easy to mistake for a natural response to receiving the most life-changing news any of us have ever heard, so I don't look too out of place as we parade back down the ramp. I'd never noticed before how narrow these hallways are. Or maybe they're not and the walls just feel like they're closing in around me because every cliché about impending panic attacks is 100 percent true.

No one here knows me well enough to assume that my silence comes from anything other than being overwhelmed. I mean they'd be half right; I'm very overwhelmed right now, because I trapped myself in a tournament that I thought would give me a taste of glory only to find out it's actually trying to shove a massive slurry of it down my throat like that mean thing people do to geese.

I want to play. I want to find out if I'm good and stand tall in front of crowds like the one that just screamed my team's name and see where being a founding player in a national league takes me. If I had anything resembling a choice, that would be what I choose. I don't have a choice, though. Thibault's announcement took that choice away from me. I really, really can't win.

And there's my answer. That's how I get out of this: I have to lose.

The clarity I was looking for early snaps back into focus. Planning mode: activated. It would be easier if we had reserve players because I could just quit now, but we don't and I still owe it to Fury to give them their best shot at winning without me. That means I have to play today.

I'll mess something up, something bad enough to lose but not quite, and Byunki will be mad enough to let me resign once the match is over.

If there isn't a contractual obligation for the teams to remain intact through the finals—mental note to check the fine print on the tournament documents we signed on entry—that gives them two weeks to find a new DPS. It will be difficult, but not as impossible as it would be if I ditched them today, or with only one week to go before Round 3. Once I'm out, I disappear. I junk my *GLO* account, say goodbye to all the sweet cosmetics I earned on this one, and . . .

. . . probably never make a new one. This has gone on long enough. I should have stopped playing the first time, when those guys made it very clear that I didn't have a place in gaming. It doesn't make them right, but once I give this up, there's nowhere else for me to go. I'll be good. I'll go to school; I'll do the things. I'll even have time to do the readings during the semester.

Jake will have to find another ride to Round 3 if he makes it.

Doesn't matter. I'm done. It makes sense to be done.

"KNOX, you're quiet!" Ivan nudges me with his elbow exactly when I don't expect it, and I stumble a half step to the side.

"I'm good," I lie, about the stumble and the holistic state of my identity. "It's just sinking in. I think I need to clear my head or something."

"I knew something was up. Byunki was so weird this morning? I've never seen him so . . ."

"Happy?"

Ivan looks sideways at me and smirks. "I was going to say stoked. He knows we got this on lock. You and me, I mean."

"Oh," I say. Please don't let this be a whole thing about how well Ivan and I work as a team. My heart is at capacity. Any additional feels would constitute a fire code violation.

"Like I honestly—and I'm not being shady or anything—but I didn't think it would work, when Byunki brought you up this summer."

"Oh." The less I say, the more room Ivan has to monologue. I don't even need to tell him that is barely an appropri-
ate use of the word "shady."

"Not because you're a girl or anything. I have a sister, and
she . . . well, she doesn't game, but, like, females are strong as
hell, you know? Just because I'd been partnered with Arjun for
so long and after Byunki kicked him, I was like 'Yo, now what?'
but you"—he punctuates his speech with a playful poke at my
shoulder; Ivan is certainly the touchy-feeliest out of all the Fury
players—"came out swinging. After Round One, and don't tell
B this, but that checkmate? I was like, 'Is KNOX our secret
weapon?' And then I checked with Han and Erik, and they
were like, 'Yo, KNOX is our secret weapon.' If we win, nah,
when we win, you and me are going to be, like, *GLO* GOATs."

What sucks is I know Ivan is right. GOATs and all. On any
other day and under other circumstances, this speech would
be the highlight of my entire year. Today it's just a reminder of
everything I'm giving up and everyone I'm letting down. Rick
Astley would be so disappointed in me.

"Hey, Ivan?" I interrupt him before he can keep going. "I
was kind of serious about needing that minute. Can you tell
Byunki and the rest that I'll be back in, like, ten minutes?"

"Oh? Yeah, sure. Don't take too long. You okay?" I can tell
he's a little hurt that I'm trying to ditch him after he's said such
nice things about me.

"Yeah. Crack a hand warmer open for me?"

"Uh, it's better if you do it yourself. Slower heat."

"Then don't." It's better if he thinks I'm bitchy today. It'll make it easier to write me off later.

I like Ivan, I really do. As much as I wanted to impress Byunki going into this, I'll feel worse making VANE look bad when I whiff this match. In an alternate universe, we could be GOATs. Forever and ever.

The crowd from the ramp has thinned out by now, with the rest of the teams splitting off to head to their respective green rooms. I've been so single-minded both days of the competition that I haven't poked around to see where everyone else is holed up, and the only other place I know besides the Fury green room is that weird spot by the craft kitchen.

Thibault's announcement will for sure delay the day's matches as the press catches up to the reality of the Guardians League, so I'll have just enough time to sneak away and kick craft's unused mountain of stackable chairs until they collapse and bury me forever. Kudos to whoever finds my skeleton many years from today.

Picking my way through the hallways toward somewhere I'm only halfway sure I know the location of feels like navigating a basement level of a game I've played before but don't really remember how to win. I definitely take a few wrong turns and wind up somewhere even more unfamiliar, hallways I'm sure lead to empty rooms that are lying in wait for when the arena plays host to bigger competitions than this, full-on

Guardians League tournaments that pull in hundreds of players on teams from all across the world. The relative emptiness
of having only four teams left in this round is great for me
because I'm not running into a million people back here, but
it also means that the signage leaves a lot to be desired.

Just when I'm about to give up and slump against a random
wall and hope for the best, I spot the stacks of chairs at the end
of a hall and charge toward them, hoping no one in one of the
empty corners behind me catches a glimpse of my red-and-
black jersey and tries to follow me. The spot is exactly as I
remember it from before, except this time there's no Jake.
That's a relief, honestly. I need a few minutes to be alone and
work this out for myself. I don't want anyone talking or getting
close to me. I am exactly who I'm supposed to be right now, an
island of a person who got herself into this mess and needs to
get herself out.

"Figured I'd find you here, Em."

I don't think islands shiver when they hear familiar voices
behind them. They definitely don't feel a horribly comfortable
combination of toasty and desperate when it's a voice they
thought they didn't want to hear.

"Hey, Jake."

"Do you want me to go?" he asks. I knew he would. The
normal, defensive thing to do would be to ask him to leave me
alone. He would if I asked him to. I tried to push him away
here a week ago and failed, which wouldn't have solved my

problem but might have made ditching the competition a little easier. When I quit *GLO*, I'll quit Jake too. As wonderful as he is, he's still a glitch in all of this. Quitting is about having less to deal with in the months to come, not more. Jake is very, very *more*.

"No," I hear myself saying even though I can't even bring myself to turn around and look at Jake. "Please stay." Hey, me, *stop*.

"Wait, really? Okay. Cool." Jake sounds as shocked as I am to hear me say I want him around. I know a little bit of that is rooted in Jake assuming I never bother thinking about him, which should not be my problem anymore but still makes me feel terrible. "Hold on a sec—here you go." Jake stretches his arms up and grabs a chair at the top of a stack and clumsily wiggles it away from its spot. He places it next to the single chair he sat in a week ago, which apparently has been waiting patiently for our next disaster chat.

Jake sits in one chair and pats the seat of the other. This boy is corny as hell. I sit down anyway.

"So, the league," he begins. It's all he needs to say. "Could be dope. Lotta money, big commitment."

I know, Jake. He knows what I'm thinking, though, doesn't he?

"But you won't do it." Yes, he does.

"I can't," I say. Won't isn't the issue here. "Winning would change everything. What I have now is perfect. I play *GLO* and I hide, and I'm a totally normal high schooler. And I hide. I can't afford to change that."

Jake clears his throat. "Listen, Em, I'm d—"

"If you say 'dumb,' I will grab this chair and strike you like a Hardy brother."

"Fine, I'm a genius. I'm the smartest man in the world."

"Eh, dial it back."

"Can you stop doing that?" He doesn't say it harshly, but I still turn to him, visibly annoyed.

"What?"

When I look, Jake is holding me in his gaze, staring as intently as he did that day in the cafeteria.

"That . . . prickly, defensive mean girl thing. You can talk your way around anyone, I know, but that's not you."

He's wrong. It's absolutely me. I wouldn't have survived this long keeping my two lives in balance if I didn't push people exactly where I needed them to be. I push them away, I pull them closer, and they stay there until I need to move them.

I've been getting progressively suckier at it, but that's still the guiding principle.

"It's who I have to be," I explain quietly.

"Nah," he says dismissively. "It's really not. I know, remember? I'm seeing you from both sides. All sides really; there's way more than two. You're, like, one of those conceptual *DnD* dice that no one can even use because there are too many sides. A tri . . . contra thing."

"Triacontahedron." Technically a disdyakis triacontahe-dron, but I'll let it slide.

"Sure, you *nerd*. Anyway." Jake reaches across me and holds both of my shoulders. Not like Connor does it, when he's trying to steer me around like a tiny girl-tractor, but like Jake is holding something small and soft that might run away before he has a chance to help it. "You still have to try to win."

"I—"

"Shush. What you have right now, it's not working, right? You think the people in school can't possibly understand why you play *GLO*, but what happened when you told Penny and Matt? Or that Fury won't protect you if the shit hits the fan, but do you hear your name coming out of Byunki's mouth, ever? We got you. So, so, so many people got you."

Well, okay. Penny and Matt were cool when they found out, and Fury is obviously fine, but that's not the important thing here. There are my parents and school and exposing my real identity to the world. These are all valid concerns.

"You do," I submit, "but I still can't risk winning. I'm going to throw this match and quit before Round Three either way. I'll stop playing; it's not the end of the world. That's bet-ter than cracking this whole thing open."

"You are so smart," Jake says kindly. He absentmindedly rubs his thumbs back and forth over my shoulders; it feels incredible, like a Vulcan chill-the-hell-out pinch. "And so not right. You know the first thing I thought when we were onstage and Thibault announced the league? First thing, like I didn't even think 'Wow, my team could go pro' or 'Muddy's gonna crap himself.'"

"What did you think?" I ask. Those thumbs are lulling me into something *new*.

"I thought, 'Emilia is about to do some real dumb shit.' And here you are, trying to quit when you have a shot at getting what you want. You do want it, right? In a vacuum, like you say."

"Of course I do! Stop touching me." I shrug away from his hands, and he holds them up on either side of him like he's under arrest. Immediately I feel more tense. That "prickly, defensive mean girl" thing is back in play, and I fully hate myself for it. "No, wait. I'm sorry. I just . . ."

Jake puts his arms down for a moment, then reaches over and hovers his hand over mine. He tilts his head experimentally: *Are you sure that's what you wanted? I'm fine either way, but I need you to choose it*, he seems to ask.

Fuck it. I grab his hand with both of mine. I touch the tough skin at the joint of his thumbs and the tips of his forefingers and feel the weird, specific muscle tone of someone whose hands burn more calories gaming than the rest of him combined. For all the thick, unruly hair on his head, the five or six hairs on each knuckle are fine. Smooth wrists, nice hands. He's a healer for sure.

"I want to try," I finally admit while I'm petting Jake's hand like a guinea pig. Penny's going to lose it when I tell her about this. "I'm good enough."

"You are." Jake doesn't know what to do with his extra hand. He's tried tucking it under his chin, messing with his hair, and in the last few seconds settled on squeezing it between his legs. Other than that, his eyes are fixed on my hands touching him. That should bother me, but it doesn't. Not even a little bit. It's just easy.

"Fury could win today if I don't throw away my shot."

"They could."

"*You* could win today too."

"That's right," Jake says gently. "Then you're gonna have to get through me."

"We'll bring it. We'll fight all of you."

"It'll suck," he agrees, but I see the grin spreading across his face. This is exactly where he wanted to lead me, and he's proud of himself for getting there. I could say something to wipe the smile off his face, but I don't want to. I like it there, and it's stirring up something inside me that I am actively choosing to identify as my, ahem, competitive spirit. "But the best man . . . woman . . . or, like, nonbinary collection of individuals, they'll win. You deserve to be in that fight. Don't give up because of what might happen."

What can I even say to that? Every time I've tried to push or pull Jake, he outmaneuvers me and slips in closer. Ordinarily I'd hate feeling out of my depth, but he's the one person I don't mind surprising me. Unless it's going to screw him over in the long run.

"Does your team know you came back for me?" I ask.

"Nope," he answers.

I felt guilty about taking Jake away from Team Unity this morning, but right now I'm content to have him here, breaking whatever social rules should keep us at odds. We've only been talking for a few days and have literally only re-met each other for a week, but just sitting and talking to him feels necessary somehow. I was prepared to do this without him, and then I wasn't, and now I'm back in the game because he's with me. That counts for more than whatever weird rivalry Bob and Byunki have.

"You want to get back to them?" Neither of us knows how much time Jake has before his match. It has to be coming up soon.

Jake unsticks his other hand from its hiding spot between his thighs and places it over mine. His hand is warm and more than a little sweaty, but it feels nice, like hugging a field hockey teammate after we've won a game. *I've got you*, Jake's wet hand seems to say. That's pretty cool, to be got.

"Yup. Gotta go beat Beast so we can, uh . . . beat you."

I try to pull my hand away playfully, but the physics of yanking anything out from between two sweaty boy palms make the whole motion too awkward to force. My fingers are Jake's until he decides to let go.

"Good luck," I reply. "I mean that literally about Beast Mode and very, very sarcastically about the finals."

"Thanks? Same? I really don't know what to do with that, but okay," Jake says and liberates my hands. I miss their warmth immediately. While he stands up and runs his fingers through his hair, I idly wonder if Jake gets his texture from touching his curls with sweaty hands all the time. Like a sea salt spray, but—no, that's disgusting. Bet his sweat smells amazing, though. *What?*

Fuck my life, he's done the thing. All Jake did was sit in a chair and listen to me, and now I want to find out what his neck tastes like. I am either massively starved for this kind of attention or exclusively nerdsexual, because Connor never made me feel the way I'm beginning to feel about Jake. I mean, yeah, I almost kissed him in the car. I can say that now; that's what almost happened, and I can name it because it was real. But that was . . . I don't know. Exhaustion. Hormones. Postgame adrenaline wearing off into ambient horniness that didn't have anything to do with the part where Jake was kind of wet and steamy behind his glasses and smelled like boy and didn't ask me to explain anything because nothing odd or secret about me could surprise him. Or make him like me less. I am clearly horny for acceptance, not for Jake.

Except he's standing in front of me now and stretching his arms to warm up before he heads to his green room, and the bottom of his Unity jersey is hiked up, like, a quarter of an inch above his beltline and—Jesus, take the wheel.

"Hey," I find myself saying as I stand up and hug Jake. "Thank you."

Jake hugs back better than he did outside his apartment building, which I appreciate. Last time I was too freaked out to touch him, and now I don't want to do anything else. I know I have to let go of him soon because we're, you know, in the middle of a massively high-stakes competition and he needs to fight his way toward trying to kick my team's ass, but I don't feel bad holding a little longer. I mean Jake *did* just tell me to go after what I want.

"Good luck today, KNOX," he whispers.

I don't know if it's his breath in my ear or hearing him go back to our competition titles that tips me over the edge of reason. Before he can get his face away from my face—and he really is too much taller than me to attempt this when he's drawn up to full height—I turn my head to kiss Jake on the cheek. For luck, I tell myself. It's a lie. I don't care.

Jake freezes when my lips hit his warm face, and for one hopeless second I think he's going to turn and catch my mouth with his. Then, I don't know, we'd make out in this hallway? Just a little, as a treat? I've never wanted to kiss anyone so badly before. When I kissed Connor in the cafeteria, I spent the whole time wondering why everything in there tasted like nickels, but the kissing itself didn't move me. Here in the hallway, *not* kissing Jake is moving me, to put an insufficient name to the good heat I'm feeling with my nose pressed against his skin.

But he doesn't kiss me. In fact he reacts more like I've stabbed him than smooched him. After that first freeze, he lets go of me and steps back, his face so red I worry for a second I've transferred my cream blush to his pale skin.

"Em," he says quietly, with some of the panic I remember from this time last week creeping into his voice.

"Good luck to you too," I reply quickly. Glad I had that one ready to go. "That was just a luck . . . thing."

"Right, you too. I gotta . . ." He jerks his thumb over his shoulder. I know, I know, he has to go. I wish I felt less giggly and triumphant having only kissed him on the cheek, but whatever. It felt good. We'll deal with it later, after the matches. Probably not on the ride home, since Bob won't let him come back with me, but sometime after that. I'm not worried about it or anything right now.

I shoo him away with my hands. "Go. I'll see you later."

Jake nods and starts back down the hallway. He doesn't get far before he turns around and looks back.

"Just a luck thing?" he asks. Anyone else would sound cocky asking the world's most obvious question, but Jake isn't anyone. As smart as he is, he really doesn't know. Not like I have a ton of high ground to stand on; I just figured it out five minutes ago.

"Nope," I say, straight-faced.

"Cool," he replies and closes the space between us in two long-legged strides. "This," Jake continues, "isn't for luck either."

As good as not kissing Jake Hooper felt, I have to say, kissing him is so much better.

PART IV

Jake!!!

BOB HAD GONE through a lot of trouble to make the Team Unity green room feel like home. He'd brought in blue curtains for all the sense that made, since none of the green rooms had windows, and had tacked them up on the walls like a college student trying to create a sexy, tasseled opium den vibe in their concrete dorm room. There was also a gold star chart pinned up with everyone's names to reward good ideas, which had quickly devolved into a black star chart marking down anyone who cussed and now functioned as an analog LanguageBot.

Ki had brought a few LOONA light sticks in a glass vase that sparkled like distracting electric flowers, and Penelope had brought a busted-looking black ottoman her sister was going to throw out if P hadn't found something to do with it. Muddy's contribution was a bag of cheddar cheese popcorn, which he ate by himself; his decor contribution could generously be described as the orange powdery marks he'd left on the couch.

Out of all the things Jake helped Bob drag to the green room that morning, half out of punishment for getting caught with Emilia and half out of necessity because the sheer volume of swag he'd packed in his trunk would take one man two trips, he liked the blankets best. They were navy blue, were extremely fuzzy, and felt amazing when he launched himself facedown into one and screamed into its fluff. It was a good scream. Team Unity's match was over. They were in the finals.

"Blue cross!" Bob bellowed when he entered the green room after Jake. Jake had skipped ahead of everyone else and gotten to the room first. He could have skipped his way around the arena eight times and still had the energy for another match at the rate he was going. He was having the best day of his entire life.

"Black shield!" Ki and Penelope chanted after him and flopped down to flank Jake on the sectional. Jake felt one of them scratch at his back in excitement. He felt like a beloved family pet. Whatever Bob felt about Emilia and Fury, this win had to have wiped it out.

"Can't lose. Apparently." Muddy strolled in after everyone. He'd been a little more leisurely in his pace down the ramps from the stage, dodging and bending to photobomb people taking videos and selfies in the halls. Jake didn't know why he bothered; someone had been backstage to take their picture the second they won the match. Thibault Adige wanted everyone in the city to know which players had a fifty-fifty shot at repping Philly in the Guardians League. Bob even stopped to say a few words to an esports reporter about his team and what they'd bring to the league.

For the second time since this tournament had started, people were *looking* at Jake. On any other day, the attention would make him curl up into himself, dropping his head to make sure no one had a problem with his face and apologizing for taking up any space in their field of vision. Today he was smiling, laughing, posing even. Look upon his works, ye mighty: Jake kissed Emilia.

And yeah, he'd also healed his ass off against Beast Mode, but that victory felt like a direct result of the one that came before. Kissing was awesome; did everyone know that? Like objectively it seemed great, but *mouths*, man. They do so much that should make them gross, but they're *not*.

He hadn't gone to their hiding spot to kiss her, honest. It would have been so much cooler if that had been his goal, though. Just like, swoop in, give the pep talk of the century, dip her like a romance cutscene, and get down to smooch town—that would have been dope, but it wasn't the story. Jake knew that Emilia would try to cut loose the second he heard Thibault announce the league, and the ridiculous, heart-tugging loyalty he felt for her wouldn't let him see her do that without hearing him out. *GLO* was the reason Emilia talked to him, the only reason she even saw him. When she got on voice chat after the Matcha Attack, he'd nearly peed himself on his dad's creaky old office chair. She was different when she talked about *GLO*; she knew *everything* about it. Emilia laughed and opened up when they talked about games. She got sparkly somehow, way brighter than he'd seen her in the month since he got to Hillford West and saw her going through the motions of being the junior class's student-athlete queen bee. Jake had only hoped to convince her to keep playing so she could stay sparkly, and, *bam*, she'd kissed him.

What were the odds of that? Batman would shoot someone at point-blank range before Jake thought he'd get to kiss Emilia Romero. *The Elder Scrolls 7* would come out on the PlayStation 79. Nintendo would reveal MissingNo as a starter Pokémon in the first generation of game consoles playable on Mars. Those were the odds, and *yet*.

Jake wasn't even embarrassed that he'd gotten his first kiss at fifteen. Quality definitely won over quantity in this case. And Emilia was . . . a chef's kiss kind of kisser. Probably the best kisser in the world. He had literally nothing to compare it to, but Jake didn't have to be a completionist to know when he'd scored a platinum trophy.

Whew, he really had to stop thinking about kissing. Now that everyone was in from backstage, it was time for Bob to give a speech. The only worse time to get a boner would be mid-match. Or walking across the stage. Or in the postgame photos. Now that he thought about it, there were a lot of bad times for boners. Really only a handful of good times for one, Jake guessed. This wasn't one of them.

"All right, everybody, circle up," Bob called. Jake wiggled around to get his face out of the blanket and settled between Ki and P on the couch.

"Great match," Bob continued. "If the star chart was still a star chart, you'd all be getting a sticker."

"And four stickers for you, Bob," Penelope yelled.

"You go, Bob," Ki echoed.

Bob shimmied his shoulders like the praise was showering down on him from above. "I'm sorry I couldn't tell y'all about the league. Wizzard reached out to the captains after Round One and told us they'd get better reactions if everyone was surprised onstage. So if I've seemed like a hard"—he stopped himself and glanced back at the black star chart—"butt lately, it's just because I knew what we were fighting for."

"And here we are," Muddy said smoothly. Jake noticed that Muddy had taken the long part of the sectional for himself and was kicked back with his feet up on the couch. Muddy's eyes narrowed when he caught Jake looking. Whatever that was about didn't matter. This was Unity's parade, and Jake felt like he was riding the biggest damn float in the route.

"One more match and we're in the league," Bob said. "Now let's find out who we're going to have to take down next."

"Let's see," Ki groaned sarcastically while Bob picked up

the remote for the green room's live feed of the competition. "I'm going to go with Fury, or maybe Fury."

Penelope squinted at the screen. "Turn it up, Bob. We missed the start of the match."

Bob obliged, and Jake leaned back against the couch's cushions to watch Emilia play. He cautioned a look at Bob, who caught his eye knowingly before turning to watch the match as well.

"Whatever happens, we have to talk after this. As a team," Bob said ominously. Jake felt his stomach twist. That parade feeling was fading out into a suspicion that winning today wasn't enough to get Bob off his back. He was also nervous for Emilia, so either way his abdominal region wasn't going to feel great.

"Chronic came out with Grendel," Muddy noted as the hairy, one-armed form of *GLO*'s resident monster type tank stomped around in the commentator's third-person screen view. "Smart of Fury to give VANE the swap so he could play Jubilee."

"Ugh, it's gonna be a monster fight." Ki shuddered. She didn't like any of *GLO*'s monster characters, preferring to ice people out as the light-footed mad scientist Doctor Jack.

"He did the mash . . . ," Penelope sing-whispered to Jake. The two of them had healed in lockstep today, and Jake could tell she was feeling cuddly.

"He did the monster mash," Jake whispered back before

Bob shushed them both. The match was getting serious on-screen.

Jake watched Emilia's Pharaoh perch up among the obelisks in the crumbling architecture of the Memphis III map before the camera snapped to an opposing player's POV. Chronic had gotten first blood, and Fury was way behind on getting enough damage to fill up their Special Attack meters. Both teams still had all their players alive, so there was still a chance either of them could win on payload.

"They're too evenly matched; they keep hitting and healing," Muddy noticed. He was right. Unless someone took a big bite out of Chronic, this match was going to be a long, tense slog. Jake knew how Emilia must be feeling on that stage, fueled by wanting—needing to win to keep fighting for her place here. He wondered if she was also thinking about the kiss in a non-distracting, subconscious sort of way. Kissing her buoyed Jake to some of the best heals of his life. Somehow, he doubted his lips had the same powers hers did.

Or hey, why not? She was the one who wanted to kiss him. Maybe she was on a "get what I want" warpath and making out with him was Step 1 in her quest for world domination. Jake had a sudden, vivid mental image of Emilia decked out in Pharaoh's gold robes, standing atop a mountain with an army behind her and a swirling ball of necromagic fomenting between her capable hands. He pictured himself as Pythia, dressed as a hospital clown, draped on the ground beside her and clinging to her leg, like the cover of so many of his dad's awful, vaguely porny sci-fi novels from the '70s. Jake's kiss could be good luck too, even if it meant bad luck for him down the line.

"Oh shit!" Penelope exclaimed. "Nobody even saw her coming."

"Black star," Bob said automatically, but leaned into the TV to see what Penelope was describing. It was a suicide move from Emilia, averted at the last second from a lightning-fast heal from JOON. She'd leaped from the obelisk and spun to land three paralyzing bolts on Chronic's healers and tank, and would have dropped from the fall damage if Han-Jun hadn't laid out a heal/harm wall parallel to the ground. The force field caught Emilia like a bunch of firefighters holding a blanket underneath a five-story window to keep her in the game by a tiny sliver of health. RIKK topped off her bar and sent her on her way, while VANE turned Chronic's tank armor into swiss cheese.

Jake looked over at Muddy, who was staring openmouthed at the screen.

"Think you can manage that next match, baby Jake?" Muddy asked.

Jake shook his head. That move was barely possible within the laws of math, let alone the mechanics of *GLO*. Once Chronic's tank was damaged, it was all over. Fury piled on the payload and defended it like the walls of Minas Tirith. Byunki

even had time to do a moonwalk emote on top of the hover-
wagon as his teammates beat back Chronic's DPS, his Klio's
flame sword bobbing smoothly as the character slid backward
in a perfect circle. That was it, payload to Fury. No tank kill,
but a way more impressive victory all around.

"Shiii-oot," Bob exhaled. Fury's colors flashed along the
arena's LED screens, red and black in a shooting loop around
the mezzanine.

"That's that," Ki said quietly. "Now we know what we're
up against."

"It was perfect," muttered Muddy. "They sandbagged the
first half of the match to keep it even and then . . . that heal.
JOON just . . ."

Penelope was staring straight ahead at a wall that was now
half-covered with one of Bob's curtains. One of the tacks must
have fallen off during the match. "Just gonna say it," she said.
"I couldn't do that heal."

"Me neither," Jake agreed. JOON and Emilia were just not
human. That combo looked harder than a zero-gravity tra-
peze routine, followed by the girl he'd just kissed shooting
three dudes in the face with a crossbow.

"You sure?" Muddy asked. "I'm pretty sure you could pull
it off for KNOX."

"Yeah. About that," Bob said. After the match, Bob had sat
down on the edge of the couch near Muddy and put his face
in his hands, but now he sat up to look directly at Jake. Muddy

was looking at him too, which only sent another stabbing feeling through Jake's stomach.

Ki and Penelope turned to look at him too, but they both wore such confused expressions that Jake was pretty sure they didn't know what was about to go down. Everything happened too much these days.

"Do you want to tell them or do you want me to, Hoops?" Bob asked. Yikes, Bob never called him Hoops unless it was serious. They'd called him that for the first few months of *GLO* before he moved on to a first-name basis, back when they still called Muddy "Matty." Jake felt oddly defensive, because if anything their victory today meant that whatever Bob was worried about wasn't true and everything was fine. Jake could fight with Fury and kiss Emilia. He was absolutely capable of those two things. Going up against her in the finals was not ideal, but it was not like either of them were going to back down to make the other one feel better. That was not what Emilia was like. It was not what Jake was like either.

"I mean, I don't—" Jake began. Jesus, there was a lot to explain. They knew one half of the story, but how could he compress everything that had happened since Round 1? Especially since he'd sort of . . . super lied to them about most of it.

"How about I do it?" Muddy interrupted. Bob jerked his head around to look at Muddy behind him. Jake's eyes widened. What did Muddy know?

"*Baby Jake*'s been colluding with KNOX all week," Muddy

said, directing his accusation to Bob. "I saw them in Crystal Cathedral on Wednesday. Lakeport on Thursday. They were playing freaking minigames in Euphrates Crater while we were in chat on Friday. I was on an alt and saw Jake hanging out with a legacy robe Pharaoh on a Diamond-tier dev server. Put two and two together. Kept trying to catch them in a screenshot, but Jake kept tossing freeze spells at me and running away with her."

Okay, it was a little funny that the pesky guy in Crystal Cathedral was Muddy, but only if Jake completely removed it from the context of the *complete shitshow* he had just earned a starring role in. Bob's jaw dropped, and Ki and Penelope each grabbed one of Jake's shoulders in unison. He felt like a prisoner about to be tossed on the floor in front of an unfeeling elf king.

"What?" Bob asked. "That's not what I was going to say, Mud."

"What were you going to say? Because I have more."

"I was going to say that KNOX—Emilia, by the way; her name is Emilia—"

Jake cringed. So much for keeping that cat in the bag, Bob.

"—drove Jake to the competition today. And he told me she drove him from Round One last week. They've been, I don't know, hanging out? Jake, what the hell is going on?"

Up on the TV screen, the arena's recap showed Emilia smiling and waving with Team Fury after their win. She looked fierce in her red jersey and her curls pulled back in a tight, no-nonsense ponytail. Emilia had her hair down when Jake kissed her. He remembered because it touched his face and smelled like Key lime pie.

Penelope followed Jake's line of sight to the screen and had the good sense to reach over to the coffee table and hit the power button on the remote. Emilia vanished along with the ambient clamor of competition. The ensuing silence quite frankly sucked.

"We're not hanging out," Jake began now that the distraction of seeing Emilia was gone, "not like that. I mean I've barely even seen her except from the car rides, so it's not like we're . . . we're . . ."

"Take your time," Ki said quietly. She knew Jake got caught up in his words when he felt nervous. He'd talked to her and P on voice chat more often than Bob and Muddy.

Jake took a deep breath. "She gave me a ride after Round One. It was raining; she was being nice. Nothing happened. She's just got a lot of stuff going on with *GLO*, so no one's supposed to know she plays. So please, don't tell anyone her name. Like you *really* can't tell anyone who she is or that she goes to my school."

"Who cares?" Muddy interjected.

"Not now, Mud," Penelope replied sharply.

"She almost got doxxed, okay? A couple years ago, when she first started playing *GLO*, there were some bad . . . guys, I don't know. It freaked her out, and she only agreed to play with Fury if they protected her identity. She didn't expect any-one she knew to be at the competition, so I've been keeping that secret for her. I didn't tell you because it wasn't my secret to tell."

He felt terrible for lying, but he'd done it for Emilia, and she was equally as important to him as Unity right now. He was going to have to figure out how to parse that in the finals, but it was his problem to work out, not something that should be decided by committee.

"Then we kept talking," Jake continued. "I didn't think we would, because why would she bother with me? But she did, and it's been a few days, and she gave me a ride this morning because she's nice." Jake felt his voice rising as he defended Emilia. He wasn't great at making himself heard, but this was too important. "She's great, and she's too good to have her motives torn apart by people who don't understand where she's coming from. So no, *Bob*, Byunki didn't send her to mess with me, and even if he did, she wouldn't do that. And I'm not an idiot who would fall for it anyway because I'm not a baby."

"I never said you were, Jake," Bob said calmly, "but the timing looks . . . not great."

Jake wasn't finished talking. "And about this all being a secret? Not even her parents know. She's an extraordinary player, and she does this in her *spare time*. If you knew half of what she had to do at school . . . and her parents . . . Person-ally I'd, like, die if I was her. I'd wake up, take one look at my

schedule, and die. And through all of that she . . . she still saw
me. She's so cool? And she has so many friends? She still
wants me—to talk to me and ask me questions and stuff.
And you guys are great, and I love you, even Muddy, but also
screw you right now, but I feel 3D around her, like I'm real
and worth looking at, and I love it. Because I—"

Yeah, no. Jake knew that was where the speech stopped.
Those were more words than he'd had said out loud to anyone
besides Emilia in months, and he didn't want to go any further. His eyes hurt, and his nose was tingling uncomfortably.
That was a good sign to stop.

Jake slid his fingers under his glasses and covered his face.
It wasn't enough to block out the fluorescent light in the green
room, but it did save his brain from processing a few of the
million stimuli that made him feel like he was about to
barf-explode.

"I'm sorry for lying," he said through his palms. He probably looked dumb as hell. "I'm not sorry for spending time
with Emilia. Sorry for not being sorry."

Jake was surprised to feel arms around him then, two sets
encircling him from either side. Ki and Penelope were hugging him, and when he took his hands away from his face, he
saw both of them smiling at each other like they'd both just
won a bet. Muddy and Bob looked less enthused.

"You're just going to believe that?" Muddy finally
said. "You're just going to believe that a hot girl waltzes back

into your life on the opposite side of a million-dollar deal because you're special? She doesn't want you, dumbass." He rubbed at his brow like he was trying to wipe Jake's airborne stupid off his face. "Of course you two buy it." He gestured to Penelope and Ki's half-octopus grip on Jake. "Bob, please tell me you don't believe this."

Bob leaned forward with his elbows on his knees. If he had a bomber jacket, Jake would think he was aiming for a full Karamo Brown cosplay moment. "I believe that what Jake is feeling is real. I also think"—he turned to look at Jake—"that you don't know Byunki like I do. He knew about the league before everyone else. I know he met with Thibault because Wizzard wants a big-name team like Fury to win. So if Emilia started talking to you on Wednesday, it's still possible that she's, you know . . ."

"She didn't know," Jake interjected. "She didn't know until this morning. We talked after the announcement."

"Where?" Muddy asked. "When?"

"Right before the match, some weird corner behind craft services where they keep all the chairs. Does that matter?"

"Because she tried to psych you out before the match!" Muddy yelled.

"No," Jake snarled back, "she didn't. She was actually about to quit when I talked to her, so if she was trying to psych me out, she must be on some next level sideways mind game shit, which she isn't."

Bob spoke tenderly, like he were trying to explain death to a toddler. "Maybe she isn't, but Byunki—"

"Hey, Bob?" Penelope spoke up from beside Jake. She exchanged a look with Ki, who nodded. "Maybe you need to let go of the idea that your ex is a psychopath out to get you and let people have nice things."

Bob's what? Everyone, including Muddy, snapped around to stare at Bob.

"We love you, B-man," Ki picked up where Penelope left off, "but just because Byunki dicked you over on *World of Warfare*, like, half a decade ago doesn't mean that every time someone likes someone it's the preamble to a blood feud. Like, yeah, Byunki is your evil ex, but maybe, and stop me if this is crazy, Emilia is a better person than him."

"Not like that's hard," added Penelope, "but your bad taste in men hasn't necessarily rubbed off on the rest of us."

"Not even a little bit," Ki riffed. "You're the only one here who likes men at all."

"Sorry." Jake's brain was exploding in slow motion. "But Byunki, like Team Fury Byunki, is Bob's ex-boyfriend? *That's* the thing? And you all knew this?"

Muddy shook his head. "I didn't. You people don't tell me shit."

Bob groaned and stood up from his spot on the couch. Now that the end of the reclining edge was free, Muddy stretched his feet up in the open spot and leaned back with his arms behind his head, clearly waiting for the show to continue.

"Yes, Jake, that's the thing," Bob admitted. Sitting, he was another member of Team Unity, but standing was Bob's signal that he was about to enter Captain Mode. "We were your age, we cocreated a guild on *World of Warfare*, there was a meetup, and Byunki and I got close."

"They hooked up in the bathroom at Amalgam," Penelope added. "Like a lot." She was never going to let Bob tell the story devoid of details. Jake loved that about P.

"Ma'am, can I talk?" Bob asked. Penelope rolled her eyes but made a zipping motion in front of her lips.

"Thank you," he continued. "We kept seeing each other for six months or so; we'd get rides into Philly and hang out. Talk all night on Ventrilo—yeah, Ventrilo, we're old—and I fell for him."

"Hard," said Ki.

"Just because you're not Penelope doesn't mean I won't tell you to zip it too."

Jake nudged Ki with his elbow as well as he could. She still had her arms around him. "Let the man speak," he said.

"There's not a lot to tell after that," Bob said. "He was long-gaming me. He wanted sole control of the guild, and I called him out, so we had a vote one night when he wasn't online and kicked him. He found a new guild and ganked all of us to pieces. It was systematic, search and destroy. None of us could log on without one of his goons ruining the game. I moved on to play *GLO*, and he followed me there. Enter Unity. Enter Fury."

"Enter Jake and enter Emilia," Muddy snorted. "Now do you see?"

"Do you still love him?" asked Jake.

Ki, Penelope, and Bob all answered at the same time: "*Hell* no."

Jake could see how the nature of the feud between Fury and Unity had colored Bob's reaction to finding him with Emilia that morning. He'd been holding his captain's behavior against him all day but had hoped that their victory might assuage him; now he saw that every step that brought Team Unity closer to a showdown with Fury looked to Bob like a move on Byunki's chessboard.

It was the world's biggest coincidence, or else a hilarious conspiracy of fate to put Bob's and Byunki's teams together with even more feelings at stake. Jake tried to press the buttons that he always did, the ones that told him he was stupid and gullible and all the bad things that could happen were entirely his fault because those were his favorite buttons. As much as it sucked to feel terrible about himself for what happened to his parents, he *knew* how to feel terrible. He'd felt like that for so long it was the only comfortable state he recognized. He was dumb as hell for not knowing Bob's story. He was a massive idiot for trusting Emilia. Inside his mind, he reached for the boxing gloves he'd been beating himself up with for years and found them missing from their hook.

Emilia didn't think he was dumb. She thought he was kind and funny. She didn't want him to curl up and disappear, and she never let him beat himself up, even when he thought he wanted to. Emilia trusted him. He had to trust her too.

"Well, I still like her," Jake said. "I'll kick her Fury butt in two weeks, but I can't stop liking her."

Ki and Penelope both sighed while Bob let out a groan. Sonically it was a mess, but that wasn't anything less than Jake expected.

"I didn't exactly factor true love into my plans for this competition, so here's an option," Bob said when he finished groaning. He sat back down on the couch and nudged Muddy's feet away with his hips. "Just to be safe, and to make me and everyone else here feel better about your choices, you stay away from KNOX, Emilia, whoever, until Round Three shakes out."

"But—" Jake wanted to interrupt. Bob didn't give him the chance.

"Nah, son. This is your captain speaking. I can tell you really like this girl and she likes you—"

Muddy snorted from behind Bob. Jake didn't let it bother him. Yet.

"Just walk it back for the sake of the team. It's two weeks. You can tell her before if you want. No talky, no touchy. Y'all are competitors and strangers until one of us wins the league spot."

"It does make sense, Jake," Penelope agreed. "Two weeks isn't that long."

"Jesus Christ." Muddy slithered off the couch and leaned down to grab his jacket off the coffee table. "Do you hear yourselves? Thibault Adige wants to give the winning team a *million dollars* and a full-time contract, and you care more about Jake's girl problems. I feel like I'm taking crazy pills. Ditch the bitch and get your head in the game! Tell him, Bob."

Jake felt his body moving before his mind could make a choice about it. He jumped up from the couch and lunged across the coffee table to grab at the collar of Muddy's shirt. A second too late, Jake remembered that all of the finger coordination he'd built up over years of gaming had definitely not transferred to the rest of his body, so he missed and almost face-planted into the table before he swung an arm down to catch himself. He would have been embarrassed if the wild feeling of wanting to stuff Muddy's words back into his mouth and make him choke on them hadn't burned his ability to feel anything else clean out of his system.

"Don't call her that," Jake snarled as he picked himself up and eased back onto the couch.

Muddy just laughed and nonchalantly threaded an arm through his jacket sleeve. "Stick to healing, Jake. It's the only thing you're good at."

"Matty!" Bob barked. "I get that you're frustrated, but you don't have to be mean. We're Unity; we put each other first."

"Whatever." Muddy rolled his eyes and made for the green room door. "Keep nursing the baby; I don't care. I gotta go talk to some people."

Jake hated that Muddy didn't even bother slamming the door. A big, abrupt crash was exactly what the moment needed. Leave it to Muddy to ignore the rules of high drama in an effort to look cooler than the rest of Unity.

"I'll go after him once he's cooled down," Bob sighed. "He wants that league spot bad."

"We all do," Penelope said, "but you don't see the rest of us going knives out on Jake's jugular."

"Our knives are in," Ki agreed, while rubbing Jake's elbow. He'd landed hard on the coffee table, and even though he hadn't said anything, it still hurt like hell. Nothing to jeopardize his hands, of course, but still. Ow.

"I don't want to be stuck in a contract with him if we win," Jake muttered. He'd put up with Muddy's asshole schtick for years, thinking it was an in-joke. Like "hey, Jake, you're dumb, just kidding!" Knowing that Muddy actually thought he was useless and stupid would make it so much harder to play alongside him. Going into Round 3, liking Emilia was one thing, but going into it hating Muddy was another.

"*When* we win," Bob corrected, "we'll have to get over it. Wizzard knows the league announcement might change the teams' strategy, so they're cool if people bring in alts for Round Three, as long as they're finalized a week out. After that, who-ever plays the final match is locked into the contract. We don't have alts; we have Muddy, one of the best DPSes in the game. We don't have a chance of beating Fury without him."

Bob was right. The Guardians League was too much to give up on account of one prick. Jake had told Emilia not to give up, so he wasn't going to give up either. He had two weeks to rally and/or stuff his now-seething Muddy hate deep down where he couldn't feel it. Two weeks without being able to talk to Emilia about it. Or anyone else. Jake felt insanely good about that. Spectacular, really.

"This is my fault," Jake said again. Not everything was his fault, but this particular snafu was totally . . . mostly on him. "I'll get it together for Round Three."

"What about KNOX?" Bob asked, for sure using Emilia's Fury name to remind Jake what was at stake.

"P's right. Two weeks isn't that long, and she'll understand. I solemnly swear not to talk to, text, or otherwise communi-cate with Emilia while she's still our competition."

Two weeks was *forever* in Jake years. He wished he knew how long it would feel for Emilia, or if she'd still want to look at him after Unity wrenched away the dream Jake loved to see her chase.

CHAPTER TWENTY

Emilia, Monday

IT'S ONLY TAKEN Mr. Grimes two weeks to turn his fish tank of an office into what I'm sure he imagines is a den of Zen but is doing way more to stress me out than calm me down. The last time I was here, the most egregious things were his wooden-beaded bracelets and my mom. Today, it's everything. The macramé dreamcatcher-looking hangings stuck to the glass wall with suction cups. The bamboo mat on the floor. The crystal collection on his desk, which includes a tiny faux-jade Chinese lion the size of my thumb, a patchouli oil diffuser, and one of those mini sand gardens in which someone (I'm hoping another student) has meticulously raked the outline of a . . . Is that a dick? I think it's supposed to be a dick.

"You can rake that out," Grimes says. It's not awkward at all that he caught me looking. "I try not to dissuade students from expressing themselves creatively, but if you wanted to make something new while I grab the folder you need, I would appreciate that."

Poor guy. How many dicks have people drawn in his garden in the last two weeks? Going by the defeated look on his face, I'm going to guess a lot. Out of pity more than artistic impulse, I pick up the little rake on my side of the desk and scratch some wiggly lines in the sand. There. Now it's an amoeba wearing a mushroom-shaped hat.

"Lovely," Grimes says when he straightens up from going through the cabinets under his desk. The folder he dug up for me looks dusty. It's not common for students at Hillford West to request what's inside it, so I hope the information inside is up to date.

"It's thinner than I thought it would be," I say to get his attention off the Zen garden.

"There's more, but this is just the list of requirements and general starting paperwork," he admits. He hasn't actually handed me the folder yet. "Miss Romero, it's my job to ask questions. Before I give this to you, I have to ask a few. Can we start with why?"

I take a deep breath and think back to what Penny and I rehearsed yesterday. "So there's a scholarship program my parents would, like, die to know I got accepted to that would require me to intern after graduation. If I wait until the summer after senior year, I'll lose the money. I just found out I'm a finalist, so I'm going to tell my parents about it soon, but when I do I want to show them I have everything planned out. You've met my mom; she'll want to know I have everything covered before I make a move."

By my ultrafast calculations, that explanation was about 40 percent true in reality, with a bump to 80 percent if we count the spirit of the statement over a more literal translation. Hopefully it dissuades him from lighting the beacons and bringing my parents into this before I'm ready to tell them.

"I remember your mother very well," Grimes replies with a little too much wistfulness in his voice. "Can I ask which scholarship program you're a finalist for?"

"I'd rather not say right now," I reply. "I think my mom would be hurt if I told you before I said anything to her." Penny and I came up with the half-lie scholarship excuse to get me the paperwork, but Matt was the one who told me to bank on my advisor having a crush on my mom to make it easier. When Matt's right, he's right.

"I understand." He smiles. I'm begging him with my eyes not to wink, but he does. "Miss Romero, I'm all about the youth of today finding what gives them purpose. Your generation has inherited a broken world. If you've found something that might drive you to do your part to fix it, I respect and admire your spirit," he intones. "But I wouldn't want you to rush headfirst into leaving high school. You're only young once; you should enjoy it before entering the working world."

I don't know; I think I'll enjoy literally playing video games for money more than going to prom, but go off, Louis. I do not say this out loud.

"I'm going to give you this folder." True to his word, he hands me the file across the desk. "But if anything happens with your internship, I want to discuss this further with your mother. I mean your parents, both of them. You . . . She did say she's still married, right?"

A tap on the glass wall saves me and Grimes from having to continue this conversation. I can now proceed with Step 2 in my plan, which is going to be a lot harder. Grimes makes some apologetic noises to let me know my time is up, and I'm careful to be very, visibly thankful for his help.

"Change the world," Grimes calls out as I leave, "and tell your mom I said hi!"

I'm halfway out the door of the advisors' suite when I hear him welcome the student into his cube with a gentle "namaste."

I riffle through the papers in the Department of Education folder while I walk over to the auditorium to prep for Step 2. Thanks to my parents toploading me in the first two years of high school, I'm well on my way to being able to graduate early without even trying. All I need to do is grab some summer requirements, pass a few Regents, and demonstrate full-time employment waiting on the other side of eleventh grade. Easy check, easier check, and significantly harder check, considering I still have to kick Jake's ass to get the league spot.

A part of me knew that we would have to stop hanging out

before the finals, but I still checked my *GLO* inbox yesterday to see if Jake had anything to say after the match. He left me a message saying he thought it was best we went no-contact for the next two weeks, which sucks but makes sense. It's my turn to be a good secret friend.

But that *kiss*, though. Did kissing Jake transport me to Missandei's home island of Naath from *Game of Thrones*? Because I got major butterflies and also felt like I was about to straight up die of happiness. Keeping it 100, I didn't even know kissing could do that. Literally haven't stopped thinking about it. I'm thinking about it right now. Yeah, that's the good shit. Whew.

The first thing I did when I got home on Saturday was text Penny and Matt everything that happened at the tournament. Matt already knew about the Guardians League because he was following the competition on a stream, but I had to fill them in on the pre-match and backstage action. Their reactions, in order, were (1) let's pick Bob up and throw him in a dumpster, (2) holy shit, that's so much money, (3) good thing Jake was there to stop you from doing something stupid, Emilia, oh my god, and (4) sorry, you and Jake *what*?

Waiting on the triple dots to resolve after telling them I kissed Jake Hooper was thrilling. Penny waived her God-given right to say "I told you so" and expressed regret that she didn't take Matt up on his bet, and Matt cobbled together an impressive emoji hieroglyph that included brown-girl-kissing-white-boy, video game controller, heart with smaller hearts inside it, interrobang, blue heart, red heart, robot head (?), and a party hat.

Then they asked me what I was going to do about Connor, which brings me back to Step 2.

When I get to the auditorium, it's empty except for Penny and Matt taking pictures onstage. Matt's kneeling on the floor with a reflective board propped against his chest and Penny's phone in his hand, shooting upward to get her in a power pose against the backdrop of the red curtain.

"Stop moving for two seconds." His whine carries easily over the rows of seating. "I'm trying to get the light to bounce off your highlighter."

"That's what the VSCO is for," Penny explains. "Just set it to portrait and zoom out. I need these posters yesterday."

"Why do we even need these?" Matt wiggles awkwardly to adjust the bounce board again, making Penny's dark skin shimmer onstage. "It's not like Connor's gonna ditch you just because Lia's dumping his—"

"Ask less, shoot more," Penny mutters. Matt obliges. I let him get a few pictures in before clearing my throat from the back of the auditorium.

"You look great, Penny!" I call.

"Lia, is that you?" Penny breaks her pose to shield her eyes. "What's it look like back there? Is the light washing me out?"

"Nah," I decide, moving forward toward the stage. "The vibe is very Duckie Thot."

"Aw, you always know what to say."

I brandish the folder Grimes gave me. "Apparently I do."

"Nice!" Matt holds up his free hand for a high five, and it takes me a moment to clamor onto the stage to accept it. "Grimes took the bait?"

"Like a guppy."

Matt checks Penny's phone for the time. "That gives you . . . twenty minutes left in free period to complete stage two."

"Be gentle," Penny reminds me, "but firm. Connor's still my VP, and I need his head in the game. And if he asks for a reason, don't let the reason be 'I hooked up with someone else at a nerds-only club in Philly.' "

"I'm just gonna tell him I have a lot on my plate and don't have time for a relationship right now. When I win the tournament, the cat will be out of the bag anyway, for Connor and everyone else."

"He'll bounce back," Matt says confidently. "Once you're gone, the line goes, like, Audra first, then maybe Lena on the volleyball team, then Holly? After that it's literally every other straight girl in school because you *know* the bi ones won't put up with him, then the girls at Hillford North—"

"Message received, Matt," I cut him off. "Connor Dimeo is a hot commodity."

"Dumb hot," Penny adds.

"Jake's really cute too," Matt offers. Penny and I both look at him sideways. "What? I'm secure enough to say that."

"I like you more every day," Penny says with a look of wicked approval. If anything, bringing Penny and Matt together as future supervillain and willing stooge has been the highlight of this entire experience. Well, one of the highlights. Sticking my tongue in Jake's mouth and pulling off a nigh-impossible drop heal with Han-Jun to bring Fury closer to a million-dollar contract was pretty great too.

"You got this, Lia." Matt salutes me. "Go forth and break up with your boyfriend so you can keep seducing a sophomore. I believe in you."

I return his salute and try to catch Penny's eye before I leave the stage. I really, really wish there was another way I could make this up to her. Her campaign has been a revolving door of VPs, and it's all my fault, so if Connor checks out because of me, it will just be another way I screwed her over since she announced her candidacy. On one level, I think she gets it; once she saw how much I stood to win, Penny understood that *GLO* had to take the top slot in my life. I just don't know if she's actually as understanding about the whole Jake thing.

"Go, Lia," she says, as if she can read everything I've been thinking. "Do one thing for you. We'll be here until second period if you need us."

"We're on your team," Matt agrees. "Oh, and"—he reaches

into his pocket for his own phone, opens it, and sends a quick text blast to a few choice Hillford West students—"the popcorn thing is go."

I use the momentum from that roller coaster of pseudo-encouragement to propel myself out of the auditorium, down the hall, and toward the library to meet my fate. Or make it.

Now, listen, I'm not a monster. I know what I did here. A simple recounting of the events in order would make me the Asshole on that "Am I the Asshole" subreddit any day of the week. Kissing Jake was a glorious emotional impulse, and Connor was the furthest thing from my mind in the moment, but I knew then and now that I have to break up with him. I didn't want to do it over text, because that's mean, and I couldn't do it over the phone, because I'm not a hundred years old, so I had to wait for free period on Monday.

I have intel that Connor's spending free period in the library and spot him almost as soon as I walk in. He's lounging on one of the couches with his feet stretched out on the cushions, his phone held up above his face as he texts with a fast-thumbed ferocity I am sure he's never applied to any of his communication with me.

I'm not nervous. This is the nice thing to do. It's not Connor's fault we're wildly incompatible people, and while it is my fault I kissed Jake, I know the only way I can make it right is to let him down before anything gets too serious.

"Hey," I begin. Connor was so involved in texting, I've

snuck up on him without intending to, and he almost drops his phone on his face before he shifts up and catches it on his chest.

"Hey, Lia," he replies quickly. I'm the one who has to do something hard here, so why does he look nervous?

"I have to tell you something," I try to start again. That seems like a marginally better way to begin than "we need to talk," which gives even emotionally well-adjusted people palpitations.

"I actually have to tell you something too," he says. He swings his feet off the couch to make room for me, but hell if I'm putting my butt where his shoes have been. Maybe it's because I come from a shoes-off kind of household, but people putting things that touch outside dirt on indoor furniture make me want to gag.

"Okay. Do you want to go first or should I go first or . . . ?"

"I'm quitting Penny's campaign."

The first thing that comes into my head is Penny's encouraging face telling me to dump Connor for myself. Buddy, I'm here to disappoint *you*; you're not here to throw my best friend's campaign into a bonfire.

"Were you planning on telling her that?"

What is she going to do? The election is right after Round 3, and the window for ballot changes ends . . . Shit, that's today. That's why he's telling me now. He probably thinks it's a courtesy to tell his girlfriend before he ruins her best friend's chances at being class president.

"Not yet. I was hoping she'd be in the library, but, like, everyone left a few minutes ago."

That might be because Matt sabotaged the popcorn machine in the student lounge to massively overload and texted everyone but Connor about it. I wanted an empty library for the conversation and he made sure I got one.

"Well you'd better tell her soon because the deadline for swapping anyone out is, like, now."

"Yeah, I know. I just got back from Klein's office."

"What were you doing there without Penny? You need your candidate to make any changes to the—Oh. Oh. Seriously?" He has got to be kidding me. I know what this is about. Connor can see I've caught on and doesn't look nearly as ashamed as he should. "Klein let you switch to Audra's ticket when Penny wasn't even there. What did you tell him, that she'd booted you off or that she already had paperwork to make her own switch?"

"Honestly I don't know what Audra told him, but I'm with her now. On the ticket."

Hmm, nope. I'm not buying that. Between the furtive texting, the last-minute backstabbing, and everything I know about Audra and Connor, this isn't just politics. It never was.

"That's not completely true, is it? You're with her, period."

"Do you want me to be?" He means it as an accusation,

but I'm stunned because it's the first time Connor's ever asked me what I wanted. "'Cause I don't think you care."

Well, no. I definitely care that my soon-to-be-ex-boyfriend is dicking over Penny's class president campaign because he's pissed at me, if that's what's really going on here. I also care that Connor leaving me for Audra means that spoiled witch wins our incredibly stupid boyfight, but there's brighter things on the horizon for me and I could be persuaded to forgive, especially if I get to wipe away my tears with the pages of my Wizzard contract.

"This shouldn't be about me. You're abandoning Penny a week before the election."

Connor rolls his eyes. "I thought joining her campaign would mean we'd get to hang out. You're, like, constantly running away from me. I never see you. We have lunch sometimes, but your head is, like"—he waves his phone-free hand in the direction of the window beyond the bookshelves—"way out there somewhere. I can't even talk to you; you ignore all my calls—"

Step 2 is not going according to my plan. Don't get me wrong, but at the end of this Connor and I will for sure be broken up. I just thought it would be calmer. More adult. With 99 percent less me telling him how I've actually thought and felt about him for the past two months, to my own detriment. Can't put the cork back on now, though. Connor, let's rock.

"Who calls people, Connor? I'm sixteen! I answer the

phone for my grandpa in Vieques and the pizza guy, and that's it! It's weird that you do that! I want you to acknowledge that it's weird."

"I was just trying to be a good boyfriend! Sorry for doing everything right when you don't appreciate anything ever."

"I'd appreciate everything more if you asked if I wanted it first! You kept pushing your idea of a good boyfriend on me without asking what I like or if I'm comfortable with you, I don't know, showing up outside my car every day with coffee I hate and walking me across the parking lot like a poodle."

"You never said anything! How the hell was I supposed to know?"

He's got me there. I didn't tell Connor about my boundaries because I was sure I could keep them up all by myself. I let him throw himself against a wall for two months instead of telling him to stop or that there was an easier way of getting through. There's no dimension where Connor and I make a good couple, but there's hopefully at least one where I get better at communicating my needs.

I have been so focused on being one step ahead of everyone else. I thought it would protect me, but staying one step ahead only means no one can walk by my side. No wonder I underestimate people, up to and including my best friend and my boyfriend. And Matt and Jake. God, who's next?

"You're right," I sigh. All the fighting energy deflates from me when I realize he has a point. It's not a good enough reason to ditch Penny, but I may as well let Connor have this. "I didn't talk to you about it because, well . . . I didn't want to. You were *way* too much, and I shut down because it was easier to avoid you than put any effort into making this a real relationship. Now it's over, I guess."

Connor swivels on the couch to resume his lounge, complete with his feet on the cushions. If he's upset, he's hiding it behind a facade of not caring about anything, which is exactly what I deserve. I did the same thing to him.

"Yeah, it's over. You'll see Penny before I do; go ahead and tell her," he says. His bored voice and his pouty voice are the same, and as bad as I feel for not giving Connor a chance, I don't want to give in to his feigned nonchalance. I'm done pretending not to care.

"I don't want to," I say as kindly as I can manage. "You should tell her yourself."

As I'm turning to walk back through the library and meet back up with Penny and Matt, Connor calls out one last time.

"Wait. You said you had something to tell me."

Right, I did. Telling him I came here to break up with him is pointless now, so I say the first thing that comes into my head.

"There was a popcorn accident with the machine in the student lounge. It's cleaned up now."

Allow me to accept my award for "worst parting line in

history" in absentia, and please, have the plaque sent to the Team Fury green room at the Wizzard-Claricom Arena.

When I talked Step 2 over with Penny and Matt, I figured it would feel like just another task on my pre-victory to-do list. I didn't care about my relationship with Connor, so ending it should have meant nothing. Did we not suck as a couple? Is the riddance not, in fact, good?

I'm supposed to be awash in catharsis by now, but knowing that Connor noticed how poorly I treated him makes me feel, ugh . . . It's one of those *multifaceted* feelings. I've had a lot of these since I started talking to Jake, and I can't say it's my favorite part of being willingly vulnerable.

I feel like . . . I've been tweaking the sliders on a character creator trying to get everything right—the face, the body, the base skills and strengths—and when I finally thought I was done and hit confirm, the character rendered way uglier than I expected and can't pass a skill check to save her life. Making her into something I can actually play is going to take a lifetime of grinding.

But that's the point, right? Just like Jake said, I owe it to myself to try. It's the only way I'm going to have a shot at the life I want.

Emotional honesty is exhausting, man. This is a lot for one forty-five-minute free period. I need to eat a baked good, hydrate, and get my butt to bio class. And warn Penny about Connor and Audra, that's important too. I said he can tell her himself, but let's be real; he's not going to. She needs all the advance notice she can get to find a new VP candidate today.

I'm trying to figure out how I can smush everything that just happened into a few pithy sentences when I get to the library door. Penny and Matt said they'd wait for me in the auditorium, but as it stands I've only given them a few minutes to get to their next class. I wouldn't blame them if they weren't there anymore, but when I push the door to the library open, they're standing right outside in the hallway— and so is Principal Klein, with my mom.

"Emilia, you're okay. Thank god." I'm barely out the door when my mom barrels past everyone else to give me a hug. This feels . . . extreme. Did Penny bring her over from the athletics office?

"I'm fine, Mom, it's just a breakup. I'll live. You didn't have to come all the way over here."

"Breakup? What breakup?" My mom pulls away far enough so I can see the confusion on her face, then buries my face back in her shoulder. "Your father offered to drive over, but I'm taking you home."

I twist to look over at Penny and Matt, who both look like they've just come down with a stomach flu. This entire situation is wrong. I have no idea what I'm supposed to be panicking about, but I start anyway, just to stay on top of things.

Principal Klein, who seems to be the owner of the missing

piece of information that completes this shitpuzzle, clears his throat.

"Miss Romero, the school received a call ten minutes ago. Several calls, actually, and there are more coming in as we speak. It appears your name and information appeared on a website calling for threats against you and your family."

"It's a misunderstanding," my mom interrupts. "Dad's working on getting it taken down. No one has any idea who these people are or how your picture ended up on the site."

No. No, no, no. This can't be happening, not now. We haven't had a chance to move on to Step 3: wipe my social media and mass-untag any pictures that could tie me to friends and family members. We would have made it Step 1, but I thought we'd have more time. I should at least have been able to do an Insta story for school election day. I lock eyes with Penny over my mom's shoulder. She needs to know about Connor. That's the normal person problem I'm supposed to be dealing with right now. Not this; this wasn't what we planned. It's too soon. This was supposed to be a controlled demolition, not an unexpected explosion!

I open my mouth, but I can't get any words out. Mom does, though. She looks ready to claw her way through an army of anonymous internet fiends and leave zero survivors.

"We're going to get to the bottom of this. It's ridiculous," she says fiercely. "I've never even heard of *Guardians League Online*."

CHAPTER TWENTY-ONE

Team Unity Chat, Monday Night

BobTheeQ: I'm going to need everyone to calm down.

JHoops: she's not answering my texts, she's not online, she wasnt in school, i dont know where she is and you want me to CALM DOWN???

JHoops: i DMed matt and penny and they won't answer me

ElementalP: our matty?

JHoops: different matt

shineedancer: you ever notice how every man in america is named matt

ElementalP: Speaking of, say it with me . . .

ElementalP: Where's muddy?

BobTheeQ: I don't know. Jake, it's going to be OK. You can't do anything to help KNOX right now. Her info is already down and I'm sure Fury and Wizzard are going to find out who organized the dox.

JHoops: everyone at school lost their shit. they put us in the gym because some idiot threatened to come on campus with a bomb. they all know Emilia is KNOX and i can't talk to her or see her or ANYTHING

JHoops: even if i knew where she lived i can't get there because my dad won't drive me in the middle of the night

JHoops: i'm losing it you guys

JHoops: she was going to quit and i told her to keep playing. it's my fault

[MUDD has entered the chat]

ElementalP: Fury will protect her, I can't imagine what B will do when he finds out who doxxed his teammate

MUDD: lmao not likely

BobTheeQ: Hey man. We're kind of in the middle of something.

MUDD: KNOX got DOXXED. sounds like a dr. seuss book.

JHoops: wtf this is serious

BobTheeQ: Muddy, this isn't funny. I told you I'd give you one more chance to not be a jerk, are you sure this is the energy you want to bring to Unity tonight?

MUDD: what are you gonna sic baby jake on me again? im shaking.

shineedancer: bob I swear to *god*

MUDD: calm your tits i actually have good news.

JHoops: what news coming from you could possibly be good

MUDD: Fury dropped KNOX.

JHoops: oh my god

ElementalP: Jake . . . breathe

BobTheeQ: Where did you hear that? Did Wizzard post something? I don't have any emails from them.

MUDD: you know its crazy, any other team would be celebrating. fury destabilized a week before the finals? in a diff world you'd all be thanking me but you're too busy crawling up Jake's ass to focus on what's important

[LanguageBot]: LANGUAGE

MUDD: i always hated that bot

shineedancer: what did you do

MUDD: blame jake he's the one who told me what to look for

MUDD: wahhh i'm baby jake i'd throw my shot at a million dollars off a cliff if emilia thought it was cool

MUDD: how many emilias do you think go to jake's stupid high school? this wasn't even hard

JHoops: it was you. You doxed her.

shineedancer: that's illegal you MORON

MUDD: lol wait wait

MUDD: how quickly do you think i found the footage
of you hooking up with emilia when i told arena
security i lost my backpack and wanted to look at
the tape of a "random corner near craft services."
which you ALSO told everyone about.

MUDD: hint: not long. took a picture on my phone and
figured fury's captain would be interested to find out
where his bitch DPS goes between matches

[LanguageBot]: Second warning, Matty

JHoops: it really is my fault

shineedancer: you threw Emilia to the wolves just so
we'd have an easier time beating Fury?

BobTheeQ: No, B wouldn't kick her for that. He needs
her to win.

MUDD: see.

MUDD: that's ur problem bob. you care more about
keeping the band together and skipping around like a
bunch of idiots than doing what it takes to win the
tournament. of *course* you think fury wouldn't kick
her for that because you didn't kick jake for it.
lol jesus, do you learn?

BobTheeQ: I just got an email from Wizzard. Tabbing
out but this isn't over.

shineedancer: while bob's gone i want to take the
opportunity to say I literally never liked you

MUDD: i know babe:)

BobTheeQ: Back.

BobTheeQ: I'm only going to do this once.

[LanguageBot Disabled]

BobTheeQ: WHAT THE FUCK IS WRONG WITH YOU, MATTHEW

MUDD: ☺ ☺ ☺

JHoops: what else did he do? i'm going to choke him either way but I want to get my defense in order

ElementalP: here for your alibi

shineedancer: seconded

BobTheeQ: At this point, thirded.

BobTheeQ: Fury isn't down a DPS for Round 3. We are.

shineedancer: oh helllll no

MUDD: turns out ole byunki would rather have a tested DPS in his comp than some chick who's sneaking around with enemy!!!!!

MUDD: if it makes you feel any better it was his idea to doxx her. I just said i'd bury the photo if he felt like writing my name in as an alt for the finals

BobTheeQ: This is next level, Muddy.

ElementalP: you and Byunki deserve each other, you're both snakes

MUDD: probably! idc we're gonna be rich. good luck finding an alt in four days ya freakssss

MUDD: fuck you all and goodnight. MUDDY, OUT.

*[**MUDD** has left the chat]*

shineedancer: we're boned we're boned we're dead in
the water we're boooned

JHoops: if wizzard just sent you that update, then
em must have just found out about Fury too.

JHoops: she's never going to play again

JHoops: even if she wanted to, now her parents know
and she's probably still getting threats. it's over
for her. oh my god i wish i could talk to her it's my
fault it's my fault it's my fault

ElementalP: we should call the cops and tell them
what Muddy did. if he's arrested Fury can't play
either.

BobTheeQ: Muddy didn't publish her name, Byunki
did. And Emilia would have to sue him to prove he
posted with the intent to cause harm in a civil
suit. Online harassment requires repeated, person-
to-person contact to escalate to a criminal case in
the state of Pennsylvania.

JHoops: how do you know that?

BobTheeQ: I got real familiar with harassment laws
after B and I broke up.

shineedancer: so because Byunki never contacted her
directly or repeatedly it's not criminal? he can
just post her name on some gamergate hub knowing
folks will go apeshit and that doesn't break any
laws? your state sucks!

JHoops: she should have the option to sue. someone has to tell her

JHoops: she's not our competitor anymore and that means my promise to stay away from her doesn't count right bob

BobTheeQ: Dude, of course.

JHoops: cool cuz if you said no for whatever reason i was gonna do it anyway.

ElementalP: we know

JHoops: matt (different matt) just got back to me. he says the romeros are pissed and they have her on lockdown. She told me once if they ever found out she gamed they'd like kill her

shineedancer: obviously they won't literally kill her

ElementalP: wait Romeros? she's latinx and she kept a huge secret from her parents for years and someone called a bomb threat to her school because of it?

JHoops: yes

ElementalP: yeah no they might kill her

JHoops: she was going to tell them after the tournament if Fury won cuz they can't really argue with a million dollars so GOOD JOB MUDDY

JHoops: to be clear i was still rooting for us but now nobody wins

shineedancer: i mean . . . unless

BobTheeQ: Unless?

shineedancer: unless . . .

JHoops: wait is this going where i think it's going?

BobTheeQ: It's the most obvious solution.

ElementalP: more than worth a shot

BobTheeQ: Up to you, Hoops.

JHoops: if you're serious i think we owe it to her

JHoops: I owe it to Em to try

CHAPTER TWENTY-TWO
Emilia, Friday

I CAN'T TELL what time it is with the shades pulled down. It's definitely daytime, but it could be morning, maybe midafternoon. About an hour ago, I heard the doorbell ring. Probably a package for my dad's business. Could also be whoever the school sent over with my homework for the week, which would mean it's after 3 p.m. No phone, can't check either way. I roll over to face away from the window and peek through one crusty eye at the rest of my bedroom.

The desk's still a mess. By the time Mom brought me home on Monday, my dad had gleaned the full story from forum posts on the website where my info turned up. Just seeing him sitting at the kitchen table with his laptop open when he was meant to be working in his office made my throat close up. He didn't let me read the kinds of things people were saying, but my firsthand experience with the nasty side of the *GLO* community tells me it was bad.

Dad wasn't mean when he marched me upstairs and made me show him how I'd been playing, but he was angry when he saw that I'd cobbled my PC together from stuff he thought he'd thrown out—the processor from the first iteration of his company computer, the RAM sticks he bought online and swore he had more of; he'd given me the external hard drives to bring files back and forth from school, but the misappropriation of storage to house dozens of 20-gigabyte games ticked him off as much as the (sort of) stealing did. The only thing I didn't rescue from his trash was the graphics card, which I bought with two years of birthday money.

When Dad saw what I'd built, I thought I detected a glimmer of pride, but it vanished when he yanked the power supply out of the wall (it wasn't turned off all the way; he knew that would hurt) and took the tower before he left my room.

He left my monitor, though, which is now sitting on top of my desk with its cord attached to air. It's worse than if Dad had taken everything downstairs. Now every time I roll over, I see Florence's dead, matte face and think, *Wow, that inanimate piece of equipment looks lonely as hell.*

And yes, I am aware that I am projecting. I am also aware that most of my parents' precautions, like taking away my computer, school laptop, and phone and not letting me out of the house, are meant to protect me, not punish me. I've never seen my mom look as scared as she did reading the comments over my dad's shoulder. Come to think of it, I've never seen her look scared before at all.

It's weird to remember that my parents, whose hypothetical reactions to this exact situation have been my own Sword of Damocles, are also, like, people? I think that's why I haven't left my room except to eat for four days. The whiplash of seeing them worried, then angry, then concerned, then angry again, but mostly worried was too much for me to resolve when I had to sit there and look at them. At least I haven't been up here crying. I just feel kind of dead. Turns out I'm a pharaoh after all, and my bedroom is my tomb.

Well, most tombs don't have en suite bathrooms, but if mummies had to pee and shower sitting down for forty-five minutes until the water gets cold and they almost pass out from the steam buildup, I bet they would. The ancient Egyptians were practical like that. They even buried people with stuff that would make them happy in the next life. Books, chariots, slaves (not great), snacks. What else did they stick in those burial chambers? Treasure for sure. Games too. Wait, is being a mummy awesome? No wonder Pharaoh's always grinning. That, and he doesn't have lips.

Sweet Christmas, I'm losing it. This is the isolation and hopelessness wrapping their nasty little tendrils around my brain and squeezing until all the logic squirts out like juice. My parents told me they would risk my perfect attendance record to keep me out of school for as long as it took to get a handle on my online security, but the thrill of missing school only lasted for the first few hours of Tuesday. I need to talk to people, to get up and move around. I need to keep eating and stretch and go downstairs to face my parents and whatever punishment they have in mind for me. I need a lot of things. What I want is Jake.

Jake would understand how I'm feeling right now. I bet he blames himself for telling me to stay in the tournament like it wasn't my choice to make. He would be self-effacing and would act surprised that I don't think he's garbage, and then he'd crack a joke about *GLO* or tell me a story about how something similar happened to Penelope one time, and before I knew it, I'd be smiling again. Jake would say something smart that gets to the bottom of everything I'm feeling right now without realizing he's doing it. He'd tell me this was all going to be okay, even if it wasn't. I'd believe it coming from him. Jake's not an optimist by any definition of the word, but he thinks I can outlive anything. I wish I had his confidence in me. I wish he was here to help me fake it.

And then, I don't know, maybe we'd make out a bunch. That would be cool too. I think I brushed my teeth this morning. Might have been yesterday. I run my tongue over my teeth, and they feel pebblier than usual. Def brushed them yesterday.

It's gross to imagine kissing Jake again with day-old mouth stink, so I swing my legs over the edge of the bed and start thinking about walking over to the bathroom. My vision darkens as the blood rushes up to reach my head, then bubbles back in a grayish tide that ebbs to the beat of my lazy heart trying to remember what it takes to keep me upright. By the time I can see clearly, my mom is standing in the doorway to my bedroom.

"You're up," she says, sounding surprised. Then she sniffs the air. "It smells like a hamster cage in here."

Like she would know. She never let me have a hamster. I had a bird when I was little, a feisty blue parakeet named Cloud, but when he died my parents decided pets were too distracting to keep around. Eyes on their prize.

"You wouldn't happen to have one of those upside-down water bottles with the little metal ball, would you?" I ask. My mouth tastes like dumpster liquid. How did I not notice that when I was lying down?

"I'll get you a Smartwater if you brush your teeth," Mom negotiates. "While you're brushing, we need to talk."

See, *that* is why I didn't want to open with "we need to talk" when I broke up with Connor. It immediately puts people, like me, on edge, like I am right now. The jolt in my chest when I hear my mom say those words is the strongest emotional response I've had since I checked Fury Discord before my parents took my phone away and saw that Byunki had revoked my access. I haven't been able to check my email to confirm that he kicked me off the team, but I knew then that

Fury had dropped me. Byunki wouldn't want to roll up to the championship with a player who brought death threats to his team. Whoever doxxed me wanted my *GLO* career over before it started.

Anyway, nothing matters! Mom can say whatever she wants. I slide off my bed, walk over to my bathroom, and leave the door open so I can still see and hear her. Turning the lights on would only blind me after spending so much time in the dark; between me developing a lamp allergy and Dad unplugging my gaming PC, the electricity bill at casa Romero is going to be one hell of a bargain this month.

"Your father and I," Mom begins, then seems to give in to an impulse she's been holding back all week and marches over to start making my bed. Come on, Mom, I was totally going to do that once I finished brushing my teeth. (I wasn't.)

"Your father and I are disappointed. This game you've been playing, the *League of Guardians*. That's time you could have spent studying or working on your college essays. I don't know where you found out about this tournament, but *lying* to us about campaigning with Penny on weekends? I called Mrs. and Mrs. Darwin, and they were *not* happy about that either."

Penny's moms are literally theater producers, so I doubt their daughter acting well enough to fool my mom ticked them off that much, but by all means, Mama, keep talking. I'm still working on my molars.

"We're appalled at the levels of your deception. Especially since the kinds of people who play this game are the same people who called a *bomb threat* to school. They threatened to come to our house! Do you have *any* idea how hard your dad's been working to scrub your name from the internet? The things these . . . boys said about you. I've been looking things up, trying to understand why. You had to know this was possible."

"Dun't blam me fur ther bullshut," I seethe through a mouthful of toothpaste. My parents can punish me all they want, but I'm not going to let them blame the victim here.

"I don't blame you. And watch your language," Mom replies without missing a beat. I can see, from one angle in the bathroom mirror, her finish putting my bed back in order. She smooths her hands down the comforter like I've seen her do a thousand times, making sure every thread in the comforter obeys her touch, then sits awkwardly on the edge of the bed.

"We've done so much to give you a good life, Emilia," she says. Are those brushing sounds echoing in my head or is my mom's voice breaking?

"You're so special. Even when you were a baby, we knew you were brilliant. I'd be at home with you all day and watch you crawl around, picking things up, trying to understand what you saw. It's like you were filling in a little spreadsheet in your head. Your dad would come back from work and ask me what new things you did while he was gone, and I always told him you did everything. You taught yourself to read when I wasn't even looking."

Should have thought of that before you taught a two-year-old the phonetic alphabet, Mom. None of this is relevant. Just say your piece and go. But come back and bring me that Smartwater when you get a chance, please.

"We bought this house to get you in a good school district. We put you in Monteronni so you would have the best foundation. Every Model UN conference, every class trip, the field hockey team—we've never denied you anything you need to succeed. You have the potential to go so far, and you're up here playing video games? What do you have to say for yourself? No, spit that out first. I can understand you either way because I'm your mother, but it's gross when you talk with toothpaste in your mouth."

Ever obedient, I spit. My mouth feels great, which makes it the only part of my body that does. What do I have to say for myself? Nothing I want to tell my mom. Nothing she doesn't already know. She has the story; I don't get why she needs to hear it from me. I did what I did, and the universe is exacting its own revenge.

I don't want to sit next to my mom on my bed. I'd rather stay in the bathroom and procrastinate by washing my face. That keeps my mouth free, and if I start crying for the first time this week, the suds will hide most of the tears.

"I only did it because I thought I could do both," I begin.

It's true; as ridiculous as it sounds now, I really did think I could keep this charade up for the rest of my life. "I want to do what you . . . you know, what I'm supposed to do. Get good grades, go to college, make everyone proud. So I was doing that. I just also wanted to play. It was fun. I liked it. So I did both."

Washing my face hasn't taken nearly long enough to keep me from going back in my room. I rinse off and start working on my hair. I haven't washed it all week, which is a smidge under fine considering my curly hair hates being washed more than once every four days, but I grab a spray bottle and start scraping it into a bun at the top of my head to hide the pillow frizz.

"You did both," my mom repeats. From her deadpan tone, I'm guessing that explanation isn't going to fly. "You lied, sneaked, and exposed your identity to online terrorists so you could play a game that has nothing to do with your future because it was *fun* and you thought you could do *both*."

My grip tightens around my hairbrush. This is the part of the movie where the smarty-pants teen claps back at her mom for not understanding, and they yell at each other in a big fight that ends with someone slamming a door or taking a long walk to "cool off," because kids can totally disappear for hours these days without their parents reporting them missing. My family doesn't operate like that. I don't yell at my parents; I can't even imagine what my voice would sound like yelling at them. In return they rarely ever raise their voices to me, but the few times they do generates this feeling of total dread, like I've just spotted a tarantula crawling up my leg. Sometimes even hearing other people yell makes me feel that way. I maneuver around confrontation as often as possible.

I can't do that today. Or tonight, hell if I know what time it is by now. I'm not going to yell because there's no point, but my mom has to know how I ended up here. My hair is up and out of my face, and I can't stay in the bathroom forever.

My mom watches me intensely as I walk over and take a seat on the bed a few safe feet away from her.

"It was more than that," I admit. Damn it, my eyes hurt. No, no, I hate this. Don't cry. Tears won't get you anywhere, Emilia. Do not cry. "I was doing so much for you." I sniff. *Come on, not now.* "And I wanted to have something for me. I'm really grateful for everything you and Dad do, but you don't leave any room for *me*."

I expect Mom to interrupt me, but she doesn't. She just glances over at my bedroom door like she's expecting someone to walk through. It's not disorienting enough to stop the tumble of words that I somehow can't stop from falling out of my mouth. They've been sitting at the tip of my tongue for so long, and they really, really want to come out now.

"I didn't choose any of it," I say through what suspiciously—Yup, no, those are tears. Despite my best efforts, I'm crying at my mom in my bedroom. I feel seven years old. "You and Dad pick everything. Field hockey, all those extracurriculars, my courses, and it's fine! I'll do it; I know I have to do it because I don't want to waste your time. I chose to play *GLO*, though. I'm so good at it, Mom. I taught myself how to be good at it. I tried really hard to be safe so this wouldn't happen, but it happened because those guys are scared of *me*. Did you see the pot for that tournament I was in? I could have paid for UPenn after the contract was up. It wasn't just a game I was wasting my time with; it was a real thing I could have been great at because I *wanted* to be."

I don't have a tissue in grabbing distance. Instead, I have to wipe my nose on my shirt.

"I took a risk to follow what I wanted, and it backfired. As long as no one got hurt, I'd make it again, though, because it was my choice to try a new path. I'm so, so sorry for lying. You can ground me forever—"

"You are," Mom interrupts kindly, "grounded forever, I mean. Your father and I decided."

"Yeah, cool, that's fine. I get it. I lied a lot, not just to you and Dad. I did it to protect you from . . . the exact thing that happened, but it was still lying."

"Emilia." My mom closes the gap between us on the bed and hugs me. "It's our job to protect you. We're going to do whatever it takes to keep you safe."

I can't say I expected that. This conversation goes almost too smoothly, and I'm not sure if my sense that Mom is holding something back is outweighing my relief that she's not ripping into me. So much of our relationship is Parent Tell, Child Do that I've never considered softness as a potential reaction to a fuck-up of this scale.

"Once this blows over, there won't be much to do, Mom. Someone else who isn't a straight white guy will piss everyone off by existing next week, and they'll forget about me, I think. They like it when they win, and I'm not going to play anymore, so they win."

"Don't be ridiculous," my mom says as she rubs my back. "Romeros don't lose."

I pull back from the hug in surprise and level my gaze at my mom. She has the same look in her eyes that she gets before a field hockey game. Someone has replaced Mom with Coach Romero when I wasn't looking.

"That thing you said about this game being your choice," she continues. "I wish you could have made it without keeping it a secret. I'm not saying we would have let you do it if we had known, but I understand that impulse."

"You do?" I can't think of a single reason my mom would understand where I'm coming from. She's super-mom, always on the PTA, always making sure I'm top of the class, all-supporting, all-dazzling, always. What could she know about wanting to try something unexpected?

"My mother never left Vieques, you know. She sent me and your titi Bea to live in Philly when we were teenagers. We didn't have a choice. We had to make money and get married. There were so many times when I told myself I should do something different, go to college, maybe get a degree, but I didn't. You're supposed to have more choices than I did. I see so much of me in you."

For the first time, the idea that I might be like my mom doesn't make me roll my eyes.

"There's your father in there too; he'll never admit it, but when he showed me that computer you built, I almost had to pull him down from the chandelier. He was so impressed. You're both workaholics. And nerds."

I knew it! Dad was proud of me. Horrible circumstances, but it still feels like a victory. When I smile, I feel the salty film of my dried-up tears cracking on my cheeks.

"I didn't understand that in trying to give you more options with what to do with your life, we were restricting you from choosing what those options might look like. I didn't put it together until that boy downstairs brought it up."

The boy downstairs. There's a boy downstairs. Is *the* boy downstairs?

My mom laughs out loud when I jump up from the bed. Totally involuntary movement, my legs just feel like someone shocked every muscle with a cattle prod. The charge carries up to my heart, setting it to a frantic, pounding beat that I'm sure Mom can see through my T-shirt. Jesus, my T-shirt. It's gross! I'm gross! No, I washed up in the bathroom. Did I put on deodorant? No, why would I? I didn't know there was a boy, potentially *my* boy, downstairs.

"Mom," I say as calmly as I can with a body biochemically primed for skydiving, "who is downstairs?"

"I didn't catch all their names; they're a real motley crew. Penny's with them. She brought your homework. We talked for an hour before I came up to get you. Didn't you hear the doorbell ring?"

Oh, she's enjoying this. Mama Romero, or Coach Romero or whoever's sitting on my bed today, is always two steps ahead. I don't know who's waiting for me downstairs, but whoever they are must have worked something far more powerful than necromagic on both of my parents. Mom didn't come up here to punish me; she wanted to hear my side of the story.

"Romeros don't lose . . . ," I say quietly.

"We don't. Emilia Romero stinks, though, so I'll give you a few minutes to change. Hamster cage, I'm telling you."

Well, what am I supposed to do about it now? Once Mom leaves my room, I rip my T-shirt off and run to my closet. The irony of suddenly having too many choices is not lost on me. Mom didn't say outright that Jake was downstairs, but now that she's opened up the possibility, I know it's true. I know it was him. No one else could have told her how I feel because no one else knew! Here's a shirt. It's blue, whatever. Bra first; don't want to show up tits akimbo in front of Jake and Penny and whoever else is down there (Matt?).

By the time I stuff my legs into a clean-ish pair of leggings, I can smell coffee brewing downstairs. One peek under my window shade shows me it's late afternoon, which makes it a weird time for coffee, but I'm not going to complain. Dad defaults to making coffee for guests regardless of whether they want some or not. They're lucky he hasn't started stuffing chunks of cream cheese and guava jelly into premade pastry; he'll send everyone home with snacks if they give him enough time. I should put on mascara. That will look very obvious. Jake doesn't care about mascara. Or maybe he does. He's never seen me without it.

Forget it, I'm too excited. I half run, half stumble down the stairs and turn toward the kitchen, and that's when I see them. All of them, up close for the first time.

Bob's legs are so long that his feet touch the ground when he sits on the counter-height stools on one side of our kitchen island. Ki's are not; her tiny feet are swinging above the ground as she cranes her neck to watch my dad make coffee with his sock drip. Penelope is sitting on the third stool, swiveled partially around to face the people sitting at the kitchen table. I have to step in farther to see who's there. Penny, looking serious. Matt, looking lost but happy to be here. Mom, spreading out a pile of homework across the kitchen table, and, of course, the boy downstairs.

Jake has his glasses off to clean them on the corner of his blue Unity jersey—they're all wearing their jerseys—so he doesn't notice me until he puts them back on. When he does, he smiles. Hello, Jake's dimples. I missed you.

"Em," he says. The room goes quiet. "Sorry I couldn't come soon—" He stops when Penny shushes him. Every eye turns to Bob. The last time I saw him, he looked like he was trying to summon enough laser power in his eyes to burn me alive, but when he swivels his stool around to face me, his handsome face is fixed in an expression of cool appraisal.

"Emilia Romero, aka KNOX," he begins dramatically. "I'm Bob Quince. This is Kiki Kim, Penelope Howard, and I'm told you know Jake Hooper."

I lock eyes with Jake across the kitchen. I haven't talked to him since he left me a message on *GLO* right after Round 3 saying Unity asked him to steer clear of me until the tournament was over. That seemed fair then. It's clearly a moot point now. Jake puts a finger to his lips. Shush and listen, Emilia. I comply.

"We each have certain . . . skills. Damage, healing; I'm a tank." Bob presses his hand to his chest.

"Yeah, you are," Ki mutters under her breath. I see Penelope gently swing a foot out to kick her under the counter.

Bob continues as if he didn't hear Ki. "I've had my eye on you. You're a top-tier DPS, specializing in ranged damage, necromagic, and some of the most impossible-looking team combos I've ever seen."

Over Bob's head, I see my parents staring at him like a

whole Martian just beamed down in the middle of their kitchen. I bet he told them he had a speech but didn't tell them what he was going to say. Totally related: I think I love Bob now?

"I'm putting together a team," Bob says. But he already has a team. They're literally right there, two healers, a tank, and— where's the other guy? Their second DPS. Muddy, Jake told me his name was Muddy. Unless he's hiding in the kitchen island, Muddy isn't here.

"Recent circumstances have left me with a place on that team for someone who looks a lot like you. Miss Romero"— Bob pauses for effect—"I'm here to talk to you about the Unity Initiative."

For a second I think I'm going to cry again, but the whole kitchen breaks out into applause and shocks me into laughing instead. They're clapping for Bob, who slides down from the stool to shake my hand.

"I have *always* wanted to say that. Look at my arm; I gave myself goose bumps. Hi, I'm Bob. Sorry about the highway, by the way. Jake explained everything. We cool?"

Words are difficult right now. I can just about handle nodding while sneaking a glance at my parents, who are pretending to look busy behind the island but are watching me intently.

Matt sees how confused I am and takes it upon himself to start explaining. "So. I was having a normal one on Tuesday when this guy"—he jerks his thumb over at Jake—"comes up to me in the library saying he's gotta find Emilia, Emilia isn't texting him back, yada yada . . .".

Penny jumps in: "And Matt was, like, no one can talk to Emilia, her parents are keeping her away from school to be safe, she's probably not gonna be at school for a few days. But Matt texted *me*, and I was like 'hey, I'm bringing Emilia's homework on Friday, so if you want me to bring her a message I could make a little something happen for our boy Jake, if you know what I mean.'"

"I didn't," Jake adds, "know what she meant. I just needed to talk to you. When I heard about the dox and Fury, I wanted to see you so—to tell you something." He glances over at my parents, who didn't seem to notice anything amiss. He didn't tell them about us. Which makes sense; there is no us yet. Is there going to be an us?

All I know is it's fantastic to hear Jake's voice again. I want to turn his voice into a lotion and rub it all over—Wow, I have been *massively* undersocialized for the past four days. I am 100 percent feral.

Matt's talking again, thankfully diverting that particular train of thought. "Anyway, Penny told me to talk to Jake about talking to her about talking to *you*. Turns out he had something more than a message to bring you." He gestures broadly at Bob, Ki, and Penelope.

"Hi, I'm Penelope. You can call me P. Unless you call *her* P." Penelope points to Penny, who shakes her head. "No?

Cool. Jake got us all to meet in Philly on Wednesday and told us his plan: we group up, piggyback on Miss Penny's home-work trip to make sure someone answers the door, and make you an offer you can't refuse."

"It was actually my idea to offer you a spot on the team," Ki adds. Tiny, bossy, pink-haired, and pretty. I love her already.

"They showed up on our doorstep at three forty-five talk-ing like they had an appointment." My mom puts one mug of coffee in front of Bob and another in front of Penelope. "Penny was with them, so I knew they weren't from the bad internet."

"My guess was carolers," Dad adds, bringing coffee to my friends at the kitchen table. "Then I remembered it's October. *Then* I thought: Halloween carolers."

"Okay, that's genius, Mr. Romero," Bob says. "I'm stealing that. Doing it next year. Watch me."

"Uh, can I come?" asks Penny.

This is surreal. It's entirely possible that I'm still in my bed thinking about Egyptian burial methods and spiraling into a wild hallucination where Jake's *GLO* teammates are best friends with my parents. I still haven't said anything. That's definitely a sign this is a dream; I never talk in any of my dreams.

"Em, why don't you sit down." Jake got up without me noticing and—if this is a dream, it's a great one—takes my hand to lead me to an empty seat at the kitchen table. His hands are sweaty again, and I love it. Damp hands for life, sign me up.

I find my voice once I've sat down. "I still don't know what's going on here. You all got together to ask me to join Team Unity? That's not . . . Don't you already have a guy?"

Team Unity exchanges an uncomfortable look.

"About that," Bob begins.

"No, Jake should tell her," Ki blurts out from the counter, then addresses me. "It's a long story. You're gonna hate it."

Mom sets a glass of water on the table before returning to Dad's side behind the counter. Thanks for remembering, Mama.

"I'm sorry, Em," Jake says. This time I think he really is. "Muddy—our DPS—convinced Byunki to dox you. He found out you and I . . . know each other. He thought I was jeopardizing the team and jumped ship to Fury knowing they'd think the same thing about you."

Jake looks nervously at my mom, who I'm sure got an abridged version of this story earlier and is getting the equally abridged recap now. I can read between the lines, though. Somehow, Muddy knew about me and Jake. I'd often wondered what Byunki would do if he found out, and now I have my answer: he'd betray me in a fucking heartbeat.

You'd think a week of processing the fact that Fury dropped me when I got doxxed would prepare me to be less angry at the revelation that the team I'd sacrificed so much for was a bunch of turncloak bastards, but I don't work that way. I put the glass down on the kitchen table so I don't squeeze it to death and grip the sides of my chair instead. Byunki may have made the call, but everyone else on Fury went along with it. Ivan could have quit when he knew Byunki was going to hurt me. Han-Jun and Erik could have tried to make him see reason. They didn't, and even if they tried, they failed me.

"It's my fault, Em. I let too much slip and blew it up again," Jake says quietly.

"No," I reply less quietly. "You were—you're the . . ." I take a deep breath to force the anger out of my voice. I'm furious, but not with Jake, or Unity, or even with myself. Muddy screwed him over too. I know where to aim my fury. "Rotten people are never your fault, Jake. It's not your job to fix what's bad in them. You're so good; I wish I could trust people like you do. I can't be mad at you for that."

I feel a sweaty hand reach into my lap and gently squeeze my fingers. Jake doesn't have to say anything else. It's super cool being real friends again, or more, who knows? No one's ever diverted an esports coup to my doorstep before, but if that's a love language, I'm pretty sure I speak fluent Jake.

"We all trusted Muddy for too long," Bob agrees. "If it's anyone's fault, it's mine for thinking we could work on him. I owe Ki and P an apology too; they weren't his biggest fans from the start, and I'm the one who asked them to try harder."

"Apology acknowledged," Penelope says. "You're gonna work on listening to women, though."

"Hear, hear," my dad interjects. "I've undone most of that little punk's damage, by the way. Got that whole forum taken down. The pictures they had were from Wizzard's tournament photographer, so I worked with the company to ding the posts for copyright violation. That Thibault guy is nice, took my call as soon as he knew what I was calling about."

Uh, holy shit, but I'll need to save the story of how my dad got on the phone with Thibault Adige for later. We still have details to discuss here, and I need to make a decision about Unity.

"They're helping us keep you safe," my mom says.

"That's good," I say, still high key stunned.

"We want you to be happy," she continues, "but you also messed up. So like I said upstairs, you are the most grounded child in America."

"The *most* grounded," Dad echoes. "You live in the ground now, as our mole daughter."

"Except . . ." Jake looks up at me. Whatever embarrassment he was feeling has obviously passed.

"Except for next Saturday," Mom admits. "The blue shirts said they need you in this tournament, and I will *not* let the people who tried to hurt my baby come out of this thinking they won."

Jake can barely contain his grin. Penny and Matt are smiling too. A quick look over my shoulder shows the rest of Team Unity looking nervous but ultimately beaming. Everyone from every facet of my life is here, smiling. Happy for me. I never thought I'd see them together, let alone happy for me about the same thing.

"If you do win, the money is going into a savings account for college," Dad adds. "We have some money saved to help you either way, but there *is* a student loan crisis in this nation and—" Mom cuts him off with a glare.

Listen, I'm with Dad here. Even when I thought the pot was 200k split five ways, I was going to put the money toward college.

"Only if you want to," Jake says suddenly, because he's just remembered the most important part in all of this. "It's your choice, Em."

"If you could make up your mind in the next thirty-eight minutes, that would be great," Bob calls out. "The deadline for submitting an alt to Wizzard is, like . . . well, it's in thirty-eight minutes."

Thirty-eight minutes? I need negative two. Mom and Dad are giving me a nod of approval, and lord knows I'm not going to be doing anything else for the foreseeable future. For now, I only have to say one thing.

"I'm in if you are."

CHAPTER TWENTY-THREE

New Team Unity, One Week Later, Friday

BobTheeQ: Ladies and gents, that's a wrap on our last practice!

shineedancer: any notes?

BobTheeQ: I have a few, nothing too big. Jake, stay snakey with Pythia. Reserve your poison tomorrow until I tell you to lay a strike trail around the payload. It might make or break our hold and we want to avoid taking this to checkmate.

JHoops: hiss hiss venom kiss

ElementalP: better not miss

BobTheeQ: Ki, I'm giving you the swap spot but I don't think we're going to need it. 90% chance we'll keep you on Doctor Jack but slot Balor just in case. I want you to have an option in case Fury plays a monster tank.

Beloveandabow: they won't. YUNG doesn't trust Bad

Matt yet. he'll stick to what's familiar. Klio
or bust.

BobTheeQ: Hard maybe. Recall that I've known him
longer than you.

Beloveandabow: you right

BobTheeQ: P, any thoughts on working with our new
DPS? Feeling good about timing your heals on
Pharaoh?

ElementalP: Yup. the timers aren't too weird and he
can sacrifice a special for a one-time self revive so
speaking as a healer i am completely in love with
this mummy. Like i ship him with Castor for real

JHoops: hey now

ElementalP: you heard me

Beloveandabow: jake you will always be my number one
girl-snake

JHoops: i literally cannot wait to afford therapy

BobTheeQ: Speaking of mummies: Emilia. How's the
stress? It's OK to be nervous, we're here for you.

Beloveandabow: i mean the team fury post-practice
ritual was getting yelled at over voice chat and
routinely DMed all day and night to make sure we're
playing to B's standard so not having that anymore
has brought my stress levels down I'd say . . .
halfway

shineedancer: is jake taking care of the other half
like a good boy

ElementalP: hey-ohhh

JHoops: permission to curl up and die, bob?

BobTheeQ: Not granted.

Beloveandabow: . . . he is

BobTheeQ: I'm gonna change the subject now.

JHoops: cool idea!

BobTheeQ: I feel great about where we are as a team.
We've only had a week to pull this together so feel
free to pat yourselves on the back for putting in
the work.

shineedancer: is this speech a screenshot of
penelope's finsta because i'm sensing a really
big "but"

ElementalP: omg thank you

BobTheeQ: BUT. We need to be prepared for tomorrow.
Wizzard only knows about the dox, not who did it.
The player swap is unrelated as far as they know.

BobTheeQ: We want to win as clean as possible, with
as little drama as possible. The payload is our first
priority, checkmate only if things go south. Fury
will try to bait us into doing something stupid. You
especially, Emilia.

Beloveandabow: why would i do anything stupid? they
only violated my privacy, basically called me a
slut, doxxed me, kicked me, and still have photo
evidence that I hooked up with your teammate before
you let me on the team. how stupid could any action

i take against them possibly be under those
circumstances

JHoops: hey em what's the countdown difference
between pharaoh's normal type bolts and the necro
piercers

Beloveandabow: .75 seconds, .6 more if his mana at
less than 50% why

JHoops: i just wanted to cut you off before
you spiraled

ElementalP: the fact that jake doesn't have a gay
twin sister is my life's greatest tragedy

shineedancer: do not feed his ego any more i am
begging you

shineedancer: he kissed emilia *one* time and thought
that meant he could win a fight

Beloveandabow: ummm when did that happen?

JHoops: hey bob how about that speech you were just
typing to all of us i was really enjoying that

BobTheeQ: Don't worry about me, I'm having a
great time.

BobTheeQ: Seriously though, get to bed everyone.
Stay sharp and follow my lead tomorrow. I have faith
in You-nity. Blue cross! Black shield!

shineedancer: can't lose:)

[shineedancer has left the chat]

ElementalP: CANT LOSE

[ElementalP has left the chat]

JHoops: can't lose!

Beloveandabow: wait what is this something we do?
nobody told me there was a call and response portion
of the program should we start over

[BobTheeQ has left the chat]

Beloveandabow: no i want to do the team thing
too! Jake!

JHoops: just say can't lose, em

Beloveandabow: can't lose

JHoops: nailed it.

JHoops: are you really ok for tomorrow?

Beloveandabow: lol no i'm freaking out. I have no
idea what's going to happen and i'm really used to
at least kind of knowing what's going to happen

JHoops: whatever does happen you got up there and
showed them you're not afraid

Beloveandabow: to be clear, i am very afraid

JHoops: i know. we got you tho

Beloveandabow: and i got you

JHoops: sleep tight. * <- that's a kiss

Beloveandabow: come on dude

JHoops: too cheesy? sorry

Beloveandabow: * <- kissing u back

JHoops: yeah wow that sucks we're not doing
that again

Beloveandabow: never

CHAPTER TWENTY-FOUR
Emilia, Saturday

A FEW THINGS I am learning at my first ridiculously high-stakes esports championship match:

1. As big as the crowd is, I'm only playing for an audience of four. To emphasize how grounded I am, my parents took my car keys and drove me, Penny, and Matt to the arena this morning. They also took full advantage of my previously unused comp tickets to get seats that are, in my opinion, way too close to the stage for comfort. I made all of them promise not to wave, take flash pictures, or make any noise that I could easily identify as coming out of their mouths, and I sincerely hope they hold up their end of the bargain. I never thought my parents would find out about *GLO*, let alone want to watch me play it, and now that they're here, it just adds another layer of

nervousness to what's already become the most nerve-racking day of my life. I want them to see me win, but more than that, I want them to understand why I'm here. Matt already understands, obviously, which is why I've asked him to be my parents' and Penny's gamer translator for the day. Matches move fast, and as nervous as they make me, I want my parents to know what they're proud of.

2. Bob must have worked some magic on Wizzard, or else put the fear of God in anyone in a position to question why I switched to Unity for the final match. Once I said yes to joining their team and got the full, unabridged story of Muddy's deception (Unity graciously withheld from my parents that me kissing Jake is what sparked his whole tantrum, for which I am eternally grateful), all I had to do was e-sign some documents. Bob handled the rest and spread a convincing enough tale that no one at the arena seemed surprised or creeped out that I showed up in a blue jersey. Jake and I are both pretty pleased about that—the mystery of the DPS swap gives our first match as teammates a little extra edge.

3. It is so, so much better going into a match with people I actually like on my side. I'm not just talking about Jake (though I did technically shove him in a broom closet and kiss him senseless when he showed

up this morning, for luck), but the rest of Unity too. In Round 1, I was petrified to meet the rest of Team Fury and worried they wouldn't like me even after I'd been playing with them for months; I've known most of Unity for a week, and they treat me like their long-lost sister who is also a highly competent digital assassin. I don't have to prove myself to them at all, which is a big weight off my back considering how awful I'd have felt coming into this match from the opposite side of the stage. Thanks to Unity, all of my current jitters are directed precisely where they're supposed to be: the match. Nothing else. We have thirty seconds until they call us onstage, and Jake is holding my hand in the wings. I'm feeling nervous and lucky at the same time. Nerucky? Lurvous.

It's possible I'd be less nervous if Thibault Adige hadn't crashed our pre-match meeting just a few minutes ago. One second we're holding hands in a circle while Bob leads us in a focusing chant, and the next, *he* was standing at the door with a small army of assistants peeking in from the hallway. It was all standard stuff, and I'm pretty sure he'd stopped by Fury's green room earlier to say the exact same thing. But shaking the hand that designed *GLO* was more than I'd expected from my morning.

"I weesh you all ze best of luck," Thibault told us. "I 'ave already designed a free champions' tabard skin to go out in a patch tonight. Eef you win, it will be blue. If it is Fury, red."

So if Fury wins, we won't be able to log into *GLO* ever again without running into someone sporting fabulous red armor in honor of our nemeses. But hey, no pressure.

If—no, *when*—we win, we'll get to spend a lot more time with Thibault. Bob says he'll be organizing the rollout for next year's tournaments, and even if the winning team doesn't compete, they get to go with him as ambassadors for the league. All we have to do is make sure those tabards go out blue.

Jake squeezes my hand and brings me back to the moment. I don't need hand warmers when I have him.

"Ready?" he whispers. From the wings, I see Fury filing out from their side of the stage. All in a row, with Muddy at the end as a surprise. Pretty boring of Byunki to pull the same move twice, but I have the tremendous advantage of not having to care.

"Ready," I whisper back. I let go of his hand just as the announcer calls for Bob (BTEQ).

The lights and sounds of the arena don't freeze me this time. I walk out after Ki (KIKI) with more confidence than I've had for the entire rest of the tournament. I'd be lying if I said I didn't feel a little thrill when the crowd whooped in shock to see KNOX here, but not even my brand-new Unity portrait (Wizzard took one this morning; they must have rushed Muddy's too) distracts me from taking my place standing with my team.

Jake, or HOOP as he goes in competition, and P (LMNO) line up next, and for a moment it's just the ten of us onstage. I keep my gaze straight ahead, refusing to look over and grace Fury with my attention.

"Finalists." The announcer booms from the speakers like a movie trailer's voice of God. "Shake hands and take your seats."

Oh, buddy, I'm not shaking *shit*. I glance over at Bob, who makes an apologetic face at me. Neither us nor Wizzard wants the drama behind this match to leak. After a beat, Bob sets the example by walking up to Byunki and shaking his hand. Byunki doesn't even look up to meet his eyes. I'd give a lot of money to find out more about what happened between them; all I know is that they dated and that's what started this whole rivalry. If Bob can shake his ex's hand, then surely I can shake my enemy's without maneuvering into an over-the-shoulder judo toss that sends them flipping into the audience.

Fury doesn't budge, so it's up to us to give ground, walk over, and show good sportsmanship to each and every one of those pricks. When I get to Han and Erik, they stare coldly at a spot over my shoulder; Ivan is the only one who looks a little . . . sad? Upset? He always was my favorite. Maybe I was his favorite too.

Muddy I have a problem with, but after seeing Bob and Ki get through him without trouble, I think I can handle him. I've never even met the guy and he tried to completely ruin my life over, what, one kiss? A misguided sense of betrayal? Long-standing issues with intimacy, toxic masculinity, and a single-minded pursuit of greed stemming from attachment issues he developed as a child? Running over the reasons he might have betrayed Unity keeps me busy while he has my hand, and by the time I'm done, it's time to let go.

Except he doesn't.

I feel Jake bump into me from the side—he was going through the line as mechanically as I was, and now we're clumped together on the stage, with Muddy holding my hand and Jake close enough to feel both of us breathing.

"Listen to me," Muddy says through a fake grin. To everyone watching, it looks like he's merely saying something to his replacement in earshot of his former teammate. There are no rules against that as far as I know. Doesn't mean I want to find out what he says next.

"If you win, I'll release the picture," he continues. From the corner of my eye, I see Jake turn white. "Everyone will know you're a slut who stole my spot. Lose and it goes away forever."

Shit. I try to pull my hand away from Muddy's grip but can't do it too violently without arousing suspicion. The audience is already quieting down, wondering why the DPS handshake is taking so long. I look down at his grip on me, hating the way his hand feels in mine, when I see Jake reach out and grab Muddy's wrist.

"Can't lose," Jake says quietly. His fingers tighten over Muddy's arm, squeezing it until he's forced to let go of me. I pull my hand back too quickly; some people in the audience gasp.

Thank god the lights up here are too bright for me to peek down and see my friends in the front row. Matt had to stop Penny from trying to pack a Taser in her purse this morning.

The Unity table is close. I just have to take a few totally normal, nonchalant steps and take my seat. It feels impossible. Bad enough that just posting my name brought the incel hordes screaming into my real life, but Muddy's photo shows Jake and me kissing in my original uniform. He's right; no matter what I say after the fact, it will look like I slept my way onto Unity and sink my reputation before I can sign Wizzard's contract.

Bob can see I'm trembling when I sit down and motions for me to put my headphones on. The tight, dim hum of noise cancellation feels suffocating in my ears. Jake rushes over to the table and takes his spot next to me, followed by Penelope.

"Jake," I say, trying to keep my face neutral so it looks like we're just checking our levels. "I—"

"Don't listen to him," Jake replies quickly. He's still pale as a ghost when he reaches under the table to touch my leg for a too-short second. "Muddy isn't getting what he wants today."

"What happened?" Bob asks. I leave it to Jake to explain; I can't find the words.

"Shit, okay." I see Bob look over at Fury for a second. "Jake's right, don't listen. Fury doesn't get a win today; Muddy doesn't get a win later. We'll figure something out. Ki, give me the swap spot."

"What?" Ki sputters. This wasn't the plan.

"I have a bad feeling Byunki wants to checkmate me instead of fighting for the payload. I want the swap in case I need to change my tank to ward him off," Bob explains.

"Okay." Ki nods. We all watch on our computer screens as Bob reassigns the swap totem to his character.

"I'm going Carrigan or Grendel." A mech or a monster tank. Bob is betting that Byunki will either keep Klio, a fire tank that would be weak against Grendel the monster, or change his tank to Lucafont the ghost specifically to target Bob's usual character, the magic type Fabella. If Bob swaps his tank to Carrigan, a mech, Byunki won't have any advantage over him regardless of the character he chooses. Something about that seems familiar, but I'm too distracted by the start of the countdown to put my finger on it.

"Mics down; let's go, Unity!" Bob yells. I can't tell if the audience heard him, but the artificially blunted sound of cheers does seem to get a smidge more intense. I chance one more look at Jake, who nods at me (not even a smile? I could really use a smile), and get ready to tunnel my vison in 3 . . . 2 . . . 1.

The map is Euphrates Crater, an abandoned city of dusty

brick towers built in the middle of a bowl-shaped depression on the surface of one of the *GLO* universe's many ruined planets. There are very few high points, which is bad for Pharaoh, but the map also has none of the environmental hazards that could jack up a strategy based around certain characters—no water sources to debuff fire and mechs or dead zones where magic gets fritzy. Wizzard wants this championship to cleanly showcase us as players with no tricks or lucky breaks.

As we beam down onto the map, I hold Pharaoh's crossbow up to take advantage of his aiming zoom and peek at Fury's lineup across the map. The others are falling too fast for me to see, but I peep Byunki falling as Klio. I alert Bob, who has an extra ten seconds in his swap countdown to change his tank. He's sticking with Carrigan. Smart choice.

Bob gives us the order to stay close and hunt the payload as a group. Getting our mark will stake our claim and put us in a good spot to defend it; our second priority is to get first blood on Fury to start our team Special Attack countdowns. Penelope sticks with me on Bob's left flank—she's playing Castor, a magic healer who gets a bonus when she heals other magic characters like Pharaoh. Jake has Pythia, of course, and is moving on Bob's right with Ki as Doctor Jack, her usual ice healer. She's better with Jack than she would have been with another DPS, so it shouldn't be a huge deal that Bob stole her swap.

These first few seconds in a five-on-five match are crucial.

They play more like a stealth game than a team-based shooter. It's hunt and hide, stun and run, just to get enough info on the map and our opponents' characters to kick the rest of our strategy into high gear. Bob's long-legged mech jogs through the city's streets and alleys with the rest of us in formation around him, eyes peeled for the first sign of Fury action or the payload's treasure chest chime.

Ki spots the flash first, a high trail of sparks that indicates a Fury player up ahead. Bob calls Penelope and me up in front of him with Jake behind us to heal if Fury tries to get a shot in. We're almost at the red brick plaza in the center of the map, and from the placement of those sparks, I'm guessing Fury is waiting for us.

"Prime a shot; they don't know we're coming from this angle," Bob whispers, even though he doesn't really have to. I get Pharaoh's bow up with a normal bolt on load. I'll need blood to charge up his better attacks, but a bolt will start our timer just the same.

P and I launch ourselves into the plaza, laying down fire to discourage Fury from ambushing us, and quickly realize we shouldn't have bothered. Fury's here all right, but they're not coming toward us in a charge. They're just standing there on the far end of the plaza, waiting as a gust of alien wind kicks up a swirl of brown dust between our teams. Ivan's on Jubilee, no surprise there. He must have gotten comfortable being a monster. Han is Glace, his typical ice healer, and, wait, why didn't they swap Erik's Jenkins for a better character? As a mech, he won't have any advantage against Bob, but mechanical characters have an advantage against magic. Does Byunki want to send a healer to do a DPS's job and have him take me and Penelope out?

I only have a second to wrap my head around that choice when Muddy and Byunki step out from behind their front line. Muddy's playing Nero, which I've never seen him do before. And Byunki—no, that's impossible. I saw him beaming down as Klio. I told Bob to pick his character *because* he was sticking with Klio. He's not Klio today, though; he's Lucafont.

Jake puts it together before I do. In the moments we have before all hell breaks loose, he spits his realization into the mic.

"They didn't base their comp around taking Bob out. They based it around drawing me and Em out."

Lucafont the ghost is weak to Pharaoh. Nero the alien is weak to Pythia and strong against Carrigan. They've completely tailored their lineup to piss off me and Jake while giving Muddy the best shot at killing Bob.

"It's bait," Ki growls. She and Bob start speaking over each other but fall in unison to deliver the new imperative: "Don't do anything stupid."

Byunki must have given Team Fury his signal, because the plaza explodes in a flurry of first-move action. Erik levels his dual pistols at me and takes a shot, which Ki deflects with an

ice shield. Muddy and Byunki zoom across the plaza to engage
Bob and Jake in melee, and the match is officially on. Half a
second later, Byunki lands a sword hit on Bob. Fury has first
blood. There's still time to make up for it.

"VANE's running! KNOX, follow. Payload is priority,"
Bob commands as he parries Byunki's first attack. Ivan's hunting the payload, and Bob wants me to sneak around him and
get there first if I can. I drop a fog cloud to mask where I'm
going and scurry after him with Penelope on my tail for heals.

"We need to drop that Jenkins," Penelope says as we leap
onto a rooftop to get a better idea of where Ivan's headed.
"He'll take us both out."

"I know," I say. Pop fog, jump to next roof. Penelope's
doing a great job staying in the radius of Pharaoh's stealth
attacks. "Up ahead, VANE's scouting that palace." From my
angle on the roof, I can see that the payload isn't there,
but now's as good an opportunity as ever to get a shot in.
"Cover me."

Penelope swings her character around to keep my back as
I ping a bolt off Ivan's armor. I watch him spin around and
spot me on the roof. Another bolt crunches through and takes
off the tiniest sliver of his health bar. It's enough to grant me
the power to charge a magic shot that will take off more than
a sliver, and as I send it sailing into Jubilee's shoulder, I see my
camera angle slide wildly to the left. Someone's hit me from
the side.

I wheel around and see Byunki swinging at me and pop another fog to try to get behind him, but he's seen me play against Lucafont and anticipates my move. He pulls his arm back for a heavy attack and—BAM!—collides with Bob's mech armor instead.

"I got him, keep hunting." Bob doesn't have to tell me twice. Penelope and I leap down from the roof and continue on street level, dashing through ruined walls that form short-cuts through the city's half-destroyed buildings.

Our payload is in another castle, it seems. Up ahead, the windows of the western palace glow with the unmistakable rainbow tint of a jewel cask. Penelope alerts the team that we've spotted the payload. Jake meets us on the street, where we see Ivan and Muddy heading straight for our prize.

"Don't let them land," Bob pants. You'd think he was actu-ally running around with how out of breath he sounds over chat. His command comes too late. Red text appears in the center of my screen: Payload Timer, Two Minutes. Fury's got the cask marked.

Before I can stop him, Jake's Pythia dashes past me into the palace and smacks Muddy's Nero with a well-placed staff strike. It's enough to knock Muddy out of the payload's radius, but it's also exactly what Muddy was waiting for.

"Jake, no!" I call out as I run in to support him. I fire off triple bolts at Muddy, hoping to land a stun. Get the hell away from my snake priestess boyfriend, space scum. Yeah, that's

right. I've decided. I'm kicking Fury's ass and asking Jake out
right after, you slut-shaming piece of shit. Penelope falls back
to swipe at Ivan while Jake and I chop Muddy's health up as
best we can before he leaps away. With all three of us in proximity, the payload quickly switches to Team Unity's posses-
sion. Flag: captured. Now we just have to keep it.

The rest of our teams have caught on to the battlefront
moving to the western palace. Bob and Ki file in quickly and
form a half circle around the payload. I see from the health
bars in the top corner that Han and Erik are topping off Fury's
health for the next phase of battle. Ki and Jake heal us as well
while we wait for our enemies to arrive.

It doesn't take long.

I'm more than happy to engage Ivan one-on-one as Unity
launches into a dense, defensive battle—a sortie, if I remember Byunki's military terms correctly—centered on the
payload. I trained with him for months, so there's nothing
he could do to surprise me. Parry, leap back, pop fog, close-
range shoot. Tap into my magic meter to cause a little pain,
dodge back, and keep chipping at his health.

To my right, I see Ki engaged in an ice fight with Han-
Jun. Neither of them has any advantage, but the giant icicles
erupting from their battle quickly begin taking up more of
the palace floor. Euphrates Crater might not have any default
environmental hazards, but player-generated ice can change
that real quick before it melts. Ki is playing masterfully,

barely taking one hit for every three she lands on Han-Jun. Her special meter fills up faster than I thought was possible, and the millisecond it's charged, Ki blasts Han-Jun across the palace with a chunk of ice big enough to bury him completely. Han-Jun drops. Fury is down a healer and is no longer eligible for a payload win!

"Nice one," Jake congratulates Ki. He's locked in a fight with Erik's Jenkins, holding his own, and still has time to toss a heal where it needs to go.

"Don't you mean ice one?" she asks triumphantly.

Her victory is short-lived. Erik dodges one of Jake's attacks and slides on the remaining ice toward Penelope, who doesn't see him coming.

No one can warn her in time. Erik is juiced up from his fight with Jake and slams a mechanical baton into Penelope's Castor. If she wasn't weak to mechs, she might have survived, but that baton attack drains health over time, multiplied by his character's advantage. Castor glows blue, briefly turns so transparent we can see his skeleton model shine bright through his armor, and drops.

It's death to look away from my screen, but I sense Penelope's movement two seats down. She leans forward and holds her head in her hands, allowing herself a moment of disappointment before she pops back up, crosses her arms, and drifts her eyes up toward the ceiling. Dropping in competition shows the dead player a third-person view of the rest of the match and cuts their audio so they can't advise their teammates.

With Penelope done, we've lost our chance to win the payload too.

"Abandon ship!" Bob shouts. With the payload strategy scrapped, we move through to our less-loved but still feasible plan of going for a checkmate.

Unity scatters like roaches, the remaining four of us each leaving from a different direction pursued by a Fury player. Byunki is after me, and a glance behind me shows Muddy running to catch up with Bob.

Byunki's Lucafont whip-catches Pharaoh's ankle, and I take another hit. I spend my leftover juice from my fight with Ivan shooting at his spectral armor but don't have enough to pull the Shatter special that won the first round.

"Heal." I try to remain calm. We still have both of our healers, and one should be free to help me out here. No one arrives. "Heal!" I try again. Nothing.

Byunki lands more blows on me faster than I can throw fog to evade them. I've shaved off about a fifth of his health, but he's easily taken three-quarters of mine. It's possible that Unity could take him from here, but I'll be damned if I let Byunki take me out of this match without taking him with me.

Lucafont's head is hidden beneath a glowing white helm, but I picture it shielding Byunki's face, salivating at the prospect of humiliating me one last time in front of my parents, friends, and Jake.

"Stand down, Em," Bob calls. I don't know where he is on the map or how he can see where I am.

No. I don't want to abandon this fight. I have maybe a quarter of his bar now and enough of a charge to pull off another necromagic attack. If I use it, my special counter will reset to zero, but it might be exactly what my team needs to hammer down the rest of Byunki's health.

"Em, don't do what he wants," I hear Jake say. "Come to me. Middle plaza."

He's right. I should have listened to it coming from Bob, but hearing Jake's concern snaps me out of the rage I was feeling just a moment before. I turn and run, using Pharaoh's superior speed to leave Byunki whipping his sword into a cloud of fog.

My call for heals went unanswered because of the situation going on in the middle plaza. Ki, Bob, and Jake are there staving off double attacks from Ivan and Muddy. I had decent luck with Ivan before but don't want to alert them to my presence, so I leap up onto a building and see if I can line up that magic shot I wanted to use on Byunki. I could aim for Muddy, since he has an elemental strength against Bob, but I see his health bar is nearly twice what Ivan has to work with.

As much as I want to slam this bolt into the asshole who betrayed Unity—and I really, really do—the smart move is to take out my former partner. Never say I don't learn from my mistakes.

Ivan's played alongside my Pharaoh for so long he's forgotten what it feels like to play against me. Remember those insanely difficult ranged kills Byunki asked me to master, Ivan? I'm about to nail one right . . . now.

He doesn't see it coming, but it comes nonetheless. Right in the back of Jubilee's head. VANE drops out immediately, and my Special Attack bar sinks down to a quarter of its full power. Worth it. Fury's down two.

A lot of times in *GLO* matches, death comes in pairs. It's a side effect of each game inevitably splitting off into a series of mini-battles that winnow players out until a final few are left standing for the checkmate. I leap down from the roof to join the rest of my team in kicking the crap out of Muddy but can't get there in time to stop him from launching his Special at Bob. *No!* I think. *Bob's weak to Nero. That's a checkmate.*

Ki slides Doctor Jack over faster than I can even perceive her (that's ice powers for you) and sucks up the hit instead.

Like I said. Pairs.

I hear the beginning of Ki's howl before her audio abruptly cuts out. Can't comfort her now. It's just me, Bob, and Jake against Muddy, Byunki, and Erik.

"Bastard," Bob snarls. "Jake, heal Em. He's mine."

I feel like I haven't seen Jake in this fight for a hundred years. Muddy's fled across the plaza to regroup with Bob in hot pursuit, leaving Pharaoh and Pythia hanging out alone just like old times. Jake showers Pharaoh with a healing spell that brings me up to 50 percent. Back in the real world, which seems further away the longer I spend in this match, I feel my body shiver with relief.

"You good?" Jake asks.

"I'm good," I reply.

"Not my daughter, you bitch!" screeches Bob.

Wherever he chased Muddy, Bob must have cornered him good. The screen flashes red with another Fury drop. I could have shot Muddy earlier, but I like the idea that he dropped off-screen to my perspective. Die like the NPC you are. That's how little you matter to me.

"Em, eyes," Jake suggests. I hop up to another rooftop and scan the surrounding streets for a sign of Fury.

"Nada," I say.

"They're coming," Bob says, sprinting his Carrigan back into the plaza. He took some serious damage in that fight, and Jake needs time to replenish his healing spells before he can help him. "Hold our ground. We're in the endgame now."

Soon after Bob comes in, I spot Byunki and Erik's Jenkins walking slowly in from the east perimeter. What they lack in speed, they make up in strategy. Erik is laboriously maintaining a force field around Byunki that shields both of them from our attacks. I land a few normal bolts on the field to jack up a few Special Attack points before Bob calls me down to join Unity's last stand.

In most cases, three players against two would be an

obvious win, but I'm the only one with an advantage against Byunki and I'm dangerously weak to Erik's character. Using Pharaoh at this point would be the same as killing him, making me completely useless.

Byunki and Erik lumber toward the three of us, maintaining their shield like a two-man Spartan phalanx. I know what we look like to them: a weakened tank, a healer too drained to heal, and a nerfed DPS piloted by the stupid girl they thought they buried two weeks ago.

"He's coming for one of us," Jake says quietly. Byunki's next move will depend on what he wants more—to checkmate Bob quickly or punish me for stepping out of line. I know Byunki. He's going to go for Bob. Fury's about winning, and that's his winning move.

"It'll be me," Bob says grimly. At least we'll lose on the same page. "Em, fire at that shield, see if you can crack it."

I oblige, slamming Erik's defense with normal bolts that do nothing but incrementally increase a Special I won't be able to use without Jenkins taking me out anyway. Wait. That gives me an idea.

"Jake!" I say quickly while firing. "Fire at the shield. Get your special up."

"May as well," agrees Bob. He's shooting too; now we're three idiots chucking bullets, bolts, and magic at an unstoppable moving object. This is good. We need to keep firing.

"We need to get Byunki out of that shield," I say.

"He won't leave until he can attack me," replies Bob. "He knows he's got us cornered."

"I almost dropped earlier because I was so mad I wanted to kill him," I reply. My Special Attack meter is so close. I peek up at the top of the screen where Unity's status sits and see that Jake's is almost done too. "We have to make him do the same thing. Jake?"

I see Jake sit up straighter in his chair. "Yeah?"

"Remember Crystal Cathedral?" Back when we talked about the ice cream incident, Jake told me to use my fire to goad that pesky player into attacking me. That player turned out to be Muddy, who is now the only person who can warn Byunki of my plan. Thanks to Bob, he won't be able to warn anyone, even if he screamed.

"Yes. Why—Oh!" Jake's catching on. "But he already sees you."

"Uh, report to your captain, please?" Bob is too cool to panic. Audible stress is a different story.

"Jake and I did this move, a combo. If I can get Byunki out of the force field, you'll both need to attack at the same time."

"Okay," Bob replies, "we can time that. How—"

No time to explain. Byunki and Erik are almost in striking distance. I shoot off the last bolt I need to charge my Shatter and step behind Jake and Bob.

The only way I can think of tricking Byunki into attacking me instead of Bob is to make him do what he almost made me

do. Something really, really stupid. He hates Bob for all kinds
of personal reasons and needs his checkmate to win. I can't
change that. I can, however, pull Byunki's devil trigger by
reminding him I'm an enormous pain in the ass.

"Get ready," I call out to Bob and Jake.

This part's easy. All I have to do is miss. I charge up Pharaoh's Shatter and aim ever so slightly over Lucafont's shoulder, just close enough to make it seem like I've genuinely
mistimed my attack. The impact doesn't take down Erik's
shield, so to Byunki's eyes, my attack is entirely wasted.

If I were a narcissistic dickweed who was threatened by a
girl's perfectly timed Pharaoh Shatter three short weeks ago,
and I saw that girl mess up the same move in a pathetic attempt
to deny me victory, I'd get a little cocky. I'd maybe even deviate
from my checkmate priority to take her down first, proving
once and for all that she's a nobody who doesn't belong in this
game. Hell, I wouldn't even notice that my force field got
nudged a half step back from the force of that "failed" Shatter,
which would totally leave me exposed to a poison attack on the
off chance that I *lunged forward* to humiliate her once and
for all.

That's how it would go if I were the dickweed here. I feel
comfortable declaring I am not. Next time you try to bury me,
Byunki, dig a deeper hole.

Jake recognizes his moment, nearly identical to the way we
stunned Muddy in Crystal Cathedral, and sends his poison

field streaming out from us in all directions. Lucafont's whole body is out of the force field now; I pull out Pharaoh's bow and shoot an endless stream of bolts to keep Erik from coming in to heal or protect his tank.

The stun reduces Byunki to a two-second window of powerlessness. Jake and Bob do their jobs and make sure he can't catch a single break. They don't even need Pharaoh for this part; Byunki's health is already circling the drain. One fragment left, less than half, Bob lands an attack and chips off a little more—honestly they're beating his ass like he stole something, and it's the best thing I've seen all day. I can drop or not drop at this point; without magic I'm basically set dressing, but I shoot a quick bolt into Lucafont's thigh anyway. For old time's sake. In one final flash of Pythia's staff, Byunki drops. Checkmate.

TANK KILL: HOOP.

The arena's screens immediately light up with Jake's name and face displayed on every monitor. I yank my headphones up and leap from my chair alongside the rest of my teammates, who are all so good and talented and worthy and extremely physically attractive. Ki and Penelope rush around their chairs to glom me, Jake, and Bob as the final three, and whoa—Jake has confetti in his hair. Bright blue confetti.

Jake remembered that silly combo and saved the day. Sure,

it was after *I* remembered Byunki's an asshole and also saved the day, but the screens don't lie. Jake took Byunki out. He had a lot of reasons, like wanting to see our names up in lights as the first *GLO* players in the Guardians League and winning a bunch of money, but I think he also did it for me.

I can't hear a thing over the crowd and the announcers declaring our victory. Not everything needs to be said out loud.

"Thank you," I mouth through the noise. Jake doesn't bother trying to respond verbally through the noise and puts his arms around me instead. We're still getting jostled all over from the rest of the team, so it's a normal-looking friendly type hug. The kind we can definitely pass off as friendly for now.

Heck. No, we can't. In the heat of the game, I'd forgotten about Muddy's threat to release the picture he has of me and Jake kissing. That's still a huge problem. Jake feels me tense up and leans down to yell in my ear.

"You okay?"

"No!" I shout. I hope no one in the audience can read lips. "Muddy's picture. They'll know we kissed."

Jake looks over my head at Fury's table, where the five horsemen of the dumbpocalypse are jabbing their fingers at one another in a useless argument. I turn my head and catch sight of Muddy staring both of us down. All my excitement drains faster than Byunki's health in the final phase of our match.

"Kissing's not that bad," Jake screams. "Lots of people kiss."

"I'm wearing my Fury jersey!" I explain. "Red, says KNOX on the back, puts the kiss before the swap."

Jake leans down to get closer to my ear and screech more intimately. "Em. He took a picture of *surveillance footage*. Black and white. All they'll see is 'KNOX.'"

Bob had to rush to get the order in, but he did manage to get me a Unity jersey with "KNOX" on the back. If Muddy's picture really is black and white, no one would be able to tell I'm not wearing my shirt from today.

"Still," I shout. "Kiss! If he leaks it, he can spin it."

"Can't leak what everyone knows. PR 101."

Now there's an idea. As I look out into the audience, there's a sea of shiny silver-and-blue sparkles raining down all over the arena. It's coating my parents, lucky as they are to be so close to the stage, and if I squint through the lights, I think I see Matt attempting to hold a sweatshirt over Penny's hair while she bounces up and down with her fists held high. Can't leak what everyone knows. That's a tactic Penny would approve of.

"Come here," I say. I don't have to yell because Jake knows exactly what I want him to do.

He reaches out to cup my cheek in his warm, no longer sweaty hand. When his lips touch mine, I see stars explode behind my eyes. Or maybe that's just the confetti.

EPILOGUE

Jake

JAKE HOOPER WAS kind of feeling his new persona: guy in a suit with a fancy-ass umbrella. He couldn't remember the last time he had even worn a suit and panicked two weeks ago when he realized the plastic-wrapped one in the back of his closet looked like it had been cut for a toddler. It hadn't; he'd just grown a lot over the summer, but that didn't help him when it came to having something decent to wear to the homecoming dance.

The suit he ended up wearing was new and blue. His dad had bought it for him. It was the craziest thing; by the time he got home from the match, his dad had fielded a dozen calls from press wanting to know about his prizefighting son, and he finally seemed to understand that Jake's gaming habit was worth a damn. He wanted to know everything, mostly about the girl Jake was kissing in front of thousands of people, and when Jake told him he was taking that same girl to a dance, he drove Jake to the mall to get his son a suit. They talked a lot that day, more than they had in almost a year.

Jake knew that one day of suit shopping with his dad wasn't worth much compared to the lifetime of relationship trauma he was looking forward to unpacking with the mandated individual therapist Wizzard provided for its league players, but it was a start.

Also, again, he looked *damn good* in this suit. There was something about being fancy in the rain with a magnificent black umbrella—one of the long ones, not the foldy ones that bend the wrong way if you look up and sneeze at the same time—that made him feel like the star of an old-timey movie. Jake couldn't dance to save his life, but while he was waiting outside the school doors, he was seized with an uncontrollable urge to jump up and click his heels. He thought it might feel magical, like tonight was the enchanted evening he always imagined school dances to be.

Perhaps tonight was not *that* magical. He nearly launched himself into a puddle on his third try. Luckily, Matt Pearson was there to catch his elbow and save Jake's suit.

"It's mad slippery, bro, watch out." Matt had an umbrella too, but compared to Jake's, it was nothing. "You got a famous face. Try not to smash it."

"Thanks, Matt," Jake replied. "I don't know what I was trying to do."

"*Singin' in the Rain*," Matt said. "I get it. I love that movie."

"It's the suit," Jake admitted. "It's really doing something for me."

"Yeah, I'm sure that's where all your newfound confidence comes from," Matt snorted. "Def not from walking around with your hand in Emilia's back pocket all week. Or the hundreds of thousands of dollars you're going to rack up next year. Or going viral, having an army of gamers declare your relationship 'goals'; can't forget *Good Morning America*, that was pretty dope. But no, you're right." He looked Jake up and down. "Suit's cool too."

Jake's face got hotter with every word that came out of Matt's mouth. Yeah, all of those things had happened, but on the inside he was still, you know, himself. He held his head a little higher these days and didn't walk into a closed door every time Emilia smiled at him, but the foundational elements of Jake Hooper were mostly the same. He was just better at being Jake. Like the suit, the fabric was all there, but the fit was so much nicer.

"Thanks, man," Jake said after an awkward pause.

"Yo, thank me for nothing. Hook me up with some *GLO* Unity merch or make me your assistant. I can't do shit, but I'm fun! Actually, could you introduce me to that Ki girl on your team? I thought she was cute, but when I saw the way she handled that ice fight, whew! The cold never bothered *me* anyway."

"Ki's gay as hell. Sorry." Jake was not sorry, but it was a

hard habit to break. He had been breaking it, though, slowly and with Emilia's help.

"Damn it." Matt kicked the ground and sent up a small splash.

"Wait a minute." Jake looked over at his friend. "Aren't you here with Penny tonight? I kind of thought you two were . . . you know . . ."

"Purely professional. I mean, political. We're here as a united front. It would be pretty messed up if the VP dated the president. Besides," he added, grinning, "she's got bigger things on her mind. We win *one* high school election and she's talking about studying political science in college. Wants to be the youngest congresswoman in Pennsylvania so she can change online harassment laws."

"Wow." Jake hadn't known Penny for long, but that seemed exactly like something she would want to do. Before he met Emilia, he thought Penny was another one of those intimidating people who thought they were cooler than everyone else. He was right, but she was also focused, passionate, and fiercely defensive of the people she liked, a short list that now included him. She'd be a great tank, now that he thought about it. "I almost feel bad for the laws."

Jake watched a light bulb switch on over Matt's head. "Wait, you think I could be *her* assistant?"

"I think you can do anything. You're the best Matt I know."

Matt's forehead wrinkled in confusion. "You mean *man*?"

"Nope."

Before Jake had to explain that, he caught sight of Coach Romero's car pulling into the school parking lot. Emilia wouldn't be driving anytime soon, but he was glad her parents agreed to lift her eternal grounding for one more night, if only because they couldn't really argue with a check big enough to cover most of her college tuition after taxes. Also, and this might be the suit talking, but Jake thought Emilia's mom had a soft spot for him. Like, yeah, he aided and abetted her daughter breaking a billion rules, but he also staged a parental coup solely to make Em happy. Maybe she was just glad he wasn't Connor. Either way, she waved at him through the window of her Jeep, and Jake waved back. Weird how much Emilia looked like her. Coach Romero basically cloned herself.

Jake hadn't told Emilia he was wearing a blue suit and wasn't surprised at all to see her emerge from her mom's car in a dress that nearly matched him anyway. Emilia and Penny shrieked in unison when they felt the rain hit their hair, which Jake picked up as his cue to rush forward and hold his umbrella over his . . . wait for it . . . girlfriend. He looked through the car to make sure Matt had Penny covered, and he did. He'd make a fine congressional assistant one day.

"I'm coming back at ten," Coach Romero threatened. "Be outside or you're walking home."

"I've walked farther!" Jake said cheerily, after he shut the car door.

"Yeah, but I haven't," Emilia muttered. With her heels, she didn't have to get on her tiptoes to kiss him. "Hi, you look beautiful."

No, come on. That's what Jake was supposed to say! He sputtered for a moment as he walked her toward the door.

"You . . . same," was what he managed to get out. "So pretty. Always." Not amazing. The power of the suit had failed Jake for the second time.

"Good thing you play better than you talk," Penny observed. She and Matt had fallen into lockstep with them once they got around the car. Jake thought Penny's dress was fantastic too. Not everyone could pull off bright gold, especially with a massive, shoulder-spanning sash that declared in glittery capital letters that its bearer was "JUNIOR CLASS PRESIDENT." He was about to feel bad for Matt when Penny pulled an extra-small "VP" button out of her purse and pinned it to his lapel.

"I would have made you guys buttons too, but I didn't know what to put on them," Penny said once Matt received his honors. "First I made 'Unity' ones, but that seemed kind of vague. Then I used up a few trying to fit 'Guardians League Champions' on there in blue glitter, but I kept spelling it wrong."

"It's really okay, Penny," Emilia sighed. She must have heard this story in the car. Jake held her hand to lend her patience and/or give her something to squeeze in case she ran out.

"Then I just kind of lost it and made ones that said 'Jake!' and 'Emilia!' but, like, what would be the point of that? Like I have *no idea*. I was really tired. Anyway, let me know when your mom wants her button maker back, Matt."

"You could have done the blue cross on a black pin," Jake offered, trying to be helpful. "You know, put it on the little circles."

"Who am I, Kandinsky?" Penny said dismissively. "Let's go in."

He really only had 12 percent of an idea of what Penny was talking about at any given time. She had the same effect as Emilia, making him feel smarter by association.

Jake took a few steps forward and was about to get the door for his new squad when he remembered something.

"Em, I have something for you." Jake couldn't believe he almost forgot. He'd found it in his room when he tore up his closet and sort of planned his whole night around this moment.

"Aw, you didn't have to get me anything. But what is it?" Emilia asked.

Before Jake could grab it from his pocket, the school doors exploded outward. Audra Hastings barreled out of them and nearly crashed right into Matt.

"Audra," Penny said coolly. "Happy homecoming."

Audra might have been a backstabbing jerk, but whatever she'd been through looked like karma had gone slightly overboard. Her face was unnaturally red from nose to chin, and her blown-out hair had already met its maker in the rain.

"Did you see him?" Audra gasped through heavy breaths. "Does he know I'm out here?"

"Who?" asked Emilia.

Audra looked up to see who she was talking to. Her face fell when she realized she'd run up to exactly the wrong crowd.

"Connor," she said miserably.

"You mean your date?" Matt asked.

"Yeah, duh," she spat. "He's rolling out his plan to make this the best homecoming ever, and if he finds me he's going to keep . . . rolling it."

"Oh. Oh no," Emilia said, suddenly serious. "What was it? Did he stuff your locker with confetti and now it's everywhere? Bring you chocolate but it's all the shitty pink stuff that's barely chocolate?"

"Yes and yes," Audra sniffed. "But throw in a giant bouquet of flowers that I am clearly allergic to; like I didn't *tell* him I can't have hydrangeas near me." She gestured to the rash on her face, which in Jake's estimation would not be going away anytime soon. "And he spilled a jar of honey on me in the car."

Emilia nodded empathetically. "Because you're his honey. Been there. If you have any alcohol, it'll get the stickiness out."

Audra brightened up. "I have vodka in my water bottle! I need to get to the bathroom. Thank you." She checked for

Connor through the door's slim rectangular window and dove back inside.

Jake thought Emilia handled that remarkably well. If Muddy turned up complaining that people were being mean to him online after Fury dumped him from their roster, Jake would kick him in the dick, not give him advice.

"Hey, Emilia." Matt tilted his head. "Vodka doesn't get honey out of fabric."

"Oh, I know," Emilia deadpanned. "But the chaperones are going to smell her a mile away. Give it twenty minutes; they'll call her parents."

Penny's eyes widened. "For real?" she asked.

Emilia shrugged. "Yup. And good luck to her, getting Klein to bend any more rules that screw over my best friend after that."

"I love you." The confession tumbled out of Jake's mouth before he could stop it. Truth was stupid like that.

He could barely explain it—one second he was watching Emilia disguise pettiness as kindness, and the next he was stuck in a time-stretching moment again.

Jake was eleven years old and completely in awe of the bossy, curly-haired girl who showed him the shield trick in *Knights of Darkness* and waited for him to get pizza. He was twelve and thirteen and feeling his heart leap into his throat every time he went to a party and saw her there, knowing she'd want to play. He was fifteen and hiding from her in the arena, and she'd found him anyway. He was caught in the rain, and she basically kidnapped him. She opened up to him, she saw him, and told him he wasn't stupid.

Jake had never gotten over his crush, not even a little bit, and having her hand in his right now was more than the culmination of everything he'd felt over the years. It was proof that he was better than he ever dared to think he was. Fierce, beautiful, brilliant Emilia Romero wanted him. Together they were champions. If anyone could stand in Jake's place and not be in love, they were lying to themselves. Jake was simply not a lying kind of guy. The suit wouldn't stand for it.

"We're gonna go," Matt whispered. He physically pulled Penny away and through the school doors, leaving Jake with Emilia in the rain. It wasn't pouring as hard as it was when she pulled up in her car and started this whole wonderful mess, but Jake thought the rain was one of those moments where life rhymed regardless.

"I love you too." Emilia said it so simply, like it was the most obvious thing in the world instead of the most wonderful.

Jake wanted to say a lot of things in response to that. What came out was "Cool."

He could do better than that. He dug around in his breast pocket to find something small and round. It used to be shiny, but whatever garbage metal they made Hillford Mall Arcade tokens out of had oxidized hideously over the past few years.

"This is for you," he said. "I mean us, technically."

Emilia took the token from his hand. "No way. Is this from my roll?"

"It was my roll. Half of my roll, you insisted."

"You were so *weird*," the girl Jake loved and allegedly loved him back crooned.

"So I went to the mall with my dad to get this suit, and I checked the arcade, and there's, like, ten more high scores on there. We're totally bumped off."

"Unacceptable. We're champions. People pay *us* to play games, you know."

Jake grinned. "I know! Huge mistake on their part. Anyway I thought . . . with everything going on, we haven't had time for a real date yet. Maybe later since you're still grounded . . ."

"You'd sneak me out of the house one weekend so we could eat arcade pizza and win the *Knights of Darkness* high score once and for all?"

"Yup." To be honest, Jake had been gearing himself up to ask her parents very nicely for permission, but sneaking out would work too. If there was one thing he'd learned about Emilia, it was that literally no one had the power to tell her what to do once she knew what she wanted. Add that to the list of reasons he loved her.

Emilia closed her hand around the token and smiled. As far as Jake was concerned, whatever came next could wait forever as long as she kept looking at him the way she was right now. Next year's tour and playing in the league. Probably the coolest thing that would ever happen to him in his entire life. It still couldn't be better than standing here with Emilia in the rain.

"I'm in if you are," she decided, then opened the door to join the homecoming dance. Jake followed her through, knowing he'd just hit start on a brand-new game.

GLOSSARY

Checkmate: A method of winning a *Guardians League Online* match in which the other team's tank is killed, ceding the victory to the killer's team.

Cooldown: The time it takes for a character's attacks to recharge.

Crit: Short for "critical hit." An attack that deals way more than usual, but they only happen a small percentage of the time (and never when you need it).

Debuff: An in-game action that places an ongoing negative effect on an enemy character, like poison, burning, freezing, or a curse.

Devs: Short for developers, as in game developers.

Dox: The despicable and in most cases illegal practice of publishing an individual's contact information online against their will. If you dox people, you are a bad person.

DPS: A character in a game who's there to wreck the

opposition. They excel at dealing Damage Per Second but have lower health as a result.

Ganking: Harassing another player by coordinating to swarm and kill their character repeatedly.

Healer: Low health, low damage, but any team would crumble without them. Healer characters have the essential ability to top up their teammates' health and keep them in the game. Underappreciated.

Loadout: The armor, weapons, and abilities a player character takes into battle. Some games allow you to change the loadout whenever, others only allow it between missions or matches.

Main: The primary character used by a player. Usually the one they are best at playing.

Mana: An in-game resource that allows player characters to use magical spells. Players start with a finite amount, but healers can sometimes boost mana along with health.

Meta: Short for "metagame," the meta is a set of rules or conditions that affect how a game is played. Updates to an online game can change the meta by making characters stronger or weaker, encouraging players to come up with new strategies.

MMO: Stands for "massively multiplayer online" game. If a lot of people play it and can interact with each other online, it's probably an MMO.

NPC: Nonplayer character. Any character in a video game that is not controlled by a player, usually referring to nondescript background or filler characters that are basically set dressing.

PVE: Player vs. environment, a game mode that disallows players fighting each other because fighting nonplayer dragons and stuff is valid too.

PVP: Player vs. player, a game mode or server that lets players fight against each other instead of game-generated enemies.

Sandbagging: A strategy in which a team holds back their best moves, players, or attacks in the first part or round of competition. Then, when the other team thinks they're weak, they unleash the fury.

Tank: A character in a game whose stats lean toward defense. Tanks can take a lot of hits, but their attack is low and they can't heal themselves.

ACKNOWLEDGMENTS

MANY PEOPLE HAVE helped me, and some of them helped me write this book. Thank you to all of them, with special thanks to those who convinced me this was possible.

To my family, Kevin Nedd, Venus Romero-Nedd, Ashley Nedd, Edythe Nedd, Uncle Pete, my titis and my cousins. Your love and encouragement made me think I could write a book and like always, you were right. Thanks for letting me use your name, Mom.

To my agent, Steven Salpeter. You saw what I didn't and I'm forever grateful for your guidance.

To Jack Heller, Brendan Deneen, and Caitlin de Lisser-Ellen at Assemble Media, without whom this book would literally not exist.

To my editor Claire Stetzer at Bloomsbury, thank you. It's so much better now. Also to Phoebe Dyer, Lily Yengle, and Alexa Higbee for their marketing and publicity support, as well as Liz Casal for her beautiful cover art.

To Thrive Ops, through all the thrives and thrivelets—Alanna Bennett, Anna Borges, Brett Vergara, Hayes Brown, and Matt Ortile.

Those who have supported my writing before I even knew that's what I was doing—David Sugarman, Margie Palatini, John and Barbara Ripton, Anthony Sellitti, and Lin-Manuel Miranda.

The denizens of Crimetown, where no one is innocent—Adam Rosenberg, Alison Foreman, Angie Han, Erin Strecker, Kellen Beck, Proma Khosla, and Levi, who is in charge.

To the essential workers of Brooklyn, New York, for keeping this city running and me fed.

To the game developers, designers, animators, QA teams, voice actors, and more who create the many virtual universes that inspire and delight me to distraction. I don't understand your magic but I'm more than happy to play with it.